PUBIS ANGELICAL

PUBIS
ANGELICAL

A NOVEL

MANUEL PUIG

Translated from the Spanish by Elena Brunet

AVENTURA

The Vintage Library of Contemporary World Literature

VINTAGE BOOKS
A Division of Random House
New York

AN AVENTURA ORIGINAL, December 1986
FIRST EDITION

Library of Congress Cataloging-in-Publication Data
Puig, Manuel.
Pubis angelical.
(Aventura)
I. Title.
PQ7798.26.U4P813   1986   863   86-40172

ISBN 0-394-74664-3 (pbk.)

Manufactured in the United States of America

10   9   8   7   6   5   4   3   2   1

Book design by Lynn Fischer

PUBIS ANGELICAL

PART I

I

STREAKS OF MOONLIGHT filtered through the curtain's lace toward the satin pillow, which soaked them up. The hand of the new bride, beside her dark hair, offered its palm up defenselessly. Her sleep appeared serene.

Then the palm suddenly clenched, not so the perfect face, which remained relaxed, made up in cosmetics from rose to blue. Minutes after, the most beautiful woman in the world sat up, trembling with fear. The face recovered expression. The natural eyelashes, so long and arched that they appeared false, shaded eyes inordinately wide open. In her dreams she had just met a grotesquely fat doctor dressed in formal attire who hung up his top hat, proceeded to put on white rubber gloves, then came toward her as she lay stretched out on gigantic wads of cotton, and with a scalpel began to cut open her chest, revealing—instead of a heart—complex clockwork like machinery. It was a mechanical doll, and a broken one, not a sick woman, who lay there possibly dying.

A deep sigh of relief concluded the nightmare. There was nothing to fear, all those perils had proven imaginary. She looked around her, everything was new to her in the darkened room, the wedding night hadn't yet given way to dawn, but by her side there was no one. Near one hand lay a mirror with a filigreed silver handle, her lips reflected back painted, as if they'd been touched up only moments before. She remembered almost nothing, a toast with her husband, his graying temples, or were they white? the monocle scrutinizing her every move, a square cup that she hadn't known how to grasp, the cool nectar, nothing more. If her makeup was intact it was because her face had been respected.

She decided to run her right hand along the rest of her body, stretched it out and pulled it back almost immediately. Her left hand, less sensitive, seemed to her better suited for such inspection. Very soon she found a patch of skin that burned, just above the collarbone. On a breast, three or four teethmarks in an arch, which by now almost didn't hurt. Her stomach, by contrast, betrayed no signs of an assault, her lower abdomen yes, wet, inflamed, with a tear deep within.

She tried to remember, the only thing that came to mind was the coolness of those sips, a drink new to her. Her eyes searched the room for the square cup but it was nowhere to be found. She tried to walk, but in so doing roused the stinging between her inner thighs. The mink rug warmed the soles of her feet, the iron structure imprisoning the Venetian glass was profiled through the curtain of flowered lace. She pulled open the curtains, turned with difficulty the heavy latch on the picture window, its cylindrical nerved shape shocked her. She leaned out over the balcony. The park reservoir, a very long rectangle perpendicular to the balcony, dissolved in the darkness and the fog; groves of trees ran along either side, their defenseless branches manipulated by the wind, however gently. Not one of the many caretakers was in sight, nor were the contours of the island, curiously carefully camouflaged by the hazy mist on the water. Suddenly the motor of a launch was heard, the ignition was dry and determined, within a few minutes the noise faded in the distance.

She turned back toward the room. The headboard on the bed, of carved multicolored wood, finished as clouds and floating angels. One of them, with a strange look, like a fish, seemed to watch the Mistress. She stared back at him. The angel seemed to blink, its eyelids lowered and raised up again, or so it seemed to the Mistress. Was someone spying on her? She glanced away and soon discovered a note on the ermine stool, "My dear: my business affairs reclaim me, I didn't tell you because you would have persuaded me to stay. I narcotized you because, if your eyes had been watching me, I wouldn't have dared do to you what I have done. Your beauty intimidates me so! I feared that you would paralyze me, that's why I couldn't accept at the same time the challenge of your intellect, as supernatural as your body. Lovingly at your feet, your husband."

A few hours later, the sun passed between those drapes imprudently drawn, and woke her once again. Nothing had been explained to her, how could she summon the servants?, she saw no buttons to push, although she did see a porcelain telephone resting on golden feet, without a dial, but with an earpiece and mouthpiece also made of gold. The voice of an older woman immediately answered. The new Mistress asked the time, scarcely eight o'clock on a spring morning in 1936. She ordered breakfast, tea with lemon, butterless and crisp toast. She was told that it was impossible for a tray to be brought to her room, the Master had ordered that she be served more appropriately in the Breakfast Pavilion. The Mistress responded that she had no desire to go downstairs. The servant limited herself to adding only that the Master had left precise and final instructions as to how her welcome should be made, for she was no doubt tired, having arrived only the previous night, after the wedding ceremony in Vienna. All had been very carefully planned by the Master to provide the maximum pleasure to his wife and, the servant insinuated, any interference would imply grave disdain.

A whimsical minibanister finished off the dome of the pavilion, it was what least impressed her, at first sight. Above the entryway of ashen marble, clouds drifted yet again with angels encircling a saint, all in white stucco. The angels revered the saint, protected her, played instruments for her, sang to her. None of them had fish eyes, and none looked at the Mistress. Next she was offered her choice either of the corner near the rose bushes, if she preferred to be in the sun, or . . . She agreed immediately, the rose bushes. The Mistress noticed that all the lackeys were quite old. And when the tea moistened her lips, at that very moment the sound of flutes and harps issued forth from the lawns. The shepherd musicians, invisible or concealed, gently soothed the beauty's anxiety, they gave her the strength to get up and begin her first tour of the island. It was flat, a few kilometers in circumference, she could encompass it in a single walk, it would be easy to discover the best route of escape. The tea hadn't quenched her thirst.

The melody grew distant as the Mistress approached the railing, marking the bounds between the park and the shore of the lake. But soon she heard the rapid steps of a seemingly young maid. "Are you the only one under seventy in this house?" The answer was yes. "And why have they made such an exception?" The answer was that they had needed someone who would be able to follow her without getting tired, in the event that she was disposed to take long walks. As she hinted a motion toward the fence, the Mistress was stopped brusquely. "Halt! . . . pardon my manners, but the iron is electrified." The fence repeated the same decorative motif—titanic arms and serpents—along its entire length, the oval perimeter of the island. It had been built recently, while the rest dated from the eighteenth century. The Mistress hated those bars, as she had always hated—without knowing why—the works of Viennese artists from the turn of the century, with their obsession for straight parallel lines, for cages. Those vertical irons feigned parallel serpents, one with a head facing up, the next facing down, all with their mouths furiously open and their tongues stiff; the horizontal lines, by contrast, were a chain of knotted arms, each taking hold of another, depicting a clutching and apparently hopeless gesture: the serpents were piercing them. The Mistress raised her eyes to the sky, she couldn't tolerate the sight of that fence. Near the sun, strange clouds changed shape with unusual rapidity. They appeared to suggest letters, a message.

The Mistress curtailed her walk, she ran toward the manor house, panting, scared. The servant followed her effortlessly, taking long strides, and stepped before her, almost closing off the path. The Mistress, desperate, looked up again toward those peculiar clouds, the message could be intended for her. The servant shifted half a step and blocked the clouds with her head. The Mistress looked at her face for the first time, the brows were thick and dark, and the eyes? The nostrils were exceedingly sharp for a woman, beneath the cover of powder the skin was no more smooth than that of a man recently shaven, "Not that way, honorable madam and admired actress, this other is the principal entrance." The Mistress answered that she was no longer a movie star. "Forgive me, it's that I admired you greatly on the screen. I saw those three films where the lead was played so brilliantly by Madam." The Mistress responded that those movies no longer existed, her husband had ordered that the negatives and copies be burned, mentioning them thus was the equivalent of lying, because no one in the world could now prove that they'd ever existed. The servant dared insist, "One will always remain engraved in my memory, where you played a woman reincarnated into another, both with mechanical hearts." "Such a film doesn't exist," the Mistress responded sincerely, "it was never shot, you're confused, this is the first time I've heard that story." When the Mistress ceased to observe her, the servant lifted her gaze from the ground and showed her eyes.

The morning light was restoring cheer to the façade of the main building, a suitable backdrop for a comedy of intrigue. The Mistress whimpered nervously, but without tears and without modesty. In effect, the typical rococo front was resolved jovially, a flat yellow wall from which protruded white door and window frames, and embracing the balcony on the third and last floor was a relief also in white portraying a cloud where more heavenly creatures floated. The Mistress examined the angels, one by one, searching for a sign of compassion, of protection. The angels didn't look at the strange but real clouds which at that moment cut through the sky, they looked only at one another, with expressions invariably beatific. "At times there are angels that don't look benevolent, aren't there? Also . . . I don't know your name," the Mistress said, trying to conceal her fears. Thea answered that all angels were good, and they defended good causes, but they proved implacable in their struggle against evil, "Whoever feels certain to be on the side of goodness has no reason to fear them." The Mistress climbed the five steps which gave access to the central entrance, from there she noticed the pier, through the electrified fence. Thea pointed toward another cardinal point, this time the north, where an unusual structure of iron and glass threatened the

Mistress, "It's the Winter Garden, Madam. Inside you'll be able to admire the most fabulous acclimated palm trees."

At last she took refuge in her room, she was exhausted by her short excursion. She no longer remembered the peculiar episode with the clouds, she felt only thirst. Immediately she descried the square cup on the malachite table. Inlaid precious stones—two or three turquoises, one amethyst, topazes—imprisoned in their settings of wrought silver, and within the heavy crystal, taking on the shape of its vessel, the fragrant amber liquid. A delicious and refreshing liquid, but without form, the square cup was there to lend it that, and in doing so imprisoned it. The Mistress took pity on the liquid and with a single swallow allowed it to become part of herself. A delicious and refreshing sleep descended on her lids.

When she was able to reopen them, the shadows of dusk had begun to cover the island. She stretched out an arm of the purest white, with blue veins delicately visible, and lifted the earpiece of the telephone. She asked to speak to Thea. "I'm sorry, Madam, but as the day draws toward evening the doors of this house are shut, you must wait until tomorrow to visit the Winter Garden. Given the difficulty of establishing total vigilance in the park at night, the Master has ordered that Madam his wife not take risks with unnecessary strolls in the dark."

All insistence was in vain. As she sat up she saw that on the malachite table someone had set small dishes with exquisite cold foods, reserving the center for a large jar of a liquid identical to that in the square cup. Hunger stirred her rapidly to consume caviar, smoked salmon, Provençal biscuits, followed by long draughts of the only beverage capable of cooling her thirst on that island. She soon fell back into her pleasant intoxication. She looked around her, she knew she would soon fall asleep, inexorably, and she asked herself what life would bring during the mysterious hours of night. She concentrated all her strength on an effort not to look at the headboard on her bed, she feared she would encounter that angel's hostile look and that it would be the last thing she'd see on her first wedded day. She lay down and tightened her eyelids, but an instant before she fell asleep, her memory

sharply reconstructed the image of fish eyes closing their lids and
opening them up again.

—I never felt alone in my life.
—It's only natural, you're far from home, Mexico is very differ-
ent, and that has to affect you.
—No, before I didn't care about being alone, on the contrary,
in those last years in Buenos Aires all I wanted was to be alone.
—When I got home they gave me your message. And I came
right away.
—Don't be scared, Beatriz, it's nothing terrible.
—I'm not scared. But what was so urgent?
—Nothing. Or I should say, I felt very depressed because I lost
confidence in this doctor, I wish I could move to another hospital.
—Ana, you've got to really think that through, if they operated
on you here you're already in their hands.
—You bet I'm in their hands.
—I mean that they're the ones who know your case the best.
—Please forgive me for calling you in such a panic, but at that
moment I had a fit of desperation.
—What brought that on?
—Beatriz, it's that they don't pay any attention to me, this
place is really expensive and they treat me as if they were doing
me a favor.
—Before you weren't so nervous, and that's bad for your conva-
lescence.
—It's that these nurses are always so busy, they never have a
free minute when I call them.
—. . .
—They don't have any patience with me.
—Everybody's on edge these days, with so much rain . . . the
season should have finished already.
—Really? . . .
—And it could be depressing you too, this weather.
—When I arrived last year it was the rainy season. But that
doesn't depress me, on the contrary, I just content myself with

being indoors if it rains. I wouldn't care if it rained through to the end of this damned '75.

—. . .

—Can you stay a while, or are you really rushed?

—No, Anita, I already told you that I can stay. But there's something that you want to tell me, and you're avoiding the subject.

—Beatriz, I'm ashamed to be wasting your time, as busy as you are. I swear to you I was never such a bother before.

—Tell me the whole thing.

—It isn't easy, I'm afraid your guess was right. I've had bad news from Argentina. But I also have to talk to the doctor, I think he doesn't know what to do with me and that's why he doesn't show his face.

—. . .

—He comes every day, but he leaves right away, and he doesn't answer everything I ask him. The thing about the sedative, for example. They give it to me every night and it feels strange, I don't think it's having a good effect on me.

—And what did he say?

—I suggested discontinuing the sedative, and waiting for the pain to come before giving me the shots, why so much sedation? . . . And he answered that it's the only one that's slow acting, because if we waited for the pain they'd have to give me a sedative with really fast results, which has bad side effects.

—And couldn't he be right?

—He's unconvincing. Because with every dose I feel worse, I feel like my head's not my own. And later I asked him what about the radiation, and he gave me a strange look.

—Couldn't it be that you're just too distrusting?

—Beatriz, everyone who's operated for a tumor gets radiation afterward, as a precaution.

—Not everyone, I don't believe that.

—That's what he said, but not with too much confidence. And he made a joke that I'd better count the Argentine pesos that I had left, because they wouldn't be enough for more. And it's always like that, as if they don't really know what to do with me.

—But it's good that they're keeping you for a while under observation.

—Another doctor might have discharged me. What would you do, if you were me?

—Ana, I don't want to meddle, but if you don't tell me what happened with that friend of yours who arrived from Argentina, I'll be completely out of it. Before he showed up, you were much calmer.

—Even before he came, I was starting to feel funny.

—But with his arrival you felt even worse.

—It's Pozzi, Juan José, the one I had told you about.

—You told me about someone very rich, and who used to give you a lot of presents in Buenos Aires. But who caused problems later on.

—No, it's not that one.

—Don't tell me that the one who arrived was your husband.

—No, God forbid. Then I really would die of horror. Also my husband has my name.

—You mean that you have his name.

—Of course. But Pozzi is the only one I spoke well of, the lawyer. For the sake of what you most cherish in this world, I beg of you not to tell anyone. That he's here.

—Don't worry about that.

—What I can't tell you is what he came to say to me.

—And what about you, weren't you happy to see him?

—No. Because he didn't make the trip to see me. He came to ask me for something, which I can't tell you about. In any case I didn't like the fact that he arrived without warning. I wasn't wearing any makeup.

—Ana, you're being so mysterious today.

—Not at all. . . . Give me your hand. . . . Really, you don't know how much I needed you to come.

—. . .

—Beatriz, could it be that I've only known jerks in my life? All the men who have come near me have been like that.

—But you do say that this Pozzi is a good man.

—Yes, he has many fine qualities . . . but the man that one needs . . . is another thing.

—What man, Ana?

—A man, not a child.

—Then I'm getting him confused with another. Wasn't Pozzi the one who defended political prisoners?

—Yes.

—Didn't you always tell me that he was very brave, that he was always taking risks?

—With me he wasn't very brave, he would never tell me the truth.

—. . .

—And I wasn't very important to him, that wife of his, and his sons, were much more important.

—What kind of man were you hoping for?

—Beatriz, you feminists are all alike, you're impossible to talk to.

—. . .

—Isn't it possible sometimes to fantasize a little . . . about a superior man?

—Superior to whom?

—Superior to the others. Superior to me.

—. . .

—I'm not that great . . .

—If you don't think you're that great, how can you go after someone who is that great? So he can throw it in your face?

—So he can throw what in my face?

—That you're a person who's inferior to him.

—No, nothing like that, and I think I see more clearly now what I'm trying to say. Listen to me, Beatriz . . . couldn't there be something positive in admiring the man who's at your side?

—I don't know what you're getting at.

—Yes, look. . . . If I have beside me someone superior, that could serve as an incentive, couldn't it?

—Yes, perhaps. . . . But you know how couples generally get together. If a man goes after a woman who's in some way inferior, it's because he likes it that way . . . am I making myself clear? I mean that he likes her because she's inferior, and not because he sees other possibilities in her, for self-improvement.

—You're very pessimistic.

—Ana, you must excuse me, but I've at least got to know if he came to ask you, how shall I put it? something having to do with things between the two of you. Whether he wants to get divorced and marry you, for example.

—No, he came because of things having to do with him. Beatriz . . . please be a little more patient with me, today.

—Whatever you say. . . . Did he at least bring you news from your mother?

—No, he doesn't know her.

—You never told me why she didn't come, for your operation.

—I didn't want her to.

—Wouldn't it help to have her here?

—Beatriz, let's not change the subject. I want to tell you something, all kidding aside. But I beg of you, please, don't use it against me later.

—What is it?

—Beatriz, the only thing that makes me want to keep living . . . is to think that one day I'm going to find a man who'll be worth my time.

—. . .

—Why are you quiet?

—What's the point of my talking, if you know what I think?

—Of course, you've got everything in life. A good husband, wonderful children, a job you like, why would you need to fantasize?

—On the contrary, I would like to fantasize a little, but I don't have the time! Look, today the whole morning spent with the lawyers in the case of the maid who was raped. Which our movement is defending, to establish a precedent. And it's like that every day.

—But that makes you feel good.

—Ana, the next time you feel like chatting, I'll come. But don't call me sounding so urgent like today, because you scare me for no reason.

—I really am sorry, but when I called you I felt bad. I really did.

—And now that I'm here, you don't want to talk.

—Yes, I do want to talk.

—But you ask my advice and I can't give you an opinion. You conceal everything, I haven't even gotten you to tell me why you left Argentina.

—Please, not today, I feel much better and if I start talking about those things I'm going to feel bad all over again. I'll tell you another day. . . . There's something . . . very serious, I admit. But that's all I can tell you in advance. You see, Pozzi sometimes exaggerates, I don't know if I should pay any attention to him or not.

—. . .

—According to him, something very important depends on me.

—. . .

—What can happen to someone very important, I should say.

—. . .

—Someone's life. But those are stories of Pozzi's.

—What's that about?

—Another time I'll explain it all to you. Today I feel a little weak, but I have no headache. So please don't spoil my afternoon.

2

IT NEVER OCCURRED to me to write a diary. Who knows why. It's probably that I've never had the time, even though for thinking, yes, I think all day long. The truth is that I'm a person, or a woman, which may not fit into the person category, who spends the whole day thinking and thinking. I do nothing but reflect the whole day, but, yes, I do that while doing something else. I don't believe everyone is like this, no, impossible. For example, if I'm picking out an apple at the supermarket, how can I put it, I'm giving it tremendous importance, as if this apple, as it's served on a silver fruit dish, or as a particular guest takes a bite of it, or as I myself digest it, could change the course of a life, or of two lives. And not to mention that moment of choosing between a handkerchief that's plain blue and one that's sky blue, well, there you're toying with the fate of all humanity. Mania for metaphysics? or boring, foolish superstition?

I used to sort of enjoy being at the mercy of these tricks of fate, but in these last few weeks they've begun to irritate me. Or maybe I'm irritating myself with so much danger. Already almost five weeks in bed. Why is it that odd numbers frighten me? I must be starting this diary for some specific reason, but I can't think of what it is.

I had to interrupt this a minute, the wind suddenly blew really hard through the window and these loose pages went flying. I could use a notebook, that would be more practical. And I called the nurse to ask her to get me those pages and she came in when I had counted up to twenty-four, which is a multiple of two, of four, and of six, so surely this diary is starting off well. Meanwhile, why this feeling that even numbers bring better luck?

But let's go back to the reason for this diary. Wait a minute, why do I say let's? could it be that I'm not alone perhaps? or is this diary an excuse to tell things to someone? who could it be? or am I talking to myself? am I splitting in two? which part of me is talking to which other part? The truth is that this plural irritates me, "it makes me fat," as they say here in Mexico when something is annoying them—that plural. In Argentina we would say it swells me up, meaning the same in slang. We would say, plural again. It seems to me that I'm hiding something from myself, my wish to speak to someone that I really, though I think and I think, I don't know who it is. Maybe Papa, if he were still alive. Not Mama, because I know perfectly well what she'd say about everything. According to her a woman has problems because she wants, she pretends to be a man and not a woman. To be caring for my daughter, to be waiting every night for my husband to come home, now, back in Buenos Aires.

And how right she is, that's the mistake, not accepting our position as women, as sentimental dolls, what can we do? But why so much trembling of the heart? Oh, how tedious, being so sensitive, or so oversentimental. Why not be made of stone, like men are. But it's futile to try to imitate them. We have to resign ourselves to envying them. Me and the others, we have to, and once more the plural tense. But it's not another woman that I want to talk to, because I know what they would say. It has to be to a man. If I really need to talk to someone, it would be because I can't predict the other person's reaction, because I'm intrigued by the response, isn't it?

It can't be Pozzi. I know him so well that I'd dare anticipate all his reactions. It must be Papa I want to talk to. When he died the world was so different, I think he would have been amused by that whole circus of my divorce. A circus, another Mexican expression, I've picked up so many, just having been here a year. In Argentina I would have said something else. That mess, or that tangle, or that bind. I like to say circus. It's a positive word, a circus has color, gaiety, emotion. I like so many things about Mexico. The accent. The tequila. Too bad you never know what those guys are really thinking about. Mystery. Or "misstory," as that little old lady used to say as a joke, imitating that comedian on the radio. I was so little and when she said "misstory" I would die laughing. How I loved her, but she didn't come to the house too often, she was the aunt of that really kind maid. How wonderful it was to like somebody so much, I felt it in my chest, this affection, I was full of that little warmth in my chest when I saw her, I carried in my chest, I don't know, a warmth, a chest full of roasted chestnuts? or muffins recently baked, I don't know, something that would be a treat for her, and that I knew she would like a lot. Is it for her that I'm writing all this? No, what a delusion, poor old lady, she wouldn't understand a word of it.

Maybe what I want is to be a little girl again, and to talk to her as I did then. Could it be that? I don't think so, no, I'm absolutely sure. I wouldn't enjoy being a little girl again. If there's something I do enjoy, it's dealing with a woman's problems but already with some experience, as bad as it may have been. No, how boring to be little again, and still not know anything. But how I do want to love intensely, as I did then.

I can't even love myself this way. Myself least of all, because first of all it's me I'm fed up with, of reactions already hyper-known, but then why am I jotting them down? Yes, I must admit it, one possible reason is fear, I write so as not to think that I could die. And how curious, now I didn't say we could die.

What's undeniable is that sometimes I feel I have to use the plural, so it's with someone that I'm trying to establish some contact. With my previous incarnation? a woman who was in her peak in the Twenties, let's say. But we're back to the very same thing, it would be useless to tell all this to a woman from another era, so different. And why not? That must have been a good time to be a woman, between the wars. How wonderful to be mysterious, languorous, stylized.

I already know what Beatriz would say: stylized, mysterious, languorous objects! to the point of yawning. But Beatriz, how mysterious anyway that existence would have been, living for themselves, lost in their own beauty. Objects, but precious objects. A figurine, a *potiche*. Although those names really sound funny now. How they used to impress me before. Now because of the fact that they're objects, like us poor women, they already bore me. Or do I pity them? Yet we're like that, it's useless to try to change us. But it has to be acknowledged that it's fine to be always taking care of ourselves, and making ourselves pretty, because it's so much fun to see someone get worked up over you. Of course, that rules out the ugly ones, that's why they bother with feminism. Now that I think about it, I really would like to talk to a woman from that period.

But no, I don't think so, I think it's Papa I'd like to talk to. But what a fruitless endeavor. Isn't it? Let's see, why this need? Of course it must have to do with what Papa represented for me. Yes, because I don't really know what he was like. To me he seemed so wise, so just, so calm, but on the other hand that someone like Mama could have made him happy makes me wonder. How could he have liked a woman who said yes to everything, whether or not he was right? For that purpose it would be better to have a little dog, or an Angora cat, meek and false to the bone. That seventh of November in '59 when he died I hadn't even turned fifteen, every time I told him that for all my friends at the party for their fifteenth birthdays, their fathers led them out for the first waltz, he would take the pipe out of his mouth and looking away he would move it to signal no. It seemed ridiculous to him, theatrical, this waltz. Maybe it was because he didn't know how to dance. I'm going to ask Mama in my next letter.

And to think that in a few years when my daughter has that party for her fifteenth birthday, her father will be delighted to dance with her. What a conventional man. I really had my fill of him. He was such bad news. Everything that has to do with him succeeds in annoying me. And what a relief to know he's thousands of miles away. If on top of this nuisance of an illness I had to add the disgust of seeing him entering the hospital and playing the role of concerned ex-husband . . . oh, what a ghastly character, always playing his role, why does he give the impression that he's performing on a stage? he's like an actor who performs well but who doesn't appear natural, there's something strange about Fito, he always has to show people everything he's feeling. And I don't think he feels anything. Nothing, that's what he's feeling!

If Papa had been alive he wouldn't have let me make a mistake like that. Who knows. Fito had his strong points. So dependable, so protective, so willful, so very, oh so very sexy. And so organized, how awful those Capricorns are. So strong, so enduring, of course, because ever since he was born he's lived—I think—stuck inside this armor, where even bullets can't reach him. And what's this armor made of? Who knows, but, ah, now I know, it's like a dead man's coffin. And that's why he feels nothing, because he's dead. And in his casket he's alone and quite comfortable. And for all the boasting he does that he's all emotion. He doesn't feel any-thing, except for his daughter. Yes, he does love Clarita, I have to admit it. That's true about him. If anything happens to Clarita he's despondent, he exists to please his daughter. So how can I say that he's a guy without feelings? He could turn around and say that about me then, because I never think about Clarita. I don't even remember her. And I'm supposed to be her mother. What right do I have then to talk about feelings?

Thursday. I continue today. That really tall blonde in high school used to tell me that her father fell apart when she brought home her first suitor. The father acted like someone possessed. He treated the boy like dirt, as if he was a thief who had broken into the house, and afterward the old man didn't talk to her for days. At home Mama couldn't sleep for weeks, when she found out that a boy waited for me outside the high school door and we then spent the hour together until my class at the conservatory. She lived in dread that he would do something to me, that he'd secretly slip a little pill into my Coca-Cola, to "excite" me, as she used to put it. During that time there was a lot of talk about those little pills. Aphrodisiacs. It's been years since anyone's mentioned them, I wonder if they ever really existed? That's another thing I want to ask the doctor.

Papa didn't live to meet any of my suitors. How would he have reacted? There she is, as Beatriz says, the main ornament of the house, with the little soul of an Angora cat, among silk pillows, until the day that someone comes and presents his intentions to take her to another house. But no, how unfair I'm being, how exaggerated, I'm letting myself be influenced by Beatriz even if I don't want to be. The truth is that those parents were delighted that their daughters were getting married. What they didn't want was for those flings to prevent their daughters from finishing their studies, so they'd be better able to fend for themselves in life, not depend so much on a husband. This is a good argument to take up with Beatriz.

Today Saturday the ninth. I take up these pages again, without any interest in reading what I've already written. I'm scared. Of what? Of seeming even more foolish than I am. I forgot to order the notebook. Fito. How I'd like to tell him off to his face. But when I had him in front of me I could never get up the courage to tell him what I thought of him. It wasn't because of fear, why was it that I kept quiet? I think I got that tumor from pent-up rage. What I don't know is if they brought him before me now, would I have the nerve to tell him what I think or not? According to him, the divorce was a step backward for me. I'd like to set the record straight, here on this piece of paper, the fact that it was a stage in my evolution. Because there were clear steps forward in all of this. And I want to list them. I don't want useless doubts. Those doubts waste time, they mix me up, they don't let me think. But where do I start, that's the question. The main point, when was it that he made me accept the fact that he would give the orders in the house? No, he made me accept something else, that it was more practical for him to give the orders.

I get furious just thinking about it. What a repulsive guy! Of course it's more practical that the man run the show in the house, because he's more stable, more rational than the woman. But on the other hand, he should be a lot better than a dope like Fito. A man, a real one. Will I ever have a real man sometime in my life? There was no one before Fito, only young boyfriends in high school. He was just finishing engineering, "What does it matter that you won't earn money with a Bachelor of Arts degree, I'll bring home the bacon, and if you want to finish your studies, finish them, but I don't want to wait anymore before we get

married." Then the first wrong step: I chose a career that didn't
pay, no, even worse, two of them! Arts & Letters and the piano,
but that was to please Papa. A career in Arts doesn't pay, of
course, not enough to maintain the style of life I was accustomed
to: two servants, season tickets to the opera, summering for three
months at the shore. The first wrong step, the wrong profession.
Or was I wrong in thinking that that standard of living was so
essential? Yes, it was essential, I was used to that. And he could
give it to me. And also I liked his looks so much. So much. And
the necking, and the French kisses, he would graze me with his
mustache. But stop right there, because he wasn't getting any
further.

Thinking it through, even if I hadn't been used to such com-
forts at home, I would still have fallen into Fito's trap. I would
have accepted whatever condition—matrimonial, of course—he
had imposed. Because I was so horny for him I was dying. Then
. . . my first bad step was not getting over that thing for him,
freely, to cool that fever inside me, to subdue it to a reasonable
degree. And only then to try to see him as he really was, to know
him! not imagining him inside my head, that he had all the virtues
in the world.

But that's not true. It's all Beatriz's influence. It's futile to try
to pass for something I'm not. Why do I write this diary, then?
To tell the truth, I think. If I start by lying to myself I'm not going
to get anywhere. What I've liked best in my life was necking with
Fito. It was what was most exciting and enjoyable. And those first
months of marriage. Then I'm not so sure I could have gotten rid
of that longing beforehand. Our wedding night, and everything
leading up to that, the marriage all in white, was like a dream.
That afterward everything got spoiled doesn't mean I should
forget how wonderful it was at the beginning, it would be unfair
on my part. When I was single it was heaven to get excited with
Fito at Mama's house, to the point of not bearing it any more,
and, after he'd leave, to stay there alone imagining what awaited
me in marriage. Alone in my little bed figuring out the pleasures
of love. And later the reality surpassed everything. Too bad it was

only for such a short while. I should content myself with that memory, nobody can take that away from me! If it had only lasted longer . . .

What awful fate! Wretched, as they say here. How would you say it in Argentina? moronic? but moronic is the opposite of smart, which is what all Argentines want to be. On the other hand wretched is to be miserable, poor. Now that I think about it, poor is what no Mexican wants to be. And it'll sound quite foolish but I'd like to believe in something the way I used to believe in love, in how good love was going to be for me. What an imagination I had then, when I was single. Well, now too, but for ugly things, to frighten myself. To imagine wonderful things, not any more. Yes, I hit the nail on the head with that, what burned out in me was that little lamp, because to want something so badly, to yearn for something, to fight for it, you've got to believe blindly in it. Well, that's what they say, to believe, but to believe in something that isn't reality yet, well, that's not believing, that's dreaming. Well, it's not dreaming either, that, that's another thing. What is it? Well, it should be . . . to be capable of imagining something. I used to be capable of imagining sensational things. Not any more. It's not that I don't want to. It's that my imagination won't do.

But I'm getting off the subject, what I want to talk about are those bad steps. We left off with that, all things considered, the first one hadn't been not having relations before I got married. What could the first one have been, then? Oh, I'm a little tired. Better to continue tomorrow. I like to feel tired, from having written so much. It makes me feel that I've earned my sleep, like when I used to work. How wonderful that was. I'd like to remember that time, but I haven't quite gotten up there yet, that comes later, I'm going to sleep.

Sunday. On the subject of bad steps, I think what I wrote yesterday may not be true, that I needed so many things to live, so much money. I could have lived with less, teaching some course in a high school would have been enough. Let's see . . . without a daughter, without having to support parents, what would have been enough to get by? To have a little apartment where I could live quietly, that's all, the way I did after I was separated. With neither a car nor special vacations. Nor the bother of expensive clothes. I had such a good figure. I'm sure I won't still look that way, after this aggravation of an illness. Just at such a delicate age, on the cusp of those terrible thirties. But maybe they won't be so terrible. On the contrary, it's when you begin to know what it is you want.

Oh, let me jot it down before I forget. Last night before I fell asleep, I realized what was the exact moment when I broke away from Fito. Because within a few months of being married I started to wake up with a headache, and I didn't know what could have made me ill, some food, I'd rack my brains thinking of what it could have been. And one day I noticed that the pain came in the morning if the night before I'd been forced to give a dinner party at home, because Fito had said we should invite some executive and his wife. Fito was convinced that it would be smart to invite the president of such and such a company, the manager of that other one, etc., etc. One day, unforgettable, he showed me a list that he'd made, with the names of important executives from the entire Republic. He was no longer satisfied simply with those in Buenos Aires. His plan was to include all of it, to be on good terms with the entire country. I almost fainted reading the list, it had been typed up by his secretary, placed in a folder with the title Mr. and Mrs. Lucarelli. And he got his way, now everyone respects him, and he's at the top of his field.

And that day we had our first fight, our first serious discussion. He forbade me from complaining about the stupidity of our guests, executives and consorts. I couldn't believe my ears, why did it offend him so much that I criticized those people? wasn't it all just a business tactic and nothing more? how ugly that is, the first time that it happens, shut up there in the bedroom, like in a boxing ring, or worse, a Roman arena, with the beast there in front of you, which at last bares its fangs. For years I asked myself why he had gotten so angry that day.

Mama gave me one explanation, at the time of the separation proceedings. According to her, if he had identified with those stupid guests, he had every reason, because he was just like them. She really made me furious because she told me that in his defense, blaming me for breaking up a home without any reason. According to Mama, he was the same as the others, and I was the one who was different, or who tried to be different, but who deep down really wasn't because I liked to live well. And according to her he had never deceived me, he had always been that way, and now I had to resign myself, because perfect husbands didn't exist. Sad, because I'd imagined him so different. And as bad as things were I allowed Clarita to be born. I imagined that this way everything would get straightened out. I imagined it so pretty, how it would be with a baby in the house.

I was interrupted because Beatriz stopped by. The thought that occurred to her, seeing me with my hair parted in the middle and loose on my shoulders, she said what no one had told me for many years. That I looked like Hedy Lamarr. It's been so long since I've seen photographs of her, as a little girl they always used to tell me that, of course now she doesn't act anymore and people don't remember. With all those stories that her husband had locked her up. Beatriz said her case should be carefully examined, because though married to one of the richest men in the world, she still chose to run away from home to make her movie career. One of the most stunning-looking actresses that ever was if not the most stunning of all. Would she still be so? I'd like to see a photo of her now, it could give me an idea of how I'm going to look at her age. Before I used to dread thinking of myself as an old woman. Not now. Who knows why one changes. Let birthdays come, let them pile up. I don't want to die young. When will they discharge me? why am I taking so long to get better? will there come a day when I'll get better?

Monday. I'm mustering up my courage. I just read what I've written. Before anything else I promise never to get dramatic again because it'll end up badly that way, if I'm keeping this diary it's so as not to get depressed. Afterward I had to laugh in spite of myself: it turns out I proposed to make very clear the stages of my evolution. What evolution am I talking about? If I took any step it was backwards, like a crab. Fito would be pleased. But stay tuned, maybe I am beginning to straighten out this whole puzzle for myself.

Well, today I'm not going to ramble on. Clarita. If something were to happen to me she'd be left entirely at the mercy of her father. I was wrong to leave her with him, I was wrong to let him inculcate her with all his foolishness. Clarita loves him, but when she grows up who knows whether she'll notice how shallow he is, poor guy. Maybe she'll turn out just like him. Anyway it's him she loves, not me, the kid doesn't love me, I didn't know how to win her over. Nor did I want to. Let's be honest. And once again with a plural, who is it that I would want to be talking to? I have to know!

Tuesday. I have a little while before Pozzi arrives. I'll have to be quite direct with him. Sad, today I wanted to deal only with pleasant thoughts. And it's going to be exactly the opposite. But when he leaves I'm going to make a list of lovely things, if I still have the strength. In the first place the year '71, how well it went for me after the divorce when I finally began to work. And later, about Pozzi, but only the good points. And what other things happened to me that were one hundred percent good? nothing more? I can't even remember who it was that told me you've got to make lists of all the wonderful things that have happened to you so you don't forget them, because human beings tend to remember only the bad ones. I want to put down everything in the year '71, from the appointment to the Teatro Colón of my instructor at the Music Conservatory. The invitation to work with him. The work, the enthusiasm, the most wonderful thing in the world. The whole day in the theater. Organizing more and more events, the lower-priced performances! If I could arrange it two thousand people would be able to see an opera sung divinely instead of three hundred. Which was much more gratifying (I picked up that expression from Pozzi) than sitting with Fito at mealtime. The separation. Pozzi. Juan José Pozzi once a week. My daughter twice a week. Oh, if only I could get that same job in Mexico. I want to do lovely things, I want to get well, I want to work. Once on my feet no one can stop me this time. It can't be that I'd have such bad luck that, I don't know, another boulder would cut across my path. It's frightening to think about certain things, the devil for example, even if one doesn't believe. Having to leave everything, country, friends, because the devil crosses your path.

—The truth is that since the day you showed up here, I haven't felt too good.

—Because you were frightened by what I said to you . . . but you're wrong, Ana, very wrong, to be frightened.

—How can you expect me not to be frightened? Starting with the fact that that man terrifies me, get it? terrifies me.

—Alejandro doesn't mean you . . .

—Don't utter that name in front of me!

—He can't do anything to you, now. You call him, you tell him the truth, that you're hospitalized, that they've removed a tumor, that you're scared you won't get well.

—Which isn't true, the doctors all say that there isn't the slightest danger.

—But what does that matter, you could be scared just the same. The point is that he would come to see you immediately, if he knew you wanted to see him again.

—You, Pozzi, what do you know? He could be with another woman now.

—We have all that well researched. He still has photos of you at his house, at the office, and he doesn't know any other woman. He's entirely devoted to his job and nothing else.

—I don't believe he would come from Buenos Aires, just because I called him.

—We're all sure that he would, you know very well that he was madly in love with you.

—And at what point would you kidnap him?

—A few days after he arrives.

—Not right away?

—No, because then one could suspect you.

—Then I would have to see him.

—Once . . . or twice.

—Impossible.

—We wouldn't lay a hand on him. What we want is to exchange him for our friend.

—They would come to suspect me, inevitably.

—No. Not necessarily.

—But they would question me, that's for sure.

—And you would tell them the truth. He was a friend of yours, a suitor, and you phoned him to tell him about your illness. The truth. Because that's the key, all you have to say to him is that you feel sick, not that he should come. You do it like this: you call him and you tell him that you're sick . . . and without the support of friends, of family. Little by little you tell him. That you need to talk to a friend. And then he's going to say that he's coming to see you.

—And what if he doesn't say it?

—Of course he will. You certainly don't have to ask him to come. Let him say it. Then you answer that no, he shouldn't come. And he will.

—And what if things get complicated? I despise him with every bit of strength that I have, or that's left in me, but I don't want anything to happen to him either. Anything serious, like that he'd be killed.

—Nothing's going to happen to him. We will promise you one thing, and I say this very much in earnest: if the exchange doesn't take place, if something doesn't work, we'll let him go free.

—That's what you say, but how about your other . . . associates? or I don't know what the word is, that you use among yourselves.

—Associates is fine.

—And you, Pozzi, couldn't you think of anything better than to get me involved in this mess?

—If you want to know something, it wasn't my idea.

—But you gave them free rein in the matter.

—Don't think ill of me.

—. . .

—Anita. This way we could recover someone very valuable.

—Don't say we, I don't even know who it is nor are you willing to tell me. You know that I don't understand too much about politics. When I left Argentina it was because of something else. But it was a personal matter, I never got involved in politics and never will. Because I don't understand it.

—By rejecting that guy you already got involved in politics.

—What does that have to do . . .

—. . .

—Did you call Beatriz?

—No.

—She's a really good person, you'd like her.

—I'm not really in the mood to see people.

—And did you go to the Pyramids?

—No, it's that I'm walking around nervous, Ana. All day long I'm waiting for you to call me.

—Waiting for me?

—Well, for you to make a decision.

—. . .

—He behaved badly toward you, yes or no?

—Yes, that's for sure.

—And you took a stand against him, to go into exile.

—I'm not a political exile.

—You can say what you like, but that's what you are.

—I don't understand you, Pozzi. If I'm not in sympathy with your leftist Peronistas, how can you expect me to collaborate?

—The very first day, I explained to you, that before you make any decision you should let me tell you about our movement.

—No, I'm not crazy, if I let you talk it's a cinch I'll end up siding with you.

—And for good reason . . .

—But it's that you're a good lawyer, and you can make me believe that white is black, I know you.

—. . .

—What's important to you is being right, no, what am I saying, winning the argument, that's what you want. You're not honest once you're in the middle of an argument.

—You have to hear me out, it's not fair of you to close yourself off like this.

—The subject doesn't interest me, that's all.

—I see it differently. You want to remain apart, as the woman of yesterday stayed out of politics.

—I'm not a woman of yesterday.

—In a certain way you are, your passivity in matters of politics, what would you call that?

—There must be a reason I'm here, and not in Buenos Aires. If I'm so passive I would have stayed there.

—You could have stayed, you could have come face to face with him there, with Alejandro.

—Will you please not say that name.

—. . .

—I see it doesn't matter to you that I'm convalescent.

—You knew you could count on me unconditionally there, you shouldn't have left.

—Unconditionally for what? for one or two dates a week?

—You were wrong to come here, exile is only justifiable when you've exhausted every possible way to take action in your own country.

—But you have to have some of that to leave everything and start all over again.

—What? balls?

—Yes.

—Say it then. Some women don't even have the nerve to call things by their name and they think they're liberated.

—How offensive . . .

—I want to be as direct as possible with you, you know how much I love you, with you there can't be any misunderstanding.

—What I know is that when you get vulgar it's because you're losing out, look how well I know you.

—. . .

—But you should take advantage, since you're here in Mexico, to get to know it a little. You should see the Aztec pyramids and the Museum of Anthropology, at least.

—. . .

—Later when you're back in Buenos Aires you'll be sorry you didn't see anything.

—Yes, it's a waste, you're right.

—A little distraction would do you good.

—It's that I'm sure that if you would only hear me out . . . I already told you that the other day, what I ask is that you listen to me. Calmly. I want to explain to you what it is that this movement proposes. And I know that politically it'll seem legitimate to you.

—Pozzi . . . you've given me a headache.

—I can't insist any more, if you want at any moment . . . I'll come and explain the entire matter. And you can decide afterward.

—But not now.

—Think about it, but tomorrow at the latest you'll have to give me an answer.

—Excuse me, but if we keep talking for one more second the pain is going to come on, I know how it works.

—Will they give you a sedative?

—Yes, but I can't ask for it every time. It's a strong drug, it's not child's play. Please, don't get me worked up like this again.

—I'm sorry.

—That's the only thing you're going to get from me, making me become worse.

3

THE PARKS IN Vienna dawned wet with dew. Despite the mistrust that her husband inspired in her, she decided to tell him everything: "You see me like this, pale, with shadows under my eyes, because I sleep but I don't rest, the nightmares prevent me. This last one was the worst, can you listen to me for a moment? will your innumerable preoccupations permit as much? will I in this way be detaining the march of the new Europe? Is Chamberlain on the telephone? the Führer? Mussolini? yes? I guessed correctly, really? at least don't deny that I was right! or is it the White House that cries out for your counsel?"

The husband stopped the flow of hysteria with a learned caress. "Thank you, I don't know what I would have done if such a feeling had lasted one moment longer, by all means, the iron of the Ruhr continues to nurture that foundry of yours, and a personage of such magnitude has a right to a private life. I'm not referring to myself, of course . . . I'll try to be brief, what I dreamed a few hours ago . . ." The husband interrupted her this time with a tender kiss on her lips, "You are the only person who can save me, because these nightmares don't leave me once I've opened my eyes. At this moment I don't have before me the monstrous character I dreamed about because your very image covers it. In the dream I was having a birthday, I was still a child, and I was being attacked by unbearable pains in my chest. The house was prepared for a reception in the early afternoon hours, a children's party. . . ."

She went on with her story, as she finished she didn't hear the expected commentary from her husband but in turn another story. "The little girl, you, didn't feel unbearable pains in her chest, nor was she taken in a carriage bound for the only doctor in Vienna who was at home that Sunday. The day you turned twelve years old that doctor was not dressed in tails, he was not obese, and after examining you he didn't tell your father that he refused to have dealings with anyone who in his turn had had dealings with the dead. What he said was something else. And you shouldn't concern yourself with that either, because I doubt that your father could have accompanied you that day to the obese doctor's home, having passed away . . . let's say a little before the end of the Great War. Do you see at last that your nightmare doesn't hold any threat? Anyway I ask you, I beg of you, not to talk about it with anyone, ever, understood?"

The young woman asked for an explanatory remark: "Yes, there is a meaning, but not an ill-fated omen, nothing of foreboding, in your nightmare. Now I'll explain what occurred. You as a very little girl must have heard talk of . . . well . . . of dealings with the dead. No, don't hasten to deny this, it's that surely your memory has stored it away in the darkest dungeon of your subconscious. Your father, the Professor, sheltered in his laboratory a lunatic, or an illuminated, species, a certain . . . I don't remember the name. And don't look at me with such a stare of incredulity, because thanks to that lunatic you and I are together today. Let me explain. During the Great War a rumor spread, among the high command in espionage on both sides, according to which a researcher had made progress in the most ambitious of all experiments: the ability to read that which isn't spoken, that which isn't written, that which is only thought. And here the lunatic enters the picture, it was he who had succeeded in this assignment! and rumor had it all was based on covenants made with the dead. But unfortunately or fortunately for humanity, the poor fellow blew up when one of his laboratory flasks exploded, without having revealed the secret. He precipitated the end of the war, the longed-for weapon had become as intangible as a dream, as your dream, my dear. And the very idea of a human being capable of reading thoughts had produced such dread that people preferred to forget all it represented. But the world isn't populated solely by cowards, and several years ago . . . I . . . became determined to decipher the mystery of the lunatic. After much searching I came across your family, only to find out about the sad death of your father, caused by the same explosion, while he was engrossed in ancient alchemy treatises in another chamber of the same mansion. All my research ended there, because the only person who had had close dealings with the lunatic had been he. Well, I had hoped for the realization of one miracle, and another one came about, in your appearance in my life."

She felt her eyelids more and more heavy, she asked what time the dance at the Palace would take place. Her husband replied that she had nothing to fear, they would arrive on time: the hairdresser, the dressmaker, the beautician and the new perfumist would appear at the proper time, they had been summoned for a specific hour, which she needn't be concerned about knowing. She looked at her bedroom in the Viennese mansion, tread for the first time that morning. Before falling asleep she noticed a number of surprising details, such as the high portal which comprised the only exit, of plain dark wood, bordered on either side by two titans sculpted in gray marble, one with a suffering grimace but not the other. Both had their eyes cast down, they weren't looking at the Mistress; they sprouted, at the height of their loin cloths, from thin columns which widened gradually as they rose, and with strong uplifted arms supported a pediment where two ladies sat smiling, serenely gazing at a little colt. They appeared figures made of flesh and bone, though pale, or dead, because of the gray marble.

It was an hour after the young woman arrived at the Grand Salon that the courtiers lowered their rapt gazes. They hadn't bothered her, on the contrary they had made her feel protected. A foxtrot had followed a round of tangos à la Valentino, now it was time for those magnificent and graceful national waltzes. These provided the musical background for the appearance of four handsome young men who greeted her husband with profound respect, they were engineers on a fellowship, personally selected by the industrialist to carry out experiments in his chief munitions plant. The young woman felt obliged to focus her attention on one of them because he reminded her of someone and she didn't know whom.

He was dark, thin, with features so delicate that they were almost feminine, but his husky voice and the near-roughness of his gestures marked him in the end as masculine. He wouldn't take his eyes off the Mistress. The industrialist was conveniently summoned once again by the Soviet ambassador and she felt free to do as she pleased for the first time in many days. The intriguing young man invited her to dance, she accepted without consulting her husband, because she'd already danced a rumba with the German chancellor and a beguine with the Austrian minister of the treasury.

For reasons unknown to the Mistress herself she asked him to close his eyes for a moment and open them up again. The young man didn't obey her, he told her that she was as beautiful as an angel. "Young man, angels aren't always beautiful, sometimes they can frighten, I glimpse evil shadows behind that empty look which painters and sculptors assign to them." "My lady, angels are children who have died before losing their innocence." "It's always very sad when a being dies without fault, even more so at such a tender age. I've often asked myself, might there not be girl angels as well?" "There should be, the ones sacrificed by those who knew the future belonged to both sexes." "Sacrificed?" "Yes, my lady, long ago it was considered an act of mercy. Those who saw the future, and knew the intense suffering that awaited such children in this world, recommended that their anguished parents eliminate them." "What a horrible story . . ." "That depends on the point of view you take. Those parents would have preferred to drown them with their desperate weeping, but tears didn't suffice, and they had to stifle their children's warm tender breath as they slept, with a pillow." "You are cruel, you would appear to agree with such murderers . . ." "Do you call those disconsolate parents murderers? Not them, though perhaps yes those who foretold the future. They almost always told the truth, but they sometimes used their powers for petty vengeance."

She couldn't effectively restrain the quickening of her fears,

leading onto the balcony the Grand Salon offered doors flanked
by narrow columns which widened little by little as they rose,
suddenly to be transformed into the folds of the golden fabric
wrapped around hips that continued into torsos of smiling women
of gold, which, with extravagant humor, held up a golden ceiling
with their coiffures of infinite curls. The Mistress's discomfort
among these mocking gazes was evident. "You speak of those who
foretold the future as if they'd actually existed." "They existed,
my lady, they had acquired that knowledge through deals they'd
made with souls in pain, pacts with condemned souls who lent
them their sight." "What sight?" "The sight of the dead, of
ubiquitous spirits which see everything." "What did those souls
stand to gain for lending their sight?" "That's easy to deduce:
they did it in exchange for prayers, in exchange for the reduction
of their punishment. In exchange for sharing their punishment
with the living, once they would all meet on the hour of perpetual
rest for the living. And thus the dead hastened the access of the
living to the sea of time, where the past, present and future flow
together." "These are all lies. No one knows the future."

The perfect pair had a curious effect on the assembly, no one
could look at them for more than a second, their magnificence so
scorched the retina. The Mistress repudiated the words of her
partner yet she couldn't help admiring his boldness, how dare a
subordinate of her husband's speak to her in that manner? "My
lady, why does it frighten you so that someone could know the
future? Aren't there those even now, for example, who are able
to read thoughts?" "I never heard of such a thing." "Predicting
the future seems to me a much more innocuous act, it doesn't
claim to change anything, but only to advance a piece of news.
While to infiltrate, in all impudence, the present, living thoughts,
of the person who happens to be before you, who suspects nothing
of the terrible danger to which he's exposed . . ." "Please, my
young friend, don't go on." The beauty disengaged herself from
the arms which were encircling her ever more closely, already too
late to give another glance at the golden insignia on the lapel of
his jacket, was it possible it was in the image of a child angel?

She took a few steps aimlessly, she caught sight of one of her personal guards, the heavy lady in gray, beneath the rococo arch-way of the exit, ready to follow her. On this occasion her presence struck the Mistress as amicable and not oppressive, she exchanged a look with the guard which the young man caught immediately. He ceased all explanation and his partner descended the royal steps, immense, spiraling, and borne, due to a lack of columns, on the shoulders of two ancient beggars who regarded the Mistress with rancor, sculpted in their entirety from a single block of granite. Those looks didn't matter to her, she obsessively con-tinued to ask herself who that young man could so closely resem-ble.

It was morning once again, the fog had turned whiter, and blacker the mansions on the narrow street. The limousine had been detained and the Mistress was escorted by the lady in gray and another bodyguard, of the masculine gender. Face covered by a blue veil which delicately caught her chin, she stopped to observe the façade of the Imperial Library, its simple entrance, the balcony on the first floor with a large planter on either end being regarded by a child angel in play, its second floor without a balcony but terminating with two languid women reclining once again on either side of a tame colt, all looking at one another, oblivious to the strangers' visit.

In the penumbrous interior her request for old newspapers was attended to immediately. She kept her guards at a distance, they shouldn't see what section she consulted. Very quickly she found those desired pages from the day she'd turned twelve years old. It was imperative to find out as soon as possible what had hap-pened on that day, she had dreamed about it for some reason. But she didn't find anything. She checked the previous days, then the days that followed. At last she uncovered a news item, in the criminal section, which probably had to do with her. A domestic servant, about whom all that was cited were initials—the same as my wet nurse, the Mistress screamed silently—had tried to kill the daughter of the house, on her birthday, by means of poison. For many years in the service of this family, whose name was omitted for reasons of courtesy, she had acted in a fit of madness, later strangling herself with her own braid, in the cell of the lunatic asylum where she had been locked away. Transcribed as a curiosity was the text of her suicide letter, found beside the body of the miserable wretch: "Goodbye, it is my destiny, as it was my poor brother's, that I should depart from this world because of having gone mad. That's what they will believe, but my brother was no more than a servant whom the Professor, to conceal his villainy, passed off as mad. It was the Professor and not the poor slave who was mad. All lies which he had told his followers, so they would not suspect it of himself. I'm departing, and I bequeath to this world the fruit of my guilt, a daughter, conceived under the worst auspices, those of unrequited love. The Professor, in worship of his deceased mother and unable to sleep at night thinking of the possible tortures that the poor old lady would suffer in the other world, made a pact with the dead. A pact which he maintained he had made with good souls. But it's time that I admit it, I was desperately in love with him, more handsome than anyone. There was no other woman in the house, the Professor hadn't wanted anyone to occupy his mother's place. And one night, knowing how I felt, he looked at me for the first time and said that his prayer had been answered: he himself would pay in the afterlife for his mother's sins, she in this way would find peace at last. But in return, in this treacherous world he had to serve the Good, carrying out very precise orders. And what did all that mean to me, all I wanted was to touch him! I repeated the words that he dictated, and I undressed silhouetted by a moonbeam, the garden of white lilies seemed like a very precious jewel that night. When he fell asleep on the crushed flowers, which just before had been shimmering in silver, he spoke in his sleep words which I didn't understand. But after that night he never looked at me again, at me! who brought into the world the most beautiful girl that ever existed, and whom I tried to kill yesterday, because I'm afraid that what this child will one day serve will be Evil and not Good, since she's been educated to serve a man one day. A slave to one man or to all men, there's no difference. And I won't allow it! my daughter doesn't have to grovel as I did! I would hate her if she did that! no and no! before that I'd rather see her dead!"

Next the newspaper editor indicated that the end of the document had proved illegible, smudged as it was by the tears of the suicide. The Mistress made an effort—superhuman?—and reread the article to assure herself that it was not a hallucination. Following that she wept the softest and most bitter tears of her life, in memory of her mother, could anyone else know the story of that unfortunate woman? No, because it was impossible to find this news item, among the millions of chance occurrences published by the newspapers in so many years, except for the date which she was given in her nightmare: the exact date of the event.

In closing the heavy bound volume, the effort proved excessive and she fainted. She was brought without further ado to her mansion, but the fateful page was easily found by the reader who next consulted the volume. Such a reader's task was simplified by an unusual fact, the tears spilled over the old chronicle still wet, hadn't been enough to smudge the printed word, starker than the ink used by the suicide in the lunatic asylum. The reader devoured the text, with an impenetrable expression, while from his lapel smiled a minute angel of gold.

—I have my plan worked out, Beatriz.

—I'm listening.

—I promised him to think about it calmly and to let him know afterward.

—You're referring to his request.

—Yes, I'm going to tell you about everything except that, the request itself, all right?

—Maybe without that . . . I won't be able to figure out the problem.

—I assure you that you will. Then . . . my plan is this: I think it through, all that he asked me, and in addition I ask your advice. I'll tell you all about my relations with him, and you give me your opinion.

—. . .

—You remind me of the doctor.

—Why?

—He keeps quiet. He doesn't make any comments when I tell him all my symptoms.

—What do you expect me to say if I still don't know anything?

—I said that as a joke.

—Don't interrupt anymore because I want to know everything.

—No, not everything, there's one thing that I can't say.

—Okay, but start right now.

—I met him at the University, when I took up my studies again. I always had a weakness for pretty faces.

—Who does he look like? think of someone you know in Mexico, that way I can picture him.

—He's fair, rosy-cheeked, the son of Italians. With chestnut hair, a very common type in Argentina, light brown eyes. He looks like a lot of people, but I don't know who to tell you. With his hair not very long, and a big mustache. His hair is the best thing about him, chestnut but pretty light. Now you ask me something, because I don't know where to begin.

—Is he tall?

—Not very, under six feet.

—And what else?

—I don't know where to start.

—. . .

—He was going to a bar after class . . .

—. . .

—Across from the University . . .

—Anita, you really don't want to tell me anything.

—That's not true.

—Every other minute you stay quiet.

—Other friends introduced us, and at the beginning he was hostile toward me, he treated me as if I was one of the privileged few, because I got real dressed up to go to the University. It must have been because of that. In the afternoon.

—And later?

—I saw him a few times, always only for a minute, because I had to go home for a meal.

—What kind of a meal? What do you mean?

—It's that back in Buenos Aires we say we have a meal, instead of have dinner the way you Mexicans do.

—To have dinner is the correct expression, isn't it?

—And at noon we have lunch, that we don't change. But there are people back there who also say dinner, meaning the evening meal. Though that's funny, because it's considered something lower-class.

—And why is it funny?

—No, I say funny because exactly that has to do with something about him, about Pozzi. But I'll tell you about it later. Well, I'm ashamed but I'll tell you now. There are words that back there are considered lower-class, like red . . . wife . . . beautiful . . . dinner, and I don't know what else. And the first day that I saw Pozzi, I said that I had to go have a meal and he cracked a joke and they all laughed at me, and it made me look like a snob.

—Go on.

—I was raised that way, at home you never said red, always crimson or purple or the precise shade of red in question. And woman instead of wife, lovely instead of beautiful. He was the one who made me see just how much it was all a question of snobbery, class, do you follow? But all the while he was making me look bad, he was hostile. He had been a Trotskyist, and later became a Peronista.

—All those things about Argentine politics you're going to have to explain to me, because I never could understand about Peronism.

—Don't think that I understand much about it either.

—The question of those on the left who became Peronistas, it still makes no sense to me.

—An important detail: I noticed how badly dressed he was. I don't mean he went around in blue jeans, because that wouldn't have mattered. No, worn out suits, pants thin and short, out of fashion, those pant legs weren't anywhere near his shoes. And I sometimes practice my textbook psychology with good results, just listen. My conclusion was this: if this man is so good looking and he walks around so poorly dressed, it's because he must be caught up in something else, that's more important. But just then came the whole tangle of my divorce.

—. . .

—The year '69. And later I ran into him again at an opening, in a theater. I was dressed to kill, really elegant, and he with the same pants as usual, and the knot in his grubby tie, the same clothes he put on in the morning to go to Court, and he didn't go back home until nighttime. And he invited me to, well, to have dinner or, even worse, supper, on the way out. He said it to me as a joke.

—And you corrected him?

—No, I told him that that was well said, because after midnight you could say supper.

—And he?

—I chose a restaurant nearby, not a fashionable one, so it would be quieter. And there he caught me with my guard down, he asked me if I classified people, or worse yet, wait . . . if I wrote off the people who said having dinner or supper instead of having a meal, beautiful instead of lovely, etc. It irritated me because he was right. He assured me that those words had stayed that way, in disrepute, because of some maneuver many years ago. By people from the upper class. A little group which had nothing to do and decided to lay a trap for the . . . what does he call it? social climbers. Then they chose words which meant the same thing, like beautiful and lovely and declared one of the two in poor taste, but in secret, do you follow? so that whoever uttered them gave himself away, that he wasn't from high origins.

—Do you think that you Argentines deserve the reputation that you have, of being snobs?

—Of course! You can't imagine what the upper class is like, I know them very well.

—. . .

—I had been raised that way, as a little girl my mother corrected me if I used the wrong word.

—Your mother's from the upper class?

—No, more or less well-to-do, but not upper class. A snob and nothing more. And I forgot the worst one, "to drink milk" rather than "to take tea." Worse still than to say beautiful.

—Which is from the upper class? to take tea, I suppose.

—Of course, from the English. But the power of one word is incredible. If someone, some classmate from school, invited me over to her house for milk, I wouldn't go, I imagined a table without a tablecloth and some broken pitchers with pieces of bread floating in the milk . . . boiled and then boiled again with a horrible scum. Which quite possibly wasn't true. Later I got to know how delicious were those big slabs of bread with butter, and sugar on top, a lower-class custom back there.

—But also very fattening, no doubt.

—The people from the upper class are all really really thin in Argentina. And it's because of stinginess, they don't want to spend money on eating, did you know that?

—And what do they spend it on?

—I don't know, I barely know them. Antique jewelry, antique furniture, that's their downfall, I suppose. And cutlery.

—I thought you knew them.

—Well, more or less. If one of them invites you to take tea, you're sure to have a tablecloth and porcelain, but not too much to eat, toast with some bitter jam, like the English.

—Go on about Pozzi.

—He came at me with this attack. And I was foolish, I got defensive and told him that it was a frivolity which didn't mean anything, that one used certain words out of just plain habit. Deep down I knew it wasn't true. And that's how he beat me in round one. Because it's a national sickness, back there, this obsession with being distinguished.

—Here people have that craziness with money.

—Which is more forgivable.

—But it makes people very ill-mannered as well. Each country has its national foolishness.

—When we talked about those things, about Argentina, Pozzi defended Spain most of all, he said that the passion there was in being courageous. And in not giving any importance to money, but to being generous.

—But they're also real male chauvinist pigs, tell your friend.

—But to me the worst is when Argentines imitate the British. Or imitate their faults, at least. All Argentines want to be cynical, the Oscar Wilde way, aloof, not at all sentimental. They love British understatement.

—And what about the tango, then?

—That's a thing of the lower classes. I'm talking about the highest levels, and what people who are scaling the social ladder aspire to.

—And did your friend think as you do?

—The truth is that I'm repeating all the things that he says. Right or wrong, who knows.

—Tell me how your relationship developed.

—The second time we went out he came back to my apartment afterward, and that's where everything started. I'm ashamed to admit it, but . . .

—What?

—Swear to me that you're not going to tell anyone. And don't laugh.

—Tell me.

—Don't say anything, but he's the only man I've known, biblically, you know? aside from my husband.

—I promise never to mention it.

—Not too emancipated, am I?

—You knew that he was married.

—Yes, and I liked that. Because I didn't want to get tied down again. I was delighted, single once more.

—But you were single with a daughter.

—No, she stayed with her father. But let me tell you more.

—I thought she was with your mother.

—And we kept seeing each other for two years.

—You had gone to live with your mother then?

—No, I went to live alone.

—And why didn't your mother come, for your operation?

—Uhm . . . Mama is forbidden to come to Mexico, because of the altitude. A problem with her heart, you know about these things. . . . In Buenos Aires I lived alone, that's why Pozzi could come to see me.

—Until you came here.

—No, even before that we had stopped seeing each other regularly, because he was occupied more and more with his politics. It was a period when there were many political prisoners. On one hand he had to work to survive, as a lawyer in a firm, and afterward everything else. The entire day poor thing in those courts.

—Had you fallen in love with him?

—No, never. Well, yes, at the beginning, but that didn't last very long.

—Why?

—I think it was because the two of us were too proud.

—In what sense?

—We had too many commitments and we didn't want to waste time. And I'll tell you that with him I never felt what I did with Fito at the beginning. With Fito at the beginning it was fantastic. Later less and less. And with Fito we talked about it. But I wasn't going to go through all that again. Never mind, it's a kinky business.

—I didn't understand one word of that.

—I'd better talk more directly then. With Pozzi I never enjoyed it the way I did with Fito at the beginning. With Fito it was superb, better than what I had hoped for, that there would be this pleasure. But it didn't last long. With Fito I got disillusioned very quickly.

—Were you disillusioned because that started to fail?

—Beatriz, I see that you don't know me at all. I'm very cerebral about these things.

—In what sense?

—I don't know how to explain it.

—Because you have a lot of fantasies?

—Speaking of fantasies. Fito got me started doing something bad. But those things are really obscene.

—If it's not because they're dirty it's because it depresses you, you never tell me anything.

—According to Fito I had to see a doctor. To find out what was the source of the problem. It could be something physical, or the aftereffect of childbirth.

—Did it bother him?

—No, he went on enjoying himself. I was the one being cheated. But I didn't want to go to the doctor.

—And why was that?

—I got stubborn about not going. And I think I was right. The bad thing is that in those cases the doubt never goes away. I'm sure that no, the cause wasn't physical.

—And what was it then?

—That I didn't love him anymore. Although the truth is, I'm not sure if I ever loved him.

—And that was the kinky business?

—No, it's that when I began to notice that I was feeling less and less, he told me that I should think about other things while it was going on, for example that we were in a park and I was a tiny girl and he a big man who bought me candy to win my trust, and afterward he took me to a clearing, on the outskirts of town. Or that I was a twelve-year-old schoolgirl on a trip through Arabia and a sultan shut me up in his palace, and things like that.

—To play roles, like on a stage. Characters.

—More or less.

—And that helped you?

—Yes, I didn't go back to feeling as much as I did at the beginning, but it helped. And with Pozzi when I saw from the beginning that I wasn't feeling much then either, I began to imagine things. That he was coming out of prison and he was a national hero, but that he had been tortured and was blind, and I took care of him. That excited me a lot. Or that I was a parlor maid.

—It's been years since I've heard that expression.

—Why?

—It's not used here, we say simply maid. But when I was a girl in Argentine movies Mecha Ortiz or Paulina Singerman always had a parlor maid.

—I'll tell you about it: I imagined that I was a parlor maid in his house, and we did things hidden away from his family. But I saw him more as a martyr, that excited me more. What excited me about him was just that, that he was handsome and so sacrificed at the same time. So good.

—If he was so good, how could he become a Peronista?

—Beatriz, many good people turned Peronista.

—That I don't understand. Perón had persecuted those on the left in his previous regime. Here in Mexico he had the reputation for being a fascist. How could he reconcile one thing with the other?

—I never understood much about that. Of the Peronistas on the left I knew only him.

—And of those on the right?

—One day later on I'll tell you.

—I'm letting you know that I'm not understanding much.

—I'll repeat what he used to say. According to Pozzi, Perón was the first to succeed in getting people to respect a national politics, or nationalism.

—Or national socialism. National with a "z."

—What do you mean?

—In German the word national, as in national socialism, is spelled with a "z." Nazional, Nazi.

—And that's where the word Nazi comes from?

—Of course.

—I never knew that.

—Go on about your friends.

—Beatriz, I'm not defending them to you. I'm repeating what he used to tell me. I used to say the same things to him that you're saying to me. You're making me nervous.

—Forgive me and go on, I want to understand.

—The point is that it seems that Perón, however badly or worse, he had organized the unions for the first time and lent importance to the workers' movement, at least he had organized it.

—As far as I know, Perón had organized the workers' movement so he could take advantage of the trade unions himself, but he didn't establish a true socialist foundation.

—Don't ask me for so much detail, I don't know too well how it was. But of course, the way things ended up agrees with what you say.

—But this last time how could the left delude itself about him like that?

—I don't know, Beatriz.

—And what is it you want me to advise you about?

—About him. If he seems to you a person who cares for me or not, I mean really cares.

—You have to tell me more, with what I know I can't give you any opinion. What appeals to me is that he would have been so altruistic, in his defense of prisoners I mean. But if he's a Peronista that makes me suspicious.

—And continues to be so.

—Then no, definitely no. If he still continues with that, after what Perón did to the left before he died, no. I don't trust him at all.

—But Beatriz, the matter is very complicated, according to him socialism has to pass through Peronism, for particular reasons, historical ones.

—Whoever plays with fascism gets burned.

—Then what would you advise me?

—Anita, remember that I don't even know why you came to Mexico, how can you expect me to give you an opinion?

—That didn't have anything to do with Pozzi.

—But it's crucial to understanding your situation.

—. . .

—You're a little pale.

—Beatriz . . . you can't imagine how tired I feel, from gabbing with you all this time. It must be that I'm still very weak.

—Try to be quiet a bit, while I do the talking.

—But I wanted to tell you so many things. Yesterday was the first time that I asked for a sedative, apart from nighttime. It's already hurting me, it's here, at the base of my neck. Like a

headache. And at the same time a strange pressure, right in the middle of my chest, below the breastbone. It's always like that, the two things at the same time.

—Lie down a little, and we'll go on talking. Although to tell you the truth, I don't know if I'll have time.

—When it starts, I can't really tolerate it, without a sedative.

—Then ask for it. Does it take effect right away?

—Yes, but it makes me fall asleep, it's a strong drug. I don't want to get addicted to it either.

—Try to be still a while, I'll look at a magazine, don't worry about me.

—No, Beatriz, I think I've got to call the nurse.

4

THEY WERE TWO ungainly shadows, those cast against the fire's crimson glare, in the vast courtyard of the foundry. Even the world's supreme armaments maker had to have recourse to a stratagem to elude hidden microphones. That's what the fact of dealing with double and triple secret agents required. Pouring tumultuously, the boiling liquid iron stifled any other sound. The armaments maker spoke directly in the ear of the British agent, on this occasion attempting to establish his innocence. The agent maintained an inscrutable expression on his face. The arms manufacturer assured him that he had never suspected his young wife to be a spy, and for the Third Reich! In fact, she hadn't sought him out, as would have happened with a professional spy, but rather he had run into her incidentally, following the trail of the Professor.

The Briton allowed himself a slight ironic grimace and froze it on his face for a moment to allow the other to notice it. Immediately afterward he added that the suspicions about the wife had begun when they had found irregularities in her birth certificate, following rigorous examination. The certificate had been rewritten, it featured as the parents the Professor and a woman from high society amidst erasures which rearranged dates and other facts, surely to make them coincide with her age and sex.

Also other more recent documents of the lady in question had been revised and the contradictions added up, all of which marked her as yet another agent on the trail of the man who would one day read the mind of the world. An agent who, believing him to be close to the great secret, had cunningly sought the favor of the industrialist. This one raised the fur collar of his

overcoat higher and pulled his felt top hat down as far as he could, in a futile attempt at self-protection.

The Briton continued, he was trying to bring logical consequence to what he was saying, but his interlocutor realized the agent's effort to string together disconnected fragments of information: whoever succeeds in mind reading, thus routing the secret plans of any world power . . . will achieve such a faculty from the day he or she turns thirty years old, and he or she has already been born. Such deductions proceeded from the study of certain ancient writings, which tell of pacts with the dead and of the possibility of hearing that which is silent.

The shadows drew apart, the crimson glare remained. To emerge from the place, the arms manufacturer chose the darkest hidden corridors, in order to conceal his embarrassment, and also the quietest ones, because he wanted to hear with absolute clarity the cavernous voice of vengeance. It suggested to him some bizarre methods of elimination, but one tempted him particularly: his wife—her guilt proving to be verified—would be executed without the blare of gunpowder or anything like it, he would shut her up in a strong-box with all her jewels, yes, he would force her to enter a very small compartment, as transparent as cellophane but as rigid as steel. He would make her enter naked, under whatever pretext, no! nothing of subterfuge, he would drug her one more time and she would awaken already trapped, in the company of her jewels. From outside he would watch her consume all the oxygen in those few cubic feet of air, he would watch her suffocate slowly, lose her beauty, turn into a toad, burst, putrefy. The armaments maker consulted his heavy pocket watch, it was three in the afternoon: that very night he would surprise her in the mansion on the island, and they would settle the score.

In the meantime the young woman was spending a rare day of wakefulness, given that her husband had been called away by urgent matters at the foundry, a bare fifty miles away. The balmy atmospheric conditions had soothed the sorrow suffered days ago at the library, somehow she seemed to have dreamed it and not lived it. It was three in the afternoon and she hadn't yet left her bedroom, she leaned out over the balcony once again, the light

seemed to caress the park. She came up with an optimistic con-
ception, if all this beauty existed it was because good spirits guided
the destiny of the universe. And as if one more brushstroke had
been needed to complete this enchanting picture, there appeared
in the park the exquisite figure of a woman, she traversed a
footpath bordered by trees along one side and along the other by
diaphanous white flowers. But the clothes, the walk, the silhouette, the face, were the Mistress's own. At this moment she was
contemplating herself walking through the park, in the clothes
she had thought of wearing to make that same excursion, a few
minutes hence. She herself in the park had a gaze lost in the
distance, seeking what? perhaps she was conversing with beings
in the afterlife, with those dead accomplices who promised to
reveal everything to her. She grabbed hold of the curtains so as
not to fall over in terror, she took a deep breath.

Someone knocked on the door, she didn't know how to respond, yes or no, at that moment everything frightened her. Thea
opened the door without hesitation, her keys gave her access
everywhere, apparently, "Mistress, if it's not too impudent, may
I suggest a stroll through the park, the light is splendid at this
hour." "It seems that you, Thea, are not alone in thinking that,"
"You too, of course," "Yes, Thea, me too." She returned her gaze
toward the park, the vision hadn't disappeared, it was still there.
The maidservant moved forward toward the picture window,
"The resemblance to the Mistress is perfect, isn't it?" "But what
is this, some sort of jest? are they trying to drive me definitively
mad, like my poor moth . . ." "By any chance is this the first time
that the Mistress has seen her double? Pardon me . . . it really
makes me want to laugh! Wasn't the Mistress forewarned that for
security reasons the Master ordered the hiring of a domestic
servant as a double? But this is unheard of. . . . You should have
been notified before anyone else . . ." "A double? but why?"
"Well, it seems that the Master wanted your double to remain
here while you were away from the island, to attract potential
kidnapers and what have you," "But I'm here today," "An error
must have occurred up in the Orders of the Day," "She looks
exactly like me, I will not tolerate such an ambiguous situation,

that woman must leave here immediately," "There is only the illusion of similarity, and at a certain distance, the resemblance of the face is lent by a mask, and the perfect silhouette is achieved through the constraint of a corset and the addition of padding. But if you'll allow me to change the subject, Mistress, this is the ideal moment for that long-delayed visit to the acclimated palm grove." The Mistress searched with her eyes once again for her double, by then already disappeared.

Winter Garden, iron and glass, the iron painted a brilliant black, the glass shadowed by the green of the foliage. An iron frame, masculine strength. Thin glass panes, feminine surrender? Such was the Mistress's musing, when suddenly she felt an imperious thirst. Thea opened the weighty padlock, removed the chains and pushed open the little door. The dry desert air kissed the Mistress's skin, therein one tread the warm golden sand; from the dunes intense beams of light projected, forcing their way between clusters of dates, until they touched the glass of the incandescent ceiling, and from there in an augmented reflection they fell again toward the branches in search of another optical adventure. Venturesome lights, intoxicated, carnous. A skillful play of mirrors made the horizon appear remote and unattainable. The music sounded Oriental, the result of undulating feminine choirs, but the rhythm stressed by cymbals and other paraphernalia of operatic percussion came across as Western, nevertheless suitable as an accompaniment to a sumptuous caravan in the desert. Pam . . . pa-pa-pa-pam, pam . . . pa-pa-pa-pam-pam-pam . . . and suddenly a violin, loo . . . loo-loo-loo, a soul wailing within its body or prison.

The Mistress couldn't help but follow those cadences with her steps, she proceeded in a royal manner to the beat of the drum, while her breathing imitated the plaintive spirals of the violin. Soon her attire proved excessive, Thea's presence made no difference to her and she began to undress. Thea followed, picking up articles of clothing as they fell on the sand, and indicated that a few steps away, to the right, they would find a Bedouin tent, authentic but scrupulously clean, where they might rest a moment. The Mistress didn't say a word but she bore right at the fork in the footpath. Within the tent, as restoration from the blinding sun, the air was almost cool. An abundance of over-stuffed pillows, on top of an upholstered taboret there was a tray and a brimming cup. She hastened to drink it, held it up to smell it before she did so to advance the pleasure, it was the same liquid as always, but Thea, with a stiff karate chop, had the impertinence to stroke the cup down, making it fall to the ground.

The Mistress looked at her, startled. Thea took a few steps backward toward the opening of the tent. It was impossible to scrutinize the expression on her face because she was against the light, behind her the glare crept between the flaps of the opening. And then it was the Mistress who drew back, in horror, when she saw that Thea had also begun to disrobe, while saying, in a voice which grew deeper and deeper, "I prepared that cup in a moment of misconduct, of foolish lust." Thea's silhouette was revealing itself to be more and more lean, the legs were profiled as muscular and covered with down, "But I will not copy your husband's cowardice, I will not avail myself of that narcotic. I want to place myself in front of you, such as I am, and allow you to decide." When the last item of clothing had been removed, with a whack she wrenched off the wig, a mane pulled back tautly in a low chignon, lifted one of the many rags off the ground and began to wipe the makeup off her face. One of these motions placed her in profile, and the Mistress, with enormous and unexpected relief, observed that Thea was a man.

And it was this man, although dressed, with whom she had waltzed at the dance in the Palace, "You've already recognized me, I hope, I deceived your husband's Guard Service and managed to have them accept me as a maid. It was difficult for them to find a woman in as good athletic condition as mine. They hastened to hire me when I offered them my services, duly disguised as a woman. Thus my name proves to be not Thea, but Theo." Regardless of having been married several weeks, the Mistress had never, while conscious, stood before a naked man, and much less in the state of erection. Theo had taken a few steps toward her and now she could observe him in greater detail. Perhaps to better examine him, she let herself fall and nearly become absorbed in an extraordinarily soft overstuffed pillow. Another tremendous and unexpected reaction jarred her: the fact of being confronted with a being as beautiful as herself, and at the same time contrasting her with his masculinity, made her feel comfortable, normal, ordinary, not a monstrosity of beauty, as she had been categorized more than once.

He sat down beside her, "But that's not all. And in telling you the following I'm placing myself entirely in your hands, as you'll see. I came in as your maidservant and guard to spy on you on your husband's behalf, and also to spy on behalf of a foreign power." The Mistress felt Theo stroke one of her hands and afterward hold it gently, she didn't withdraw it, she didn't know whether it was from fear or something else, "I am a Soviet spy. Those who give me orders suspect you to be an agent for the Third Reich, but I'm sure that it's not so, that you fell into a snare set by that dreaded armaments maker through who knows what devices," "You're not mistaken. I'm innocent." Theo took her other hand, "I don't have any evidence of one or the other, but . . . I've . . . fallen hopelessly in love with you, I've lost all my defenses, I'm entirely at your mercy . . ." She was also at his, and she was beginning to admit it, "Theo . . . you must help me escape from this prison, I hate my husband. I married him for the sake of protection, without knowing that what he wanted was just another item for his collected works of . . ." "Of art, yes, don't be afraid to say it," "Me, a work of art? Do you think so?" The rosy tips of her breasts were already grazing the young man's hirsute chest, "I will give my life, if necessary . . . my Mistress. . . . But may I call you something else?" In response she placed her lips gently on Theo's. It was thus that he was no longer able to talk, but with his entire body, with his hands, his arms, his tapering pubis, he swore to her until he was breathless that he would give his life, if it was called for, to free her.

The bodies remained exhausted. Naively she endeavored to find words, images, metaphors, to explain to Theo all the pleasure with which she'd been filled. Thus she revealed her condition of novice as a lover, because the young man, more experienced, knew that "Certain heavens, my Mistress, escape all description." The only thing that was able to cloud over her happiness at this moment, however gently, was the sound track in the greenhouse, it repeated the passages of pseudo-Oriental music, *Scheherazade* by Rimski-Korsakov, *Lakmé* by Delibes and *In a Persian Market* by Ketelbey. For a moment she succeeded in distracting herself and heard nothing more than the voice of her lover, "We should leave this place this very day. One thing occurs to me: you could pass yourself off as your double, and request permission to leave for a few hours, the skipper of the launch is indulgent with the other members of the serving staff," "My treasure, I have complete confidence in you, but isn't this scheme a rather risky matter? They could recognize me . . ." "Forgive me, but it's the only thing that occurs to me as possible. We should get dressed and put the plan into action. It will be necessary to eliminate your double beforehand," "A murder?" "Not necessarily. We should gag her, put handcuffs on her, but if she resists there will be no other solution but to kill her. She's a filthy spy, and her career history a long list of betrayals and base actions characteristic of this occupation," "Theo, you too are a spy, does your work deserve such low esteem?" "I am that no longer. Because of my love for you I've renounced my country and my political ideals. It wasn't my decision, simply this immense admiration . . . and desire . . . and tenderness . . . that I feel for you proves much stronger than everything else. I despise injustice, that's why I waved the socialist banner, but neither can I allow atrocities to be perpetrated on you, it's more powerful than I am, I won't allow you to continue in the clutches of this monster," "But now we will have not only his bloodhounds pursuing us, but also the intelligence service that you'll be abandoning," "Which I have already abandoned. I want to be with you for the rest of my days. To see you grow old beside me. . . . You will always be beautiful. . . . I think that at thirty you'll be more lovely than ever," "How strange that you should say that, I live in dread of reaching that age, I always have, and I don't know why. . . . For a woman it's really passing forty that's alarming," "My love, you have nothing to fear, because I solemnly promise you that I'll be with you the day that you turn thirty years old," "You understand me so well that

sometimes it almost seems to me that you're able to read my
. . ." "Speech, why do you interrupt yourself? . . . Well then, we
must get going. Soon it will begin to grow dark, it's my daily
charge to connect the nighttime alarm in the park, it lights up
the park, as bright as in daytime or even more, in the event that
foreign elements should intrude there," "And me? what will
become of me in the meantime?" "You will go to your room, you
must choose your most subdued street clothes, you will look for
an inconspicuous handbag, yet large enough to hold all your
jewels, and you'll wait for me. Ah, and the hat must have a light
veil, remember you must pass for your double."

When she saw herself alone once again in her room, she began
to shake with fear. She should have been behaving completely in
cold blood, instead she couldn't even manage to work the zipper
on her dress. She didn't know if it was due to the trembling of
her hand, but the fastener got stuck, she had to rip it along the
seams, rending the crêpe-de-Chine. She turned to the adjacent
dressing room when the door slammed violently before her, the
safety latch was locked from the inside and she knew not how to
open it. She was consoled to think that the jewelry container was
right there in the bedroom, she removed it from its hiding place,
but the small latchkey—not fully inserted in the lock—fell onto
the mink rug. She passed her hand along the dark chestnut fur,
without result. Overflowing with hysteria, there on her knees, she
began to strike the delicate platinum jewel box, uselessly. She
hurled it against the wall tapestry of braided satin. It opened in
the air and scattered her jewels, it wasn't locked! One by one she
gathered the pieces, which dazzled her, made her dizzy with their
constant twinkling.

She pulled her forces together and managed to stand up, she
searched for an answer in the large Venetian mirror, she sought
for a change of expression in herself, any sign that would soothe
her. The luminescence of her face astounded her, she had never
seen herself look thus, a new light had been kindled in her breast
and radiated its brilliance through her sky-blue eyes, through her
rosy white skin, her blackish hair. She looked again at the jewels
held in her hands, gathered in an overflowing fistful, which proved

dull by comparison. She looked at herself in the mirror again, and that was all it required to loosen from its frame and fall, smashing to smithereens. She immediately suspected that the dead had made their presence felt, and not in an amicable fashion, decidedly hostile, what did they want? perhaps those dead were in her husband's service? why did they want to delay her escape, now that it was impossible to prevent her? She leaned out over the balcony for a breath of air. Thea, and not Theo, could be seen in the same place where hours before she had seen her double. There, on the edge of the reservoir, she stood immobile, staring toward the place that her double had also contemplated fixedly. What were they looking at? What did that posture signify, that gaze lost in the distance? did they hope that before late afternoon one of the dead would give them the appropriate sign?

Thea left the park and headed toward the basement of the main building, where the double's lodgings were. In the corridor she encountered one of the older servants, who invited her to join a group of them, at tea time they would savor a delicious torte, that famous one, the favorite of the archduke of . . . Abruptly Thea, forgetting to disguise her voice, interrupted him saying that she had much to do. But the old man was deaf, he didn't notice it and insisted that the island's pastry chef had been employed by the archduke Rudolf, and she was the only person who knew the recipe for that famous torte. The disguised one chose to join them for a moment, he might encounter the double in the group and would make some excuse to take her aside. The elders welcomed him jovially and seized the opportunity to complain that the only other young person in the household staff had spurned them. They talked of the new employee, the double of course, and they predicted a bad sojourn on the island if she didn't accept the company of the elders. Thea devoured one slice of the torte and excused herself. At last she could carry on with her plan.

She knocked on the double's door, her intention was to bind and gag her so she wouldn't be able to leave her room while the Mistress and he escaped. The woman opened the door grudgingly. A few minutes later Thea emerged from the room, with her hands clean. She had wiped them on the dress of the one with

the slashed throat, the seasoned spy had resisted ferociously, there
had been no alternative. It was the first time that Theo had killed,
he felt his heart pounding in his throat. There was no one in the
corridor, the feast continued, he got ready to take the elevator to
meet the Mistress in her room. The slow apparatus was already
arriving at the basement when the shrill ring for service could be
heard. Theo looked at the number on the bell which was sounding, it was his own. He had no choice but to pick up the telephone
and respond. It was the Mistress herself who was calling him, she
couldn't bear to wait anymore, she implored that Theo come up
immediately, and she used her masculine name. The response was
shortened to a "yes, yes," in a disguised voice, but it had been
terribly indiscreet of the young woman to express herself thus,
someone could be listening on the line, as was customary.

Thea stepped into the elevator, the sluggishness of its progress
amounted to torture, she thought that only the archduke's torte
could have distracted the old switchboard operator from his work.
In fact, she thought she remembered seeing him among the
festive revelers. When she reached her floor, the Mistress threw
herself into Thea's arms, in spite of the effect which the maid's
disguise had on her. She had been ready for some time, her coat
pockets almost giving way from their load of jewels. He was
lowering the veil on her hat to assess the result . . . when the
telephone rang. Was it advisable for her to answer it or him, or
Thea, the faithful guardian? He decided that she should answer.
It was her husband. With an affectionate voice he ordered her to
prepare immediately for travel to Vienna, where he would await
her. He also ordered her to bring all her jewels. She was scarcely
able to respond, but her astonishment was appropriate under the
circumstances. The arms provisioner added that she would have
no practical difficulty, he would speak to Thea immediately so
that she could attend to everything, the maidservant would accompany her on the launch to the private wharf in Vienna, he
would expect her there. His wife said that Thea was right there
and the billionaire ordered that she be handed the receiver. The
instructions were the same as usual, not to allow the Mistress out

of her sight even for a single instant. He cut off the line without
further ado.

Could such a stroke of luck be possible? If that call had come
only a short while earlier Theo wouldn't have had to sully his
hands and conscience with a bloody act, if only he hadn't hurried
so! But on the other hand, wasn't it strange to order her to carry
all her jewels?

The afternoon had drawn to a close. The imposing launch
quickly made its way across the waves of a Danube more and more
violaceous. The old skipper had smiled his welcome in receiving
them on board, his conduct appeared normal. Thea feared that
someone had overheard her brief telephone conversation with the
Mistress and had immediately notified the Master, that's why he
had summoned them both to come before him. But scarcely one
or two minutes had elapsed between one call and the other, would
such a swift reaction be possible? Why not . . . wasn't he a man
vastly admired for his extraordinary talents? with him such speed
in reflexes would come as no surprise. Thea excused herself and
descended into the cabin. The Mistress noted the skipper's surprise, the guardian wasn't ever supposed to leave her alone. The
Mistress attempted to strike up a friendly chat, the skipper didn't
divert his attention from the helm and clearly felt uncomfortable:
perhaps it wouldn't be well received to converse with her. At that
moment it occurred to him that the person traveling with him
could be the double and not the Mistress, he immediately pressed
a button and contacted the private dock that was their destina-
tion, he wanted to ask the guard service posted there if there was
any irregularity in the operation.

The barrel of a revolver prevented him, Thea was pressing the
weapon against a back which was bent with the years. Immediately the old man was ordered to change the course, he made an
unexpectedly vigorous attack, with one arm he succeeded in
knocking the revolver from Theo's hand. They became locked in
a struggle, fell onto the deck, the weapon lying a few feet away,
the old man stretched out his arm to reach it, the Mistress sensed
the serious danger and before she knew what she was doing she'd

shot a bullet into the skipper's back. The black smoke from the gunpowder hid her for a moment.

Theo pushed the tiller and set the course for Hungary, barely a half-hour's navigation away. "And where do we go from there, dearest?" "In Budapest I will contact the Soviet secret service." She trembled, he brought his arm around her waist and drew her toward him, he kissed her cheek without taking his eyes off the route, "Don't be afraid, they will provide the necessary documents. I will lie to them, I'll tell them that with your help I've uncovered a trail that will require our traveling to America. Once we're there we'll go on wherever you please, because at that point we'll have escaped your husband's clutches, and those of my ex-coreligionists." They kissed, shutting their eyes, wanting to forget that their flight had already cost two lives. She opened her eyes again and saw Theo's enormous hand still gloved in silk, pushing the tiller. She shivered with pleasure and fear, she remembered a saying, the one about mistrust strangling with a silken glove. He on his part didn't open his eyes, but that black gunsmoke from which the Mistress had emerged, wielding a weapon that was hot and fatal, flashed in his memory.

Thursday. It isn't fair what I did to Beatriz. You can't call someone to ask advice in all seriousness, and later tell them little or nothing. I didn't trust her at the last minute. And without reason. And I'm the one who comes up losing, because I really wanted her opinion. Although Beatriz was unfair in what she said about Pozzi. Or was she right?

Oh how ashamed I am, that lie I told her! Why did I have to invent that stuff for Beatriz that in my home we said meal instead of dinner? My home was a home just like all the others from the middle class, however comfortably middle class it was. When I switched to that private secondary school was when I found out I wasn't as privileged as I'd thought. It was there that I learned those distinctions. An expensive school where there were some girls from the upper class. It was their scorn that taught me the difference. And instead of telling those idiots to go to hell I imitated them. Who knows what they're up to, some of them were nice enough, but I didn't stay in touch with any of them. The classes stay separate on their own. According to Mama they were jealous of me, because I was prettier than all of them.

Another thing that makes me furious is losing arguments with Beatriz. I promise never again to discuss anything if I'm not absolutely sure of what I'm going to present to her, of having my defense well prepared. And another thing, another lie that is, the stuff about Mama's illness! I solemnly swear to myself that I won't tell any more fibs like that. It's only to deceive myself. If Mama isn't here with me it's because I don't want that, because I can't put up with her, she gets on my nerves. And it's shameful to tell Beatriz that she couldn't come to Mexico because of the altitude, because of her heart, when hers is far stronger than mine. Why don't I tell the truth? Mama never did me any harm, she was always out, with plenty of friends, going from house to house playing her canasta, but as far as I'm concerned she gets on my nerves. I can't stand her. It's shameful to have invented that heart ailment.

Anyway we chatted for a good while, Beatriz and I, what a good friend she is, with all she has to do, still coming by the hospital for a while. But something bothers me about her. I realized it when I kissed her goodbye. I don't feel the affection for her that I used to feel for my friends before. Can't I feel anything for anyone anymore? I even got envious, in a quite vicious way, to see her go and me stay here sick. I'm a hyena. And she's a saint. But maybe that's what it is, that she should be so saintly with me. She treats me with real fondness, but I don't know, there's something that isn't really characteristic of friendship, there's something almost maternal, or, I don't know if I even dare write it, there's something in the way she deals with me . . . which isn't like an equal with an equal. It's from a person who's above another. But in a maternal way, because a mother has enormous superiority over her infant. Of course, on one hand it's natural, she's in a far superior position with respect to me, she has money, a family in perfect harmony, and health. It frightens me to go on. There's something, I don't know, something excessively devoted in her. I hope it's not what I'm thinking. That it's not that she knows that my illness has no cure. She's my best friend in Mexico, and the doctor could have told only her. Don't let it be that. Maybe they all know it, except me.

Well, I promised not to give free rein to that pessimism anymore, and I'm going to hold to the promise. Here comes the doctor, I have to stop.

The transatlantic luxury liner departed from the port of Southampton, elegant passengers hailed from the deck, waving, with less conviction every time, their hands, which were gloved. A somewhat older gentleman, of low stature, stocky, was an object of particular attention by the crew. He happened to be a producer of motion pictures, "the owner of that fabulous Hollywood organization in whose firmament more stars shine than in the sky," remarked one tough porter to another. The producer declared to the newspapermen in attendance, who would quickly descend in boats to their writing haunts in the editorial offices, that he had discovered marvelous European talents during his exploratory journey, all of course already under iron-clad contracts of seven years with his office. But he didn't seem relaxed, there on board he kept looking around him constantly, as if looking for something, an object which was precious but nearly irrevocably lost. Once free from the reporters, he put out the Cuban cigar which he smoked only when he felt uneasy, he sunk into a sofa in his suite and called the steward, "I promise you a juicy gratuity if this very night you find me the most beautiful woman in the world, I saw her go up the gangplank and afterward she disappeared. But I know that she remained on board, I'm an expert in star quality and I detect her radiant energy in the vicinity, her whole being is crying out for a camera to film her. I hear this cry."

The travelers were asleep when the sun rose that first morning of travel. Some had happy dreams, others didn't. The luck which had befallen the Mistress was the most blissful of the entire packet boat. She was dreaming that when she woke she would be lying beside a sleeping young man. She was getting up with the utmost care so as not to awaken him, and she was going toward the mirror. The enormous bull's eye—even with arms spread wide she couldn't encompass it—illuminated her, they had admired the sea and the moonless sky from their bed until late into the night, and they had fallen asleep without closing the curtains. She was dreaming that the light at daybreak was awakening her, the mirror was telling her that she was still the most beautiful woman in the world and therefore worthy of her companion. She breathed relief and lay down again, she adored these Irish linen sheets and this coverlet of fur, from what animal? it was a fur thick as a bear's, silky as she didn't know what. She felt her eyelids grow heavy, she would doze again, but scarcely for a few minutes, because if it wasn't one it was the other who recommenced those ventures of one across the other's body, nocturnal excursions, a territory smooth and white, the Mistress by night, a hunt for larks, and in a while the big game, wild beasts roaring with hunger emerged in the dark, during the dangerous safari into the jungles of the male body, which at this moment were suddenly lit by means of an impertinent round sun ray, issuing from the bull's eye. Perhaps the ship had turned gently and the light almost hurt the face of the young man, who couldn't help but awaken.

She told him that they were both dreaming, that the dream consisted in their waking together and remembering the pleasures of that very night whose death was almost complete. Then he contradicted her: first, each night that passed didn't die, but instead it passed . . . to live forever in the memory of both, and finally . . . they weren't dreaming, they were awake, she should grow accustomed to happiness and not confine it to the realm of dreams. She blushed with embarrassment, Theo was right, they were awake.

As dusk fell, the first-class deck could be seen deserted, possibly due to the cold wind which was blowing. The couple took advantage of that and sat there in comfortable recliners, covered with Scottish wool blankets. They wanted to see the first stars appear on their second night aboard ship. He whispered, "My dear, I'll tell you something, so that you don't feel so alone with respect to your apprehensions. I too sometimes find it difficult to believe that such happiness has befallen me. To aid myself in keeping reality separate from dreams, well . . . I'm keeping a diary. But

I ask a favor of you, and it's that you never read it, do you promise me that? . . . Thank you."

A messenger interrupted them, he was carrying a note for Theo, under the assumed name on the documents with which he was traveling. She trembled, she asked that he not open it. "Distinguished Sir: I ask that you contact me. I would like to engage the services of Madam your wife for the seventh art, I could make her the woman most highly admired in the world. Respectfully yours, . . ." The name which closed the text struck her as well known, but she couldn't place it regardless of how hard she strained her memory, Theo, on the other hand, decided it was a question of simple misunderstanding. She disagreed, but he wouldn't listen to her and threw the paper into the sea. "But why are you making such a decision without consulting me?" "The man of your dreams can't be a fop who will obey his woman in whatever she says. If a woman isn't ruled by a man she will be ruled by her caprices, wouldn't you rather that I rule you?"

Night fell. Perhaps affected by the message from Hollywood, the young woman felt the need to lie down a moment on the bed, before dinner. Theo lay down beside her. A while later she got up, although still sleeping. If he had been at her side he would have restrained her. She walked somnambulant, she went out into the corridor, from there to the deck, went up small step ladders, down ramps, almost as if someone were leading her by the hand after having blindfolded her. But who was it that led her thus so quickly, without hesitation? what unknown powers were concerned with her fate? Crew members and passengers saw her pass and thought her an apparition, with her negligee seeming ethereal in the wind. Finally she entered a narrow passageway, she stopped outside a small cabin, a service office. She brought her ear close to the ventilation shafts in the door, within which Theo's voice could be heard, "At what time shall we moor at the island of Funchal?" The harsh voice of a sailor answered, "Before daybreak," "Well, that will help us, darkness is auspicious for disappearances," "The passengers will disembark to make their visit after breakfast, and their names will be recorded inexorably," "And inexorably those whose names don't appear on the list will be assumed to be on board, no one will suspect that they've remained on land," "You've got it, buddy," "This earring of genuine pearls comes as an advance, you'll receive the other one on completion of these . . . off-duty chores."

She bit herself hard on a finger to make sure she wasn't dreaming and it was then that she woke up. But this time it wasn't a question of a nightmare, the voices which she had just heard were real. Immediately she brought her hands to her earlobes, someone had removed her earrings while she slept! She returned to the first-class area holding her breath, immediately Theo's footsteps could be heard inside their suite. She pretended to awaken on receiving the kiss on her forehead, "Were you able to rest? You know, tomorrow we'll get off to take a walk on the exotic island of Funchal, so it's advisable that you gather your strength," "All right, my love. Wouldn't it also be advisable to take a small dose of a sleeping draught? The doctor on board could furnish you with a little flask, that way we would have it for another occasion. . . . Thank you."

Shortly after she wanted to dine, right there in the antechamber of the suite. The only thing still to come was coffee, they were holding hands, suddenly a feigned chill ran up the beauty's back, she asked her lover that he bring her a shawl, stored there a few steps away in the trunk. Seconds were all she needed to dissolve the sleeping draught in the silver coffee pot, "Theo dear, now drink up your two customary cups of coffee and let's go out on deck for a moment, I want to confess something to you." He obeyed, "And you know, my Theo, I won't need to take anything in order to sleep, because I'm already dying of drowsiness. . . . Look at this sky, think that it could be the last night of our lives, why not?, the ship could collide with an iceberg and sink within minutes. Allow me to guide your steps this time, look . . . there is absolutely no one there toward the rear of the deck, completely astern. What fresh air, isn't it? It will help me clarify my thoughts . . . because I must tell you some very serious things. I . . . I'm not a woman like all the others, and you know it, isn't that so? Let's see . . . look me in the eye, you know it, don't you? You yourself told me that one day, but at that moment I wasn't paying attention. After musing over it I realized that you knew everything. You told me . . . that you wouldn't leave my side, especially the day that I turn thirty years old, because on that day. . . . Come now! why does that startle you? are you afraid that this could somehow separate us, the fact that you now know that I know you know it? Well, well . . . this simple confession makes you stagger? are your knees getting weak? . . . I, on the other hand, feel more tranquil than ever, because if you can love me in spite of knowing that I'm a monstrosity, that at once . . . does away with all my fears. . . . Yes, that's better, lean on the railing, look at the sea there below, how dark! isn't it? This place is so intimate, no one can see us, only the sea and sky. . . . But why this doubling over that wet railing? you must try to stand up straight, like the consummate man that you are. . . . And let's see . . . now that you can hardly open your eyes, that your hands and arms and legs have all gone to sleep, now that you can no longer utter a sound, allow me to remove from your pocket, there close to your heart, that notebook where you jot down so many things. . . . Let me see? Yes . . . how good you are to me, you already allow me to do everything that I want, uhmmm, yes, just these last pages will suffice. . . . Let's read a little. . . . 'How despicable I feel tonight. . . . To think that tomorrow she'll believe that I don't love her, because I've handed her over to my coreligionists. I am a Soviet agent, and will be so until death. I couldn't tell her the truth, I'd be risking that she would leave me and that was unbearable for me, somehow I had to keep her by my side. No, I didn't play dirty, could she possibly respect a man without ideals, without honor? There was a moment when I weakened and decided to follow her to the ends of the earth, and from there to more and more bliss, beneath whatever latitude. . . . But there's a fear that lurks inside me, and won't let me alone. A fear even stronger than love itself. Stronger still than the remorse in betraying my cause. And it's the fear that the day will come, that terrible day when she'll turn thirty and in reading my thoughts she will find out that. . . . No! before disillusioning her in this sense I would rather she thought me a spy and her betrayer. But I love her so! Never again will I feel such immense tenderness and desire for any woman, but let's give up this chimera, it would be unbearable to wait for that ominous birthday, knowing that. . . . She would even prefer that I kill her rather than disenchant her. And I will kill her if necessary. Yes, the worst would be to disillusion her and that would be inevitable if she found out that all men . . .' " Theo mustered what strength remained in him and succeeded in giving the notebook a smack, but his trembling hand couldn't hold on and the wind swept it away, flung it against a coil of rope. With another great effort Theo opened his eyes again slightly and looked at her, it seemed to him that the young woman was brandishing a smoking weapon. She had nothing in her hands, nor did she need anything, given that the young man's parting energies had finally abandoned him and he remained doubled over the side of the ship. She thought she heard footsteps, she turned around but didn't descry anyone. She took hold of her lover's ankles and lifted them. There was no need to push him, the young man's own weight made him slip over the railing, and fall from there to the sea.

She immediately ran to find the notes, but a gust of wind outstripped her and swept the notebook along the deck. She wanted to know everything, desperately, what did he fear she would read in his thoughts on turning thirty? She leaned down to pick up the black diary, and once again the wind snatched it away. The notebook flew through the air, hurdled over the banister and fell to the sea. She let out a cry of hatred against the loosened elements of nature. "Never fear, I didn't see a thing." The beauty swung around, horrified. A few steps away stood an older man, small in stature, stout, smoking a Cuban cigar, "I repeat, I didn't see a thing. I am the motion picture producer who sent you the telegram, or should I say the most important maker of dreams in this century," "Dreams? . . . Dreams terrify me . . ." "Let's get to the point, esteemed Madam. Let's pretend we're in my office in Hollywood. I didn't see a thing, or, better said, yes, I saw a desperate youth throw himself overboard. And I've heard you accept a fabulous contract—for a lifetime—with my glamorous studios. You'll be very well paid, I might add. Of course, your private life will have to follow certain rules, and the company will supervise your activities, above all those goings-on having to do with moral judgment. Does Madam find these conditions to her liking?" "I'm expecting a child, by the young man who just killed himself," "I'm already making a note of this, the board of directors of the company will decide what to do with him, or her, wouldn't you like to give birth to a little girl who would perpetuate your beauty?"

Without answering, what need was there?, she set off to return to her cabin, she thought that those few minutes which had passed would have sufficed to bring on Theo's death by drowning. Now he would have joined that legion of bodiless, idle spirits, who played with the destinies of the living.

5

FRIDAY. TODAY I'LL turn my thoughts to Pozzi's strong points. Was the first day important? I don't think so. In the University café. Oh! Last night I couldn't stop thinking about one thing, was I paying Fito with my body or was he paying me with his? While I could have that kind of pleasure with him, I thought I loved him, at night. But it's too bad the days were so long, and that stuff didn't last more than a few minutes. Well, on Sunday mornings it was longer, almost all morning, enjoying it without any rush. But all the rest of the day there was a price to pay. So high. How could Beatriz think that I stopped loving him because that stuff started going sour? I'm quite sure about that.

And even if that pleasure of the first months had continued, why was it me who had to pay afterward, by taking charge of the house? He should have paid me! I was attractive enough, or still am. Yes, of course I paid, because looking after the house exhausted me and those nighttime activities came to be compensation, the payment that he gave me. But this is all mixed up. I'm contradicting myself. He didn't pay me, I paid him, that's what I want to make clear. If I had been single I would have passed the time much more enjoyably, the way I did later when I was divorced. Therefore, I'm not wrong when I say that I was paying him. If he'd wanted to have a woman as valuable as me in his house, he'd have had to be the one to pay. Yes, he took care of house expenses, but I was the one who had to keep things going, to have a well-run home you have to be on the alert all day long, even with a staff of servants. Then I came to be the housekeeper during the day, and the hooker on duty every night. And what he gave me was food and clothing. And that worked well in the open when I separated from him, because since I was the one who wanted to leave I had to accept the fact that he wouldn't give me a cent. So I had to put up with the dinners with those stupid people he invited, and do everything he wanted me to. And the only thing I got away clean with were those good moments of intimacy. So really I was paying him with my work, with my devotion to the house, I was paying him so that at night he would do me that little favor. The more I think about it, the more furious it makes me. I want them to pay me! Since I'm a woman, and an object, according to the latest thinking, I want to be paid, and well. At least that! When I leave this hospital I have to define myself, or I'll turn butch like the feminists, and never that, or I'll dedicate myself to being paid well. Of course at thirty it's not the same. If I could only go back and start at twenty again! That way I'd really get full value. Let them pay, if not with money, which doesn't matter that much to me, let them pay with attentions, with time devoted, because I'm not going to squander myself any more for free. And least of all that I myself should be the one to pay.

I keep going off on tangents. And misleading tangents. Instead of jotting down agreeable things to lift my spirits. A wonderful moment: when I understood all that Pozzi explained to me about those latest theories of psychoanalysis. It was during the first month that he'd started coming to my apartment. Another wonderful moment: the new tie. But that happened before. Let me see if I can remember these things in order. It wasn't the first time we went out. The agreeable things get erased from my memory, why? I'm going to make an effort and I'm going to remember. The first time he came to the house: he arrived with a new tie! he gave himself away, he wanted to impress me, what a wonderful moment! But I'm not being accurate, that wasn't a wonderful moment. There weren't so many wonderful moments. With him there never were, except for that night after the seminar. And it wasn't because of him, it was because of the ideas he explained to me.

When Beatriz was asking me, that's when I realized that he'd never won me over completely. Why? Isn't it undeniable that he

has all it takes to win a woman over? He's extremely good-looking,
he's pleasant, he's intelligent, he's sensitive, he always has something to say, he's sexy, he has a good heart, then what does he
lack? Nothing. Then there's no doubt that it's my fault, that I
can't feel anything for anyone. But no, that's not true either! I
do feel! I feel desperate to find someone, the man who will change
all this! And if I start thinking about it, and searching for what's
deep inside me, and if I concentrate, as I'm doing right now, if
I concentrate totally, I can almost see this man. It's a man whom
I admire, and I'm walking along a street, I'm going to my house,
or to my job, or going shopping, and I see him and I forget what
I have to do, I forget where I'm going, and I ask him, and he
realizes that I'm lost, I've lost my way, I've forgotten everything,
because I don't remember who I am, I don't remember that I'm
attractive, that I'm proud, that I'm not going off with the first
man that I find, and he takes me to his house, an old house full
of books, and with a grand piano, bay windows looking out over
a dense garden, half in shadow, and someone's playing the piano,
his mother? his wife? And that's where he realizes that I can't go
into the house, and he leaves with me, making sure no one
recognizes him, and we go to an unknown place, and one day he
gets lost on the street, as I did, because he doesn't know the place,
and he forgets where he was going, and he asks the name of the
street and no one can tell him, because he doesn't remember
where he was going, and they ask him who he is and he can't
remember that either, or it's that he doesn't want to say, who
knows. No, if he gets lost on the street I won't like him that much,
it's possible that I'm not feeling that much for him by now, no,
I'm sure, I don't feel anything for him anymore.

I'm crazy, writing things that make no sense. But the truth is
that while all that was occurring to me . . . I was sure I loved this
unknown man with all my strength. What's Pozzi's defect? I'll go
on to see if I can figure it out. That first visit to the house: he
praised the way the apartment was decorated, he was no fool, he
realized which things were valuable. It was easy to draw the
conclusion: he dressed badly out of carelessness, because he had
good taste. He made me tell him everything about my life. He

left very late without anything else happening, just talking and talking. I was very cold to him, why did I pretend? Because I was dying for something to happen, and to have an experience which wasn't Fito. But I kept up appearances. I froze. When he left I regretted it.

The next encounter: I didn't know how to go about calling him, then I had a brilliant idea. I rang him up to offer him tickets to the ballet for the entire family, box seats, on a Saturday afternoon. I left the envelope at the ticket office so it would all happen very elegantly, I didn't have to meet his wife or anything like that. He called me afterward to thank me and we arranged to meet at home. To avenge myself I decided I would be the one to ask the questions, about his life. Ah, now I remember why the first visit at home ended so coldly. It's that he asked me if I'd gotten divorced because another man had entered the picture, and he refused to believe it had been for other reasons. As if there always had to be a man in the middle, he made me very angry, I assured him that there hadn't been a third person and he looked at me with a little smirk, incredulous. And after that I lose the thread, I don't remember where we saw each other next, if it was in the same restaurant as the first time.

At "dinner," he told me everything, about his town half an hour from Buenos Aires, and he got irritated because I said it was a neighborhood of Buenos Aires. Quilmes a neighborhood of Buenos Aires? I envy those people who feel such affection for the place where they were born, and while we ate Pozzi was telling me about his life, that his father had owned a delicatessen, that he and his wife had been boyfriend and girlfriend since they were fifteen years old, she was the daughter of a notary. That he had begun to work before graduating from law school, in spite of the fact that his family had enough money to pay for his career. And that at present in addition to his practice in a commercial firm he did other work. And he didn't want to tell me what. Social work, I think he said. All of a sudden he said it, defending political prisoners who couldn't afford a lawyer. I couldn't restrain myself and gave him a kiss on his greasy mouth, I think from the chicken cacciatore. I wanted to answer one generosity with another. Because what he had just said did seem to me proof of generosity. Then I stepped down off my pedestal and kissed him. How stupid I was. But isn't it good to follow your impulses? But the truth is that for a woman, the more passive the better, more elegant, isn't it? Anyway I don't remember that moment happily, no, it makes me embarrassed to remember it, I should be honest, I see myself as being ridiculous giving him that kiss. Why? was it really ridiculous? why am I ashamed about that kiss? Everything's dripping with grease, his father's delicatessen, the chicken cacciatore, or is it me who can do nothing but paint everything ugly, even memories? That night we went to my apartment. After that came the misunderstandings of the following date, which wasn't enjoyable, and then the stuff having to do with the seminar, which was. I don't want to write down disagreeable things. One night he had to go to the seminar about Lacan, it was once a week. I asked him to skip it, what foolishness. He invited me to go with him. I went and didn't understand a single word. From there straight home, I had something cold ready to eat. I burst into tears, I was ashamed because I hadn't understood a thing. He explained everything that they'd discussed in the seminar from the beginning of the term and I understood it perfectly. We talked, I made some observations that he thought were intelligent. We tried to apply one of those theories, something having to do with a child and a mirror, to people we knew, and it got to be daytime, just talking. We saw the dawn break. And now I don't remember those theories anymore, at that time I bought a book which explained everything, but then came the mess of the trip here and there the book stayed. How wonderful it is when you're overwhelmed with that desire to learn. To improve yourself. I think that one of the most denigrating, filthiest moments of my life was that one particular day with Fito. When he yelled at me because sometimes at the table I didn't remember what the company's name was of the executive we had invited. And I begged his forgiveness and promised him always to keep informed. What a way of humiliating me that moron had. How I'd like to kill him this very minute. I'd strangle him. What garbage he is, and stupid me being left with this rage because I didn't answer him as he deserved. What was

I, scared of him physically? Why does one sometimes tolerate being treated contemptuously like this? where do we get that dread that paralyzes us? from where? fear of being struck? but he never hit me or even threatened me! where does this degrading fear come from, then? I don't see any other explanation: because a man, even if he doesn't threaten to, can still beat you, and he's much stronger. And a woman has no choice but to be afraid because face to face she hasn't got a chance of winning, nature willed it that way. Filthy, rotten nature, why does it have to put a woman in a shitty position like that? huh, why?

What do I gain by making myself nervous? Nor is there any need to exaggerate. "Everything about you is exaggeration," one of the sentences that Mama has repeated most to me in her life. Especially when my daughter was born. Because with Clarita I went from staying awake all night in order to take care of her, to doing nothing, to letting others care for her. During the first months of her life I couldn't sleep, worried because something would happen to her, is she breathing all right, is she cold, is she hot. Mama predicted it, that I would go crazy if I kept worrying that way. And yes, I did go crazy, the thing had to give way at some point. Or maybe not, maybe I did go sane. During those first months my brain was overdoing it around the clock, I always had such an imagination, but so misspent, wasn't it? the illnesses, I imagined all sorts of things that could attack Clarita, those treacherous drafts, windows which could open mysteriously during the night and now the chill of pneumonia would sneak in. If it hadn't been for Pilar. . . . Forty-odd years old, from the province of San Luis, single, whose mother had just died. That's the only thing I've got to thank Fito's family for, a babysitter. What would have become of me without her? I saw her take hold of Clarita, like a lifesaver. They say such things, these provincial women, according to her, month after month she'd been dealt a card of death in hand after hand, and she had lost, that was why she so loved caring for a little baby, after having cared for a dying old woman. How long did it take me to catch on? A few days, I think, or a single minute, and now I knew that Clarita was safe, and not another minute went by before I decided to go back to the

University, after almost three years! Sometimes my brain works like a computer, how shameful. When it's said that a person is scheming, that's what it means isn't it? I don't like admitting it but it really happened that way.

But it's one thing to be organized and another to be calculating. Pozzi said that to me, that I was a machine and that I organized my week like, I don't remember how he phrased it, not like an ant, but something unpleasant like that. Of course, he could organize his week but I couldn't. Another expression he used was "manipulator." That I wanted to handle him the way I handled scheduling those regulated meetings with Clarita. For instance, he accused me of planning the days I was to see Clarita to coincide with days when there were matinees at the Theater. It wasn't in order to be at work and to see her in passing. My job didn't require me to be there during the performance. The truth is that I wanted to educate her tastes, starting with ballet, and later, if she liked it, to go on with a little opera, and after that concerts. A little girl of five can already begin to appreciate music. But Clarita had no interest. She did enjoy sitting in the best boxes, with me and Mama, the three of us alone in a box seating six, however we pleased. But I saw that she got distracted, that sometimes she wasn't looking at the stage. It was Pozzi who said it to me, when I told him, he was the one who guessed the reason ahead of time. He proposed that I give Clarita tickets to go with her father. I had taken her to see the *Nutcracker*, *Sleeping Beauty*, performances geared more for children, which she'd have to like better. The following week there was only *Giselle*, which has less variety. Fito told me that the little one went crazy with delight. And when I asked her she told me that it was much prettier than the other ballets. Need we say more. And it was the same with her clothes, the things I bought her . . . she would rarely want to wear them. And to make matters worse, the things that Fito's mother bought her were in extraordinarily bad taste. What torture to see my own daughter dressed so badly. And I let Pilar keep taking her to the Theater, in my place. That's why it makes me so angry when they say that children have an intuitive sense, infallible, in knowing who loves them. I loved her, because a mother can't help but love her little girl, and she was the cutest thing, and if I wanted her own good ahead of everything else, why did Clarita have such problems with me?

Pozzi never understood that. According to him the little one couldn't forgive me for leaving the house. What did he know? As far as Clarita was concerned Pilar had always been her mother, I always knew that, but she should have been more affectionate with me anyway. Fito, on the other hand, always behaved well in matters having to do with his daughter, and he let me see her as often as I liked. Pozzi sometimes talks just for the sake of talking. One good thing about Fito was that he liked the fact that I had everything planned ahead of time. Maybe if I'd known how to deal with him, if I'd known how to talk to him, he would have changed. But no, he simply was the way he was, and just you try to change that. No, my mistake was marrying him. But in a way he was a reasonable man. And Pozzi sometimes isn't, the way he's set on the idea that if Clarita had been a boy I would have wanted to keep her with me, what stubbornness. The next time he comes I'm going to be very firm with him, I swear it. And the truth is, I don't think that Fito would have wanted to annoy me, he really believed the business of the executive meals was important. I was the one to blame for not telling him what I thought. And that's where the bile began to collect. There's nothing worse than not talking. But for me when something makes me angry I just freeze up and that's all. Maybe that's the difference between men and women, that the woman is all impulse, all sentiment, and allows herself to be consumed by rage, instead of saying what she thinks. But the truth is . . . at those moments I can't think. When someone is telling me what to do I don't think. The blood rises to my head and that's all. A typically feminine reaction. By contrast a man, where someone tries to boss him around is exactly when he rises to the challenge. That has to be recognized, that one is born that way. Beatriz says that that's not the way we're born, that's how we're trained to be. I think it's a matter of temperament.

And it's only logical, because if one is attractive to them it's because of one's sensitivity, of how tender one can be, and for that one can't be all intellect. It's either one or the other. Otherwise there wouldn't be any attraction between the sexes. One contributes one thing, and the other another. But then it shouldn't make me furious when they try to push me around. And furthermore they succeed. But here's the critical point, what happens is that a real man, or a superior man, let's say, not superior to me, because then Beatriz would be right, and she's not right, but superior in another sense . . . Well, I'd better start again.

Anyway, it's bad for women to get it into their heads that they're just like men, it's bad, it's bad, and it's bad. Because we're different. The trouble is that you need a very special man to be able to appreciate us, to understand us. The plural again. And if there's something I'm sure about it's that I'm not interested in talking to women, by any chance would you talk to a flower vase? A man who understands us, I was saying, and doesn't take advantage of our weaknesses. A superior man. It's him I want to talk to, it seems to me. And will I have the luck to know one like that sometime? Because as far as existing, of course he exists.

Beatriz can't understand me, she's into something else. It's also true that she can't understand me because I don't tell her everything. Why is that? could it be embarrassment? or because of the same stuff as always? the way I couldn't get roused to talk to Fito face to face, I haven't got the nerve to talk to her either? and with myself? I've never talked about Alejandro in this diary, so not even just to myself do I have the courage to talk when . . . when what? Maybe if I knew who this person is that I want to talk to, maybe then I would dare. That superior man. But where is he? Why doesn't he give me any sign of life? If Papa hadn't died so young, maybe he would help me at this moment now. Papa, I have to ask you something, is it true that the dead can see what's going on with the living? I think they can, something tells me yes, but then why don't I get any word from you?

Though I'd rather that no, that the dead wouldn't see anything, so that Papa wouldn't have seen what went on with Alejandro. It makes me ashamed, that must be why I don't want to tell anyone, or even to think about it myself, so that Papa won't hear it, or read it in my thoughts. I will never tell anyone, let me even forget it myself.

Friday. Papa, I'm scared. Today I felt those same pains again that I had before they operated, what's going on? not as severe but the same pains, maybe they didn't remove what they had to remove? I don't feel well.

Later. They gave me a sedative and I feel a little better. The worst is being scared. Papa, I don't have to be frightened by a little pain. I have things to tell you, I don't have to be frightened about that either, because you'll understand. Papa, without my realizing it, everything got started. In the very Theater, which brought me such satisfaction, such joy, that's where it began, how could I have known what was coming? Two great singers, the best Lucia and the best Edgar at that time, were in Buenos Aires for *Lucia di Lammermoor*. What a marvel it was, but between the first performance and the ones that followed they had five days free, they asked me if they could visit an Argentine cattle ranch. A friend of friends suggested an acquaintance of his, who owned a ranch in the province of Buenos Aires, no more than five hours away by car, a big music lover. They called him by telephone. Half an hour later Alejandro was already in my office.

I didn't like him, I felt repulsion at first sight. Milky white, of strong build but a little fat, bald. Of strong build, but spongy. An evasive glance, a rat's glasses with the frame made of gold. Always looking down. Do you understand, dearest Papa, what kind of person he was? His grandparents Spaniards and Italians. His father had been the town auctioneer, he prospered by buying land in the countryside. He was studying medicine when his father died, he returned home to be with his mother and stayed there. The mother had always been sick, all her life. According to him, from chronic anemia, from the time that he first had the power to reason he saw his mother ill, a very religious woman. His father had a constitution as strong as iron, but one day he died suddenly of a heart attack. The mother is sure to bury all of us, me at any time now, if I go on like this.

My first impression was negative, I should always follow that first impression, isn't that so, Papa? that weekend on the ranch the weather was perfect, a cavalcade of horses, the sun on the winter plains, everyone bundled up warmly. The living room of the ranch house lit up with fires in the chimneys. The foreigners delighted. Me nervous and tense because of the excessive attention of the owner of the house. On my return to Buenos Aires I received flowers and bonbons. The first time we went out he took me to the most expensive French restaurant. Me always on edge, due to the exorbitant attention. An unbelievably timid man, but contemptuous toward the servants, it disgusted me. In that you were exemplary, in the respect and dignity that you showed those people.

I was determined not to see him anymore. He'd leave me several telephone messages every day. When I acknowledged these he invited me to the ranch with Clarita and Mama. I thought it would be unreasonably selfish on my part to deprive them of this, the place was a wonder. Big mistake, Clarita got bored and Mama didn't get along with the old witch. Clarita didn't want to go anymore. The old woman really was of broom-stick material, talking to me the entire time about her son's goodness, of his sacrifice on her behalf. As a matter of fact, his only real interest at the ranch, where he spent half of each week, was his record collection, a splendid one.

That very Monday I had a call at the Theater, from Paris: the Saint-Laurent office was informing me of a credit note in my name. But I turned it down, with deep-felt sorrow. In spite of that, a few days later the packages arrived from Saint-Laurent, and I just couldn't return such lovely things. The fit was perfect, my measurements had been taken by a maid, the one who did alterations for the mother. She had measured my clothes, when I was at the ranch. He'd heard me tell the soprano that I adored Saint-Laurent's things. We agreed to see each other some night that week, but strictly as friends. Papa, my big mistake was not telling him of my involvement with that young man Pozzi, Juan José, from the beginning. Maybe I was greedy for more presents. I should also admit that with this Juan José, we were seeing each other less and less. And Papa, you probably can't understand this part, but a woman who doesn't lose her head over an item of high fashion just isn't a woman.

I hadn't known what it was like to stay awake all night just out of anxiety, and he succeeded in making it happen. More than once. I remember the first time very well. We'd had dinner together that night and he brought me home. I didn't think that he would stay there and hide spying on me until he saw that young man Juan José arrive, and also how could he know that he was coming to my apartment, if I had my curtains drawn? Undoubtedly Juan José guessed correctly, Alejandro had set a detective on me. I chalked it up to paranoia on the part of Juan José, who thought he was being watched by the police, or whatever you call it. He was right, Juan José I mean. That night after Juan José left I was sleeping very nicely, without suspecting anything. See Papa, there I do admit that I was in the wrong, because I enjoyed playing two cards, do I seem very cheap to you? But Papa, a woman has to make her own way, it doesn't mean lowering herself to have these kinds of relations, I assure you, these are different times. I understand that what I did wouldn't seem right to you, having relations with Pozzi, but it's not promiscuity. Yes, I understand that in your times a man couldn't respect a woman like that. But now it's the opposite, a woman without experience, of a priggish sort, isn't respected, would you want to have a prude for a daughter? As I was telling you, that night the telephone rang really late. Alejandro was threatening to commit suicide if I didn't see him first thing in the morning. I'd never heard someone say that he was going to kill himself, and I got scared, I felt enormous pity for him. I made him swear that he wouldn't do such a foolish thing.

In the morning I called him early, I hadn't been able to shut my eyes. He, on the other hand, was sleeping like a dormouse, for sure, because he took a while to come to the telephone and his voice sounded like he was still asleep. He came over, it occurred to me that the best thing to get rid of his passion was . . . well, to have sex. I said it out of an impulse, and I said it quite earnestly, I thought I was being very modern suggesting that to him. I told him that this way he would realize that it was only a physical attraction, because there wasn't any real spiritual communication between the two of us, we didn't understand each other at all.

Well, I didn't believe an Argentine was capable of saying it, but this is what happened. He said that he was Catholic, but seriously, not as a joke. He would never have sexual relations except with a woman who loved him. And if I didn't love him, never that. Because to him, sex without love was something for animals.

By then I think that the trouble at the Theater was already starting. It was the season of '73, the Peronist government of Cámpora had already come to power. Pozzi was overjoyed with the atmosphere of freedom, especially the freedom of the press, and amnesty for prisoners. Before that twenty-fifth of May when Cámpora rose to power and let all the political prisoners go free, poor Pozzi had been incredibly busy with his prisoners. Now that he had some spare time I was already mixed up with this guy. But how can one make sense of something like this, that I should have offered myself to this person, despite the repugnance that he stirred up in me? I feel such aversion toward him that I can't write the name. Alejandro. It's that his name doesn't suit him at all. For me that name is associated with grandeur, with Alexander the Great. I'll have to find him a nickname. Pozzi called him Beelzebub. Not bad, is it? A devil, but a strange devil, a melancholy devil.

And the intrigue at the Theater. During a performance of *Rigoletto*, at intermission, some thirty or forty hooligans came in through a passageway and began to sing several stanzas of the national anthem, at the top of their lungs. The audience, as always when the anthem is sung at a public ceremony, stood up, from a combination of respect and fear which was nauseating. Respect toward the anthem and fear toward the intruders, do you understand? But how had they been able to get in? Someone in the management had to have been in complicity, no doubt about it. Without even finishing the song they started shouting in unison that the Teatro Colón was for Argentine performers, and out with the foreigners. It was a group of nationalists. Of those who loathe anything foreign. And who wanted to demand that we engage only Argentine singers. But that was absurd. Because for example we did have classical ballet dancers, for all the parts, but not voices. There are good Argentine singers, but not to fill all the roles in a season like the one at this theater, which is the third most prestigious opera house in the world. In short, an absurd demand. Furthermore in no opera house of any importance can they get along with singers from only that country, not even in the United States or in Italy itself. They always have to import someone. And in those days the officials appointed by the new government began to appear. One said one thing and the other another. Among those who arrived some wanted to continue to maintain the Theater's reputation, and others wanted to cancel all the contracts with foreign singers who were already rehearsing.

Beelzebub. Pozzi was the first to ask me what his politics were. I didn't think he had any. That same night of *Rigoletto* Beelzebub waited for me at the door to take me out to eat. The first thing I did was tell him about that atrocity. He defended them. He said that we had to go back to our own roots, those of a healthy Catholic country, and I don't know how many other things. Such a hatred for any customs that weren't ours, I couldn't believe it. A hatred for everything that came from outside which was, as he saw it, a degeneration of our customs, stemming from the European corruption which we wanted to imitate at all costs, because we were fools with an inferiority complex, and everything that came from outside seemed better to us. In other words, a horrible puritan.

A horrible puritan, yes, I'm writing it here on this page, but I didn't say it to him. And that's what makes me furious. It wasn't because I was scared of him. On the contrary, he was a man whom I could destroy with one word, if I felt like it. But I didn't say those things to his face, what I thought of him, for other reasons. I wish I knew what those real reasons were, maybe nobody would ever know. Couldn't it have been that I felt tremendous pity for him, and that's all? Right, Papa?

We had this chat shortly after the first suicide threat. How could I get up the nerve to tell him what I thought of him? But I don't want to come off as a saint either, those presents played a significant part as well. What power a person can have with a lot of money, that really frightens me. All her life Mama had dreamed of having a mink coat, how, where was I going to get up the courage to return it to the furrier the day it arrived at my house? It was Mother's Day in '73, October. "For your mother, for having brought such beauty into the world," or something like that. Beelzebub. Only a devil is capable of thinking of something like that. How could I be so cruel as to deny Mama this joy?

But why didn't I get worked up to confront him about the private detective who was following me? this was a concrete fact, not a feeling or something vague like that. And why didn't I have the nerve to tell him? there I do think I was scared. But of what? People with a lot of money always scared me, or is it something else? it inspires respect in me? I don't think it's just in me, I don't have to be so stupid as to accuse myself of things as if I were the only one guilty. Though it's not talked about it seems to me that someone very rich has that effect on everyone. And the truth is that a wealthy person can buy whatever he wants, a person, the police, even a judge, if we're not careful.

He told me, that to kiss my hand, for him, meant so much more than who knows what for someone else. And that he would never kiss me on the lips, if I couldn't tell him that I was beginning to love him. And now I have to confess something else that I will never understand: despite the repulsion that I felt for him, the day of Mama's mink I told him, with sheer brazenness, that I was beginning to love him. Dear Papa, I won't try to lie to you, but it's true: I was moved by that expense. And he gave me the first kiss on my mouth. That thin mouth without lips, and saliva that was so cold. How disgusting. And how disgusting of me, to let myself be influenced by this gift, when I knew that three thousand dollars didn't mean a thing to him. But oh no, this fetishism of furs and expensive dresses, so gorgeous! No, why be unfair to oneself either, just because it's a woman doesn't have to mean it's a question of frivolity and superficiality. No! and I want to emphasize this to Beatriz. The subject of garb is very complicated, because in this, Papa, the matter of art enters in. And I don't mean craftsmanship, I mean art! creations of unbelievable artistic value. Saint-Laurent is a danger for the world, Papa. And of course, a woman, having a greater artistic sensibility, which is unquestionable, don't deny that, well, being more sensitive she values these rags more and loses her head. But she doesn't lose it just because, she loses it because a Beelzebub knows what weapons to attack with. If the truth be told!

It was in October of that Mother's Day, or November, that many of the officials resigned from the Theater and the Ministry of Culture, those appointed by Cámpora's government. I think they hadn't even lasted three months. And then came those from the new regime, Perón and Isabel's. He hadn't sent me a single word in advance, Beelzebub. One morning a list arrived of the two or three new Theater officials, really high up, and there his name was. Why, if he had never been involved in politics before?

Mama noticed it, and Pozzi also noticed it, through things heard on the line, but, of course, because at that point he called on the telephone infrequently or not at all, he was late in letting me know. I hadn't believed Mama. My telephone was tapped. And Mama's was also tapped. Pozzi didn't even want to tell me at home. He thought even the apartment might be bugged. We agreed to meet in a café. It was more or less at the same time of Alejandro's election to the Colón's board of directors. No, because at that point he hadn't started the business about marriage yet. It must have been in early December, because it was already Christmas when Beelzebub brought up the subject of marriage. For us to get married at the end of the year, and to spend the summer on a honeymoon in the Orient, Europe, wherever I wanted. How confused I get about these dates. He could have offered me a trip to Mars, and I would have still told him no. A kiss is one thing, a wedding something else again. The truth is that I would only consider marrying again if it was to a superexceptional person. Well, you can't really be sure about that. You only need to fall in love to make a mistake like getting married. But there I think I'm safe, because unless it's a really exceptional man I couldn't fall in love, stay calm, Papa.

My trip to Mexico really began there, in that café where I met up with Pozzi. He told me that he'd found out everything he could about Alejandro. That he was an extreme rightist, that he'd taken some political action in the small town near his ranch. That he'd had something to do with a protest against a pair of teachers in the town's high school, who lived together without being married, and had had them dismissed on the grounds of immorality. And that he had bad acquaintances, people on the extreme right, ultra-Catholics and nationalists. And that those people were in league with Perón's new cabinet. That Alejandro was dangerous. It was at that moment that I began to feel claustrophobic, a feeling that I couldn't breathe anymore in Buenos Aires.

There's one thing I'd like to know, but how? It's this: after that conversation with Pozzi, I was already quite clear on what Alejandro was all about, and the next time that I saw him, instead of making any accusations as to what he was, I was more gentle than ever with him. If I'd told him to go where he deserved, just over there, could I have avoided what came next? But it's that I'm also confusing myself, the truth is that when Pozzi told me all of this, I wasn't convinced that it was true.

Yes, that's exactly it, because the day before Christmas eve, when they raided Mama's house, I went to him to ask for help, to Alejandro, at no time did I think that he could be behind all of that. He came to see me right away, he accompanied me to the Ministry of the Interior. According to him, they had discovered that you, Papa, had belonged to a lodge, a secret society, to which a personage unsympathetic to the new regime had belonged, and that they needed all possible evidence. They didn't say anything about it to me at the Ministry, they were full of apologies, that it was an inexcusable error, that this and the other. It was Alejandro who told me about the lodge. Poor Mama almost died of fright. And the two of us lavishing thanks on him for the protection he was giving us.

But subconsciously I was rebelling in some way. During those very days I asked to have my passport renewed. Somehow I had a foreboding of what was coming, and what was already going on, with Alejandro. To top it all off Mama told me that there had always been something odd about you, Papa, something about secret meetings, about things that had never been explained. That scared me. And now that I think about it, it makes me laugh: it's that you may have had a mistress somewhere, and you gave Mama all sorts of excuses. I understand you, I see no wrong in that. But afterward there was no escape, once the January vacation was over, the whole month at his cattle ranch with that crazy mother, my mother sort of crazy too, and Clarita getting bored, at that point I felt there was no other way out, and I told him that I would never marry him.

But as I resumed my activities, the worst happened. I called Pozzi, whom I hadn't wanted to see, partly because of that vacation, but mostly because Alejandro absorbed me more every day. But I called Pozzi and told him the latest developments. Alejandro had told me that there were people in the Ministry who wanted to arrest Mama and interrogate her thoroughly, so that she could tell them about your activities, Papa, from twenty years ago. According to Alejandro, if it hadn't been for him things would already have turned ugly. Pozzi agreed with me, that these were all Alejandro's lies. But lies that he had the power to convert into truth. It all became even more obvious if one other matter was added. Alejandro told me that if we had already been married by the end of the year, all that unpleasantness with Mama would have been avoided. It was blackmail, without a doubt. But I couldn't muster the nerve to say it to his face, and it wasn't entirely from fear, it makes me angry that I can't make that clear, I wasn't scared of him, Papa, I swear it, it didn't frighten me to say things to his face, it made me feel sorry for him, because he was so madly in love with me.

It was around then that I agreed to consider the possibility of marriage once again, that he should give me six months' time. He added it would be suitable to announce the engagement. I brought up the excuse of Clarita, that I wanted the little one to know him better, to grow fond of him. More or less around September we could have the wedding, I told him. A spring bride. The truth is that the whole thing seems like a nightmare, it being impossible to see Pozzi, now the terror was all-encompassing. But at the same time I had a hope that everything would right itself, that yes, that Alejandro would realize his mistake on his own.

More or less toward the middle of the year I came to believe that things were more calm, because it was so obvious that I was dying of boredom with him, with that querulous Beelzebub, that we had nothing more to say to each other, and that he was bored out of his mind with me. But the worse I treated him, the tighter he hung on to me. And a little later, the greatest horror, the greatest surprise, the termination of my job at the Theater. They were dismissing me because they no longer needed my services. According to him it was the work of someone in the Ministry who hated him, and was avenging himself through me. What a lie, they were his orders. What doubt can there be, don't you think? Now I couldn't put up with it any longer. Without saying good-bye, without anything, I came up here. I came with all the presents. With jewelry that he had given me in the meantime. And in recapitulating all of this, I think and think about it, and I don't hate him. I feel tremendous pity for him. Papa, what am I made of? I swear to you that I feel not hatred, but pity. But I should feel even more pity toward myself, right? Papa . . . I feel that you're so far away. As if you weren't understanding me.

6

THE NEW SCREEN sensation, also known as the most beautiful woman in the world, battled captive in her bed against a very high fever. In the distance she seemed to hear the cry of a baby girl. She wanted to sit up, but wasn't able to lift her head up from the pillow, she tried to stretch her hand to grasp the handle of some mirror nearby—she lived surrounded by them—but neither was she able to secure one. She brought the hand to her forehead, she withdrew her fingers, aghast, as when one unintentionally touches a white-hot iron, but her fingers had already caught fire and were quickly being consumed, they crackled as they burned. The intense pain of scorched flesh woke her, the clock read five twenty-five. Her nightmares again, the worst thing was that shadows showed under her eyes when she hadn't rested well the previous night, and the camera relished picking them up. On those occasions she received threatening messages from the management, she was accused of settling in to read all through the night, instead of sleeping. Because all she was allowed to do at night, under the present circumstances, was to read.

One minute later the hand bell rang impertinently, as it did every morning and the actress arose. Good morning! the lady-in-waiting cried hoarsely, from the bungalow's kitchenette. She didn't respond, she had accustomed that Cerberus to her early morning ill humor. Thus she recommenced the daily routine for shooting, but she far preferred this to the program which awaited her between one film and the next: lessons in the dramatic arts in the same studio, followed by gymnastics, ballet lessons, futile attempts at voice instruction. She washed her face and put on any old trousers and any old blouse, a kerchief on her head. The hated

Betsy already had a cup of tea ready. Back to the bathroom to move her bowels, as she was in the habit of doing after several sips of the hot liquid, and next five minutes of breathing exercises in the garden in front of the porch. In the other bungalows everyone was sleeping, perhaps some young husband—all spread out beside his spouse—dreamed of the actress after having seen her the previous night in her latest film. The nestling cottages were scattered along the slope of one of the many hills in Hollywood, the two women descended along a footpath which zigzagged downward until it reached the street.

At six o'clock sharp the studio chauffeur arrived, "Good morning, Miss Star. Good morning, Miss Betsy." The women didn't answer, as was their custom with the black chauffeur. In the mirror the actress and he exchanged an odd glance. Betsy immediately opened up the typewritten script and read the dialogue aloud from the scene to be shot that morning. As she usually did, the foreigner tripped over the consonant "w," when followed by a vowel. At six thirty-five they entered the studio, already in the midst of bustling operation. The company required the actresses to have breakfast at home, but she couldn't eat anything solid until well after an hour had passed since she'd awakened. The company had relented and served her a magnificent breakfast in the large commissary every working day. Fortunately, at that hour she was the only luminary present and the others wouldn't envy the portion of rolled oats, ham and eggs, milk, bread, and butter which the divine Viennese—as she was promoted—was able to ingest without losing her figure.

At seven o'clock sharp she entered the makeup salon. Each actress had access to this area through private passageways, they were few who wanted to be seen scarcely awake and without cosmetics. With the most beautiful woman in the world the work required very little time, something more than an hour and a half. First her hair was washed, afterward the celebrated part in the middle was marked and the ends of every lock of hair curled. Next the nineteen different cosmetics were applied, with which her face would defy the reflectors. Meanwhile Betsy, without rush and without interruption, continued reading her the dialogue.

The scant half hour that remained before entering the set for filming she spent walking to her dressing room, already within the very set at the filming location, and dressing as the first scene demanded.

At nine o'clock sharp she arrived where the set for an Oriental café had been built. She was wearing a suit jacket in the European style, but she was covered with a light black veil, hanging halfway down her legs in length and placed directly over her hair. Her beauty obtained ahs in admiration. Looking at her were—satisfied —the Hungarian director and—envious—the brawny leading man. After a brief general greeting, she, grievous mistake, began to speak in German with the director. The robust actor, who spoke only Californian, threw the demitasse of coffee against the ground as protest, breaking it. He was outfitted in a white uniform, as an officer of some indeterminate army. The splashes of coffee stained the immaculate trousers, but it made no difference because in the first take the camera found him seated behind a table.

She would enter the small room, with a tragic expression, searching for her lover. The shadow of an old-fashioned fan, which hung from the ceiling, should stroke the perfect face, the pride of cinematography worldwide. The plot stipulated that she had deserted her legitimate husband, a high-ranking colonial dignitary, for the love of the handsome hero, but fate had chastised her by causing her to lose her little daughter in an accident on the road. That misfortune was interpreted as punishment for this adulterous idyll and she had come to bid farewell to her true love because her husband, deprived of his little girl's love, needed her now more than ever. The director wasn't pleased with the actress's interpretation on her first try, he found her cold. They rehearsed the scene again, without any appreciable difference.

The actress wasn't bothered by such repetition because the scene ended with both of them getting up from the table, the camera angling up to frame them from the waist up, they embraced each other and kissed. She found her co-star professionally insufferable but physically attractive. During rehearsal the robust fellow neither really kissed her, nor did he show any sign of arousal. The director decided to film the scene with the hope that as the camera rolled the actress would immerse herself in the drama, "Lights, sound, camera, action!" She went through the motions precisely, but not a single emotion crossed her face, she was only thinking of that revenge implicit in the repeated kissing, condemned as she was not to see any man until the company's executives allowed it. She reached the table, spoke her lines without phonetic difficulties, she got up for the kiss and was gratified to notice that, duly concentrating on the scene, the actor was overcome by an erection as he kissed her. The director ordered the take to be repeated, and she was delighted. During the second take she dared to do something more, in complicity with the folds of her black veil she put her hand on the part of the handsome lead which stimulated her curiosity most. He reacted in an unpredictable manner, murmuring between clenched teeth, like a growl, "Filthy whore, I'm not like you, a mere sexual object, I want to captivate with my intellect." To avenge herself she continued acting exactly the same in each take, fingering included.

After the tenth unsuccessful take, rage thundered forth from the producer, who had disguised himself as an Arabian waiter so no one would discern his presence on the set, "If you are an actress, prove it well right now!" He stamped his foot with a deafening noise, shaking even the career foundations of several of those present, he lit up his Cuban cigar and left. The director interceded, "Don't worry, Madam. Perhaps this is a kind of emotion that you've never experienced in your life, that's why you find it so difficult to express it. . . . But let's see, perhaps you might remember something similar, the loss of someone dear to you, or even of a little lap dog, or of a purebred cat. . . ."

She couldn't restrain an outburst of sincerity, "I have indeed experienced a similar emotion, precisely the same one, that very loss of a daughter . . . who was torn away from me, and I don't know where she is. I don't know and I don't care, do you hear me? I don't care! I never think about her! . . . and it's not hard to understand why, because her father was a traitor, and I hate all things that bring me back that memory!" The director suspected that such mental agitation would register well on celluloid and he called once again for action, lights, camera. She thought of nothing more than her own situation, she sunk into herself and interpreted the scene with a mysterious dimension of maternal suffering, deeper than the human. The critics failed to appreciate how exquisite her achievement was.

At noon the filming stopped to allow the crew to have lunch. Betsy escorted her to the commissary. They occupied the most isolated table they could find. Betsy made no comment about the performance completed that morning, the actress interpreted it as a sign of disapproval and consequently gloated. In fact Betsy had very mediocre tastes, she delighted in the visceral style of the actresses at Warner Brothers. The star surveyed her equals (?) occupying various tables. The sphinx, the greatest one, never came to the commissary. Struggling with caloric counts which involved a knowledge of higher mathematics, there was the company's darling—overindulged because of her discipline and her pull at the box office—with her protruding eyes and her immense mouth; further on was the cheap blonde in vogue; beyond her was the company's ex-darling, now humiliated at every turn by the producer with the cigar, implacably she was the last to get served, and the very first to have her hair and makeup done, forcing her to get up even earlier than the rest. What a cruel world, the most beautiful one said to herself.

The Cerberus noticed the subsequent melancholy and to distract her showed her a magazine for lovers of motion picture gossip, released only this morning. The Viennese actress appeared on the cover and her article was proclaimed in large letters, "I enjoy working because that way I'm free." She gave a glance to this false interview, prepared by the studio's publicity department. The text seemed almost a mockery, it told of her independent spirit, of the sheer enjoyment she had from working and providing for her own needs without being accountable to anyone, and last of her happiness in California, only threatened by the shadows of war which hovered over her distant native land. She then asked herself whether those readers wouldn't have preferred to know the truth, that she had been manipulated all her life by forces of evil infinitely superior to her own, that she had always been placed in deluxe glass showcases for the delight of the passers-by, that she had been dressed and undressed by cold hands which respected her as much as they would a mannequin. From the very depths of her being she begged for help from those who at other times had succored her, those from the afterlife who had taken pity on her at other dark times like the present one. But there was no sign that someone was answering her call. The stars were eating, only the company's ex-darling seemed as distraught as she herself was, continuing to hope that the waiter would serve her, while a tear ran down her cheek in slow motion.

Betsy accompanied her to the set and there bid her farewell until later. It was the companion's duty to go back to the house to have dinner prepared by the actress's return, exactly half an hour after the filming had ended. From one in the afternoon until six they shot various scenes. The actress changed quickly to gain minutes and even seconds, and without removing her makeup— to gain more minutes, more seconds—got into the automobile which would take her back to the house. The black chauffeur risked smiling at her in the mirror. They speedily traveled the usual route, which included a short detour on a back street which was a dead end, very wooded and solitary, where an elegant country house was being built. By that time it was already night in Los Angeles and the masons had departed from their jobs before dark. The chauffeur possessed the beauty at top speed, if they reached orgasm after five minutes of fornication they would manage afterward to arrive at the bungalow within the time constraints established by the company.

At six thirty-five she entered the house, after running up the zigzagging footpath. She removed what remained of her makeup after the forbidden embrace, she showered and at seven-fifteen sat down at the table. From eight to nine she took a nap. At nine-ten she reviewed the dialogues with Betsy for the following day. A dead calm settled on the city, spread across smooth and friendly hills. This wasn't an auspicious setting for a decisive change in her life, for the intervention of foreign powers. The city of Los Angeles, the angels, those very angels who had always persecuted her, entrapped her, spied on her, betrayed her . . . "Enough, enough!

why am I punished in this way? What evil have I done in my life
to deserve this torture? . . ."

Betsy pretended not to hear, she went over to the gramophone
and turned it on full blast to silence any subsequent indiscretion
on the star's part. Violins became enraptured with a tropical
passion, drums feverishly pounded the rhythm of a Hollywoo-
dized rumba. Shortly thereafter voices were heard accompanying
the refrain, but they didn't originate from the recording, they
were those of the happy couples' inhabiting the other bungalows
on the hillside, who joined the entertainment leaning out their
windows. The enthusiastic chorus gave way to a crescendo of
drums and at that time the couples stepped onto their respective
patios, to surrender themselves to the spell of the dance. Seen
from the top of the hill, where the most beautiful woman in the
world justly belonged, the ensemble of those dancing youths,
abandoned to the sensuality of such music, shaped a colorful
musical number, sizzling with suggestion. The women were
dressed in sheer negligees, the men only in their pajama bottoms.
The actress confirmed that everyone in the world was happy and
that it fell to her to be the notable exception which proved the
rule.

—I asked you for three days to think about it, but I couldn't
come to any conclusion, there's so much I don't know! how can
I decide?

—We'll clear up everything that you want, that's why I'm here.
That's also why they sent me.

—I see total confusion in this whole business, of Peronists on
the left, on the right, and the Socialist Party by itself.

—Ask me whatever it is.

—Well, let's see. . . . How could you, a leftist, get involved in
this Peronism?

—I got involved in this Peronism, but it was later that I became
a Peronist.

—Don't get complicated, what do you mean by that?

—I never told you why I got involved in politics.

—You did, a little.

—No, before I didn't want to talk about it because I didn't want to load you down with information. It could have been troublesome for you if they'd questioned you about me, which could have happened.

—What don't I know?

—It was at high school. During Perón's second government I was rabidly anti-Peronist. When they ousted him I was fifteen years old, I had already joined the Socialist Youth and the Federation of High School Students.

—And what was that?

—Don't you remember? the headquarters for the anti-Peronist high school students. But when Perón fell I remember many things happening. I was riding one day in a bus, the 229, and as we got close to the Plaza Falucho, in front of Regiment 4 there was a shabbily dressed group of workers who cried and shouted at the military and demonstrators who were passing them in cars, celebrating the fall. And during that period having a car in Argentina was something for people with money. And inside the bus I noticed somebody who was clearly a cleaning woman.

—How old?

—Typically dark, from the interior, of Indian blood, some forty years old. Suddenly she started screaming at all of us. I was happy that day, but that stayed with me. It surprised me. It occurred to me then that something wasn't working, that I was celebrating with the oligarchs and that the poor were defending the tyrant. At that time I didn't work it through, but it stayed with me. The year '55.

—Yes, I get it.

—Ah, and another thing. I was riding along later, still in those days, in a demonstration along Santa Fe Avenue, on top of a truck. And along with us there was a worker, dark-skinned from the Socialist Central, to which I belonged. A worker who had fought very hard, and who had gotten screwed during Perón's regime. And a lot of people insulted him, among the demonstrators who went by, "Indian, you must be one of them," half in jest and half seriously. We had to defend him. And it was unbelievable, every once in a while someone would pick a fight with him, because you could tell he was from the working class. The guy got tired of it and he left. I in the midst of that euphoria didn't think anything more of it.

—And why along Santa Fe Avenue?

—That's where the demonstrations took place. Why? It was a wealthy neighborhood, the winners' zone. No one was eager to hold them in working-class neighborhoods, not even in middle-class areas. And right after that came the agitation in the Socialist Youth, which began to take a stand against Ghioldi.

—Wait, he was a Socialist, wasn't he?

—Yes, but he was taking stands which were more gorillalike, more antiworker, against calling elections. And I'll tell you something else. Another moment of surprise in my personal experience, with respect to Peronism. There was an advisory board which counseled the new military government, and it was formed of various political parties. A group of us were summoned because the advisory board was preparing a gigantic parade to show that the military had a popular consensus. They sent us to advertise in station wagons, showing off flags—the Argentine flag—using loudspeakers. And it was symptomatic, if it fell to you to go to rich people's neighborhoods nothing happened, declarations of support but not too many, in middle-class areas there could be an isolated incident, and also isolated support. But invariably when we went to the working-class neighborhoods it rained bottles, insults, and sometimes they even stopped the station wagons with knives, to make the guys riding inside get out. I got slapped in the face, in Quilmes itself, which at the time made me furious. There was clearly a problem between the classes. The revolution against Perón had been a class movement. And now after that came the Frondizi period.

—The first president who was elected after Perón. That I know.

—The Socialist Party began to disillusion me around then, because it was a movement of the middle class, and in being democratic it was splitting up continually, and getting weaker. It didn't even have a party line, or political power. The Communist Party, on the other hand, was caught up in the issue of Hungary.

The Argentine communists fully justified the Soviet intervention without the least objection, and that was enough for me. I began to believe more and more in solutions of a revolutionary sort, but not in Stalinism. I wanted solutions that rescued socialist humanism, but those weren't being practiced in any communist country. And that's how I grew apart from the socialists and the communists, for being antihumanist. That left me adrift on the left.

—What year was this?

—The period of the '58 electoral campaign, that's when I entered law school. I decided to study and to work, not to depend on my father.

—But the delicatessen must have made money, why wouldn't you let anyone help you?

—I don't like to ask for things. I didn't like it then and I don't like it now. You don't know how much of an effort I have to make to ask you, for this favor.

—That part, that you wouldn't let your studies be paid for, seems exaggerated to me. It seems to me that you go too far with this spirit of sacrifice.

—It's that I always felt I had a lot in this world, while there were people who didn't have anything at all.

—Go on with what you were telling me.

—Of all the groups I was drawn most to Praxis, it tried to bring back socialist humanism. But it was a study group, it had no practical application, there was no contact with workers. But I began to grasp their ideas, at school. A period of tremendous confusion, on one hand the rise of Frondizi, and let's not forget the Cuban revolution, harassed by the communists.

—I don't believe it, were they against Castro? That I didn't know.

—The Trotskyists said that Castro was a reactionary. The socialists and Praxis defended him. They saw him as a liberal who in some way was fighting for his country. But this is the Castro of the year '59. Now I want you always to keep this in mind: I never lost nor would I ever want to lose my roots in socialist liberalism, which is what makes me hate intolerance, totalitarianism.

—And violence?

—And violence as well. And it's because of hating violence that I began to sympathize with Peronism.

—And you're asking me to get involved in this intrigue with Alejandro, as if that weren't violence.

—That's specific violence in a specific situation.

—Pozzi, don't talk like that to me because you know that I don't understand.

—In politics as in life one doesn't exist in utopia but in reality. And sometimes reality forces one to go along with violence even though we're against it. But let me go on, that way you'll understand why I stand before you now, asking you what I'm asking. Frondizi was a disappointment for everyone.

—Why?

—Because he did exactly the opposite of what he'd promised in everything. He got into the government by making an agreement with Peronism, yet within a few months he had introduced the Conintes Plan, to persecute the labor unions.

—What did they want, the labor unions?

—They were asking for raises. Let me give you as an example the case of the bank strike, everybody was imprisoned. The meat packers' strike, repressed with tanks. The foundation of private universities, which handed over power to the Church, because it allowed Catholic universities to be created. At about that time the Praxis supporters began to visit shantytowns, trying to talk to the people. The first thing they asked us was whether we were Peronists. But we couldn't propose anything specific. At that moment the extremism of the Trotskyists began to annoy me, I began to see that a proletarian state didn't make sense in Argentina, where there was already a middle class. With them we would be getting a horrible dictatorship, and little else. At that time, in addition, Peronism had lost its more offensive connotations for the young people on the left. Frondizi had beaten it down, he had sent it into the opposition.

—But what had Peronism meant, in a nutshell, to you?

—Let me go on. Peronism, with all its contradictions, was being transformed into a symbol of popular resistance.

—But I won't understand it without knowing what those contradictions were.

—The basic contradictions were between its composition, virtually working class, and the bureaucratic structures that controlled it, plus the confused ideology.

—Nazi?

—Not Nazi, but yes with a large ideological grab bag which one could never fully understand. But let me leave this analysis for later. There are two central conclusions that led me to Peronism. First, it represents the only specific instrument to make policy, to alter reality. How can one explain this to someone like you?

—A fool, a cretin, no?

—No, someone depoliticized. If you want to talk seriously don't annoy me with that business. To deal with politics is to deal with power. Politics is equal to power. Only those who win are correct, because they're the only ones for whom it's possible to alter reality. You can win without ever becoming a part of the government, by being in the opposition all your life, but you can never win just from knowing you're right sitting at a table in a bar. Second, I came to the conclusion that what Argentina needs, given its structure, what would be suitable is an interclass movement, a national movement.

—What, national socialism?

—No, national national. Those that raise the question that you mention don't take into account that Argentina is a marginal country, underdeveloped, dependent on imperialism. The European examples from other times don't work, why should Perón be seen as a Nazi or a fascist, and not a Labourite from the southern hemisphere?

—Do you say that because Labourite sounds better?

—No, because Labourism is providing an experience that is a model for Europe as well, that of trade unions which constitute a political party and provide its backbone. In England the *Daily Telegraph*, which is a reactionary newspaper, put together a political cartoon of Perón depicting him as a Labourite of underdevelopment. What happens as well is that there's no malady more universal than provincialism. One tends to situate other realities within the parameters of one's own reality. That's why Europeans can better understand the Chilean phenomenon, which is similar to those of Western Europe, but not Argentina, which doesn't present any recognizable political spectrum.

—But then sum up Perón for me in one word, or tell me whom you would compare him to.

—Inasmuch as you like labels, here comes the word: populism. He was a populist leader, the head of a popular movement. If you want a name, only one occurs to me, and that's Nasser. But that's another story.

—But you take me around and around, and we don't reach any . . .

—We don't reach what? I'm starting to tell you.

—But was he a person on the right or not, to you?

—He was a populist.

—Stop with that.

—Yes, stop. He had an intellectual framework formed by his military training and by the experiences that he lived in Mussolini's Italy, but he was first and foremost pragmatic, that is to say he sought power wherever it existed. It's of no importance whether deep down inside he was a rightist.

—But how can it not be of any interest, you have there what he left as a legacy, a woman president on the ultraright.

—I agree, it is of interest, for a few months I've begun to suspect that it's of greater interest than I'd thought. But don't wear me out. The legacy is a result, a finale. But politics is practiced through choices, it's the same as when you go to vote, you have to select from what's available. The same thing happened to me, and on a different level I also asked myself the same questions that you're raising. I can even confess to you that I don't have all of them entirely answered.

—What I don't understand is how you could get involved with a party that has all those groups of thugs, and very much on the right that they are, puritans and all, like the one I had the misfortune to get to know at close range.

—I didn't join a party, I got involved in Peronism, which is something much bigger than a party. Peronism is a movement:

parties, unions, organizations of businesses, students, all diametri-
cally opposed ideological tendencies. Combined only in the idea
of a national movement and in the figure of Perón.

—And now that he's dead, what keeps them united, would you
say?

—Now that Perón is dead, the party as such can no longer exist.
Today all that's left of it is the government and that for only a
short while. Afterward what will remain will be the working class,
the struggle and whatever happens. I don't want to play philoso-
pher but I believe that a stage of defeat will come and that from
there the fundamental elements of a new movement will be
established, and the only thing that will remain of Peronism will
be the name.

—There was one thing that you told me to leave until later, the
thing about violence.

—Was it violence or not, to banish Peronism from the election
to prevent it from winning? The other party gained the presi-
dency with Illia in 1963, with 27 percent of the vote. Wasn't that
violence? Later in '66 came the military coup by Onganía which
sent politics on vacation. That's what he thought at least. And
destroyed the universities. That violence of Onganía's which shut
down all the escape valves for the people's self-expression . . . was
really what created guerrilla fighting. It's curious that the guerrilla
war starts in Argentina, when the experience of the Cuban revolution has already failed, at least a year earlier, with the death of
Che. Don't forget that the Montoneros were born in 1968 with
a deed so dark as the kidnaping and murder of ex-military President Aramburu, or do you believe that I don't think about such
things as well?

—What things?

—You know what the Montoneros are, don't you?

—The Peronist guerrillas, while the ERP are the Marxist guerrillas.

—Precisely, Anita.

—And the Montoneros, aren't they in sympathy with you?

—Let's say not entirely.

—But I know from a reliable source, or no, what reliable source, why should I lie to you, I imagine, that's all! that if you're a Peronist and you're involved in this kidnaping intrigue, wouldn't you perhaps be dealing with the Montoneros?

—I'm dealing with them, but I'm not one of them.

—Pozzi, we're friends, aren't we? why then don't you talk like a regular person and not like a politician? I want to know the truth, not win the argument.

—Let me go on. Let's not make everything so rational, either.

—I'm curious about one thing, why are you getting involved with the Montoneros and not the ERP, who are more to the left?

—Because the Montoneros always stood firmly behind the preeminence of things national, and at least in their early phases they upheld the interclass ideal of Peronism. Whereas the leaders of the ERP held that Argentina had to bring about a Vietnam, which is crazy, because Argentina is a country with a standard of living and institutions half a century ahead with respect to Vietnam.

—I follow.

—Argentina reminds me of the trouble between the Arabs and the Jews and the civil war in Ireland: everyone is right. The military claims that the guerrilla war brought on the violence, the guerrillas that they came into being because the military had established a dictatorship. The military throws the blame on the parties, because it had to take control of the power due to the incompetence and illegitimacy, in substance, not in form, take note, of the political parties, which is certainly true. The heart of the problem is that Argentina doesn't have a ruling class, on all levels, business, intellectual, bourgeois, proletarian, it's a country without a political culture. It lacks a basic rule of operation, not one sector has managed to seize power and thus the country exists in a permanent state of instability, no one has managed to develop a viable political scheme.

—Yes, I agree, but in the meantime you're collaborating with the worst people.

—Within Peronism there are some of the worst people, but if it disgusts you to belong to the same movement you leave them a lot of room. And I from Peronism can attempt to take action, but from within. From outside, like you, like anyone who doesn't belong to a movement, you can't do anything. And from within I can try for whatever I want, which is to improve Peronism.

—But in the meantime, you agree to something horrible like violence, though it be provoked. It's that it doesn't matter to me whether it was provoked or not.

—If you don't react in the presence of violence, the violence of those who want to perpetuate a state of injustice, the only thing won is more violence and more injustice.

—Also I'm setting myself up to discuss the matter with a lawyer . . .

—A lawyer who spends his time defending political prisoners, protesting for those tortured, searching for the disappeared with useless habeas corpus and presenting writs which are even more useless, so he can uncover the name of the murderers of the Triple A, who in effect are employed by the government.

—The government which you elected.

—Mea culpa. But one has to change things. In '73 you had to choose, the routing of the military dictatorship was implicit in the vote for Peronism, beyond the personality of Perón. We didn't look for violence, we found ourselves immersed in it.

—And like all those shipwrecked souls who are totally about to drown you want me to drown too.

—Don't be insulting.

—It's the truth, that's why it offends you.

—Look, you succeeded in what you wanted, that I'd get fed up with your stupidity.

—What? You're leaving?

—Yes, I hope it goes well for you.

—Shut that door.

—I'm going.

—If you go, you're not setting a foot in here anymore.

—Whatever you say.

—I mean it, if you go you're not coming back.

—Ciao. . . . Get well soon.

—And with that business about Alejandro forget it, I would never get involved in something like that.

—Fine.

—And don't plan on coming back here.

—Ciao.

7

MOCKED BY NIGHTMARES once more, the actress said to herself in her bed, and still she couldn't rouse herself completely. This time the plot of the dream proved simple, easily interpretable. She had seen herself standing before a producer, one of the new recruits, successor to her extinct discoverer, now deceased, to discuss a contract. At one point she was asked to refer back to past achievements to support her quoted price, but inexorably she would forget the titles, the name of each director, of each male co-star. Neither would she remember the names of her chauffeurs.

A strange lament, or the cry of a little girl, finally let her return to her wakefulness. It was in fact the song of an unidentified Mexican bird. Certainly her seven years in the Mecca of Motion Pictures hadn't left any significant trace on her life, but, yes, a number of names and dates easily dispensed with; neither was she proud of her own work, the incomprehension of the critics had convinced her of the banality of her performances. But why the darkness of the past rather than the diaphanous present that the Mexican terrain offered?

She was exceedingly pleased with such a coquettish bedroom in a colonial style, she was seeing it for the first time in the light of day. Having arrived at the sumptuous estate after night had already fallen, she had confirmed with relief what her generous hosts had promised her: she would be alone, surrounded by discreet servants. The other guest in the estate inhabited a far-off pavilion and, like the actress, wanted to see no one. He happened to be another motion picture personality, a young, award-winning screenwriter from the United States. How tedious, the actress had said to herself when she was told. Tedium. She pictured tedium having the appearance of a peacock, as in the words of a lovely song. She leaned out over her balcony railing, where a representative sampling of subtropical flora—a banana tree, a date palm, hibiscus, bougainvillaea—offered her a profusion of pattern and color. And among these there wandered, with magnificent tails spread, more than one peacock. "They bring bad luck!" the star said to herself, searching in vain for a horseshoe to touch. "Bah . . . in other places these vermin weren't present and even then bad luck wouldn't let me be."

She picked up the telephone to order breakfast, given the number of dishes from which to choose and how incomprehensible the names it was recommended that she descend to the patio, where various foods would be served: bad memories made the actress shiver. The grand oaken staircase took her to a drawing room where she saw nothing but the overwhelming fresco which adorned it, in triptych. Over the wall on the left was depicted a peasants' rebellion, burnished Indian-like faces were reddening with fury, set off against the green of the cultivated fields, the yellow straw of their hats and the white of their characteristic garments. She didn't see the central wall now that her gaze was mesmerized by the luxuries that burst forth on the right, the brilliant festival of the rich. As she came closer the better to examine this panel of the mural, an audiovisual mechanism was set in motion which explained to her in three languages that it dealt with the enemies of the people and of life. Finally it indicated that situating oneself in a certain strategic place, whoever looked could see that the faces of those bejeweled personages were in fact skulls, and furthermore, that by situating oneself a few inches from each one of the dead, whoever was looking could see his own face reflected. The actress approached the figure of the most important woman, the most venerated one, who was holding the arm of the president or commander in chief. She then saw herself, dressed in black lace down to her feet, bejeweled in pearls and platinum. She decided to have a dress made exactly like that one upon her return to California.

The merry tinkling of a hand bell indicated the way to the balustrade with a view of a baroque chapel, invaded by humidity and climbing vines. She preferred the scene from the table itself, where a breakfast of many colors was already served. The red of those *mameyes* proved fantastic, bright Alhambra red or coral, ruby, vermilion, garnet, magenta or carmine, and the avocados were sea green or malachite or forest green, she said to herself, while the papayas proved either sulphur yellow or khaki or cinnamon or saffron, and the dates brown, umber, maroon, chestnut or bronze, depending how the rays of sunlight hit. The temperamental actress felt nostalgia for the color blue and she looked up toward the sky: turquoise, indigo blue, sapphire, cerulean or iridescent, depending on how more or less ajar those internationally acclaimed eyelashes were.

She had asked to be alone, but the silence forced her to listen to her own voice, "What will become of me now that I'm not bound by any contract? The world has changed, the head of the Studio is dead, in Europe the war has already subsided, I could return to the old world and begin another life. Only one film remains to be shot, the most important one of my entire career, the role that all the stars covet and which has caused me to receive anonymous notes threatening my life if the movie is made. Hah! those women don't know what risks I've run in my life . . . and I say women precisely because it's the other actresses who thus endeavor to frighten me. But they needn't concern themselves, because after this film perhaps I'll retire, who knows, fate will tell, I believe it's futile to plan what will happen . . ." She didn't dare continue, it all depended on a certain day both longed for and dreaded, within a very short time, less than a week, she would turn thirty.

She had spent several minutes devouring a variety of little dishes when an infectious tune caught her interest. Wearing a white organdy dress and a transparent picture hat with loose, floating ribbons, she set off in search of the musicians. In this way she reached the river bank, along waters almost covered by floating flowers. The male chorus became more and more strong, in a bend in the stream there appeared a small boat with a roof thatched with more flowers, steered by an elderly boatman wearing an enormous hat; a second boat followed, carrying graying musicians in white vestments complete with buttons and halberds. A nod of the head was all that was necessary, the actress went on board delighted and her enchantment would have been complete if she'd been able to understand the words of the song, she disliked having anything concealed from her, she couldn't help but project needless fears on the unknown.

The small boat glided quickly, the musicians continued with variations on the same melody. The actress saw on the right bank the longed-for landscape of cactus, and in English she ordered the boatman to dock there. The man was signaling no, as shadows hovered over his weatherbeaten face. She insisted, the man uttered a terror-ridden word, but since she had never shot a Western she didn't recognize it . . . *"bandidos!"* The aggregate of rock, desert and spiny plant contrasted violently with her appearance. She insisted on going ashore alone and entering a sinuous path. She admired those steep rugged rocks, the restive dunes, the giant cactuses.

The landscape suddenly became entirely rocky, with rises and falls which concealed what would appear a few yards further along. On this terrain one didn't just watch out for the danger of bandits, snakes attacked with even greater accuracy and speed. And a snake strategically placed on that narrow path by the hand of man—or woman? it was unclear because it was gloved—left a minimal margin for survival. The actress's ultrasensitive ear perceived a slight rattling, her fondness for imagining mishaps did the rest. She lifted her ample skirts and set off running. Her own sharp breaths prevented her from hearing the frustrated cursing which shot forth from the reduced group of assassins, exactly two, a man and a woman. She with a foreign accent and perfect diction, he with local, rough tones.

After her exploration, the actress decided to spend the afternoon in her lodgings on the estate. Due to the plentiful lunch she felt drowsy, she slept for several hours. She didn't dream. A perfectly tuned whistle awakened her. Someone was whistling a familiar melody, the same as the old men had played! the one she had tried to remember before her nap, to no avail. She had

the notion that it was a song bringing her luck. From the balcony she saw no one, she descended swiftly, driving off those
supposedly ill-omened birds. An enormous patch of bougainvillaea—the color violet, royal purple, plain purple or ultraviolet—
appeared to hide the whistling. She was only trying to hear it, it
made no difference to her who it was whistling. Inadvertently
she stepped on a twig, and this crack sufficed to interrupt the
music.

Very soon she had before her an unexpected surprise. The
young man who was making his way between the gigantic leaves
of the banana tree very closely resembled someone, "How strange
it feels to see you without first having the lights dimmed and the
curtains drawn. . . . Anyway, I consider it a rare privilege to be
able to admire you in flesh and blood," "You're also involved in
show business, it shouldn't impress you to meet just one more
actress," "You of course aren't that, but . . . perhaps you're not
feeling well? you've grown pale," "And with reason. You look very
much like someone I knew. There are phantoms without faces,
men whom a woman's memory has preferred to forget. You have
just brought back the face of one of those phantoms," "The least
significant one?" "The one most loved and the most traitorous,"
"Then I resemble two different phantoms . . ." "No, only one."

For the first time in a very long while, she found pleasure in
speaking with another human being, she told him her idea of
giving up the movies, "You're thinking of your Europe and of
leaving us. I'm happy for you and sad for myself. Actually, bad
times are hovering over the Factory of Dreams, and I'm not
referring solely to your absence, which I'm already lamenting.
Evil forces are preparing to take the business by storm, as soon
as the postwar euphoria takes hold. There are already demons
preparing lists of the people to be marked, and the accusation will
amount to only one, whosoever thinks is dangerous! We will all
be stigmatized as the Antichrist, they will embark on a hunt and
even within the White House bonfires will be raised to burn the
new witches. I am already being persecuted, because I'm preparing an important manifesto. That was precisely the reason why

I came here to draw it up, and I hope to have shaken off my
pursuers, although strange shadows have been cast over these
gardens at times. If you were to tell me that you too are being
pursued by some force of evil, I could breathe more restfully and
believe that it's you they're trying to find." The actress feigned
levity, "It wouldn't surprise me, even here I've received death
threats. But the motive couldn't be more unimportant. They
simply want me to give up the role of the year, I don't need to
tell you what it is, the whole world knows. And it's all foolish pride
on the part of vacuous actresses, who have nothing in their lives
but their careers. There's one in particular who's consumed with
hatred, and I won't say who she is because I'm afraid that naming
her will bring me bad luck," "Give me just one detail and I'll
identify her," "That's simple, she's the one forced to cover her
face with a thin rubber mask, to hide the pockmarks left by
smallpox," "A woman famous for her cruelty and determination,
I would advise caution," "Oh my dear fellow, I have had far more
fearsome enemies . . ."

The actress noticed, unexpectedly, that simply looking at the
young man was enough to conjure up that favorite melody again,
and now that she so enjoyed the music she didn't lift her eyes
from him again. Night was beginning to fall, the young man
suggested that they walk over to the mother-of-pearl pond, called
this because at dusk it blushed. She accepted, without saying so
she decided to observe the scenery only as it was reflected in the
eyes of her companion. And therein she contemplated the rosy
waters of the pond, the cyclamen-tinted swans and the scarlet
flowers, and it was thus that she saw herself reflected as well,
rose-colored. As if they were being dictated in her ear, she repeated words which she had already heard in some song, ". . . play
the assassin, sensuous eyes, like a pair of knives, against my melancholy . . ." to which he didn't know what to answer. She continued, ". . . I have lost all hope, grown fainthearted and faithless,
fear is a peacock who in the afternoon sun grows restless . . ." and
he then at last declared that ". . . as peacocks fanning each other,
in the blue garden of your wanderings, not far from the enemy

spear . . . there emerges in your pupils . . . the fear . . ." This time
she didn't see anything more, because the intensity of his kiss
forced her to shut her eyes. And in the total darkness she heard
from within him a broken murmur, something about the unre-
strained eloquence that her beauty inspired. She interrupted him
to say that it was naught but a phantom poet reciting the precise
words to her. Then he saw her smile for the first time and endeavored to define it, ". . . there appears a carnival behind the crystal
. . . your abundant multicolored laughter, princess of masks the
color of rose, Mistress Mirth, queen grandiose . . ." at which she,
realizing for the first time the terror of her loneliness, implored
"Remove from my path all thorns of such occasion, illumine with
your light my desperation . . ." but he could no longer imagine
that pain would touch them again and able to conceive of nothing
but her, he confused her with the swan which at that moment
was reflected in her pupils, ". . . swan that God painted on crystal,
give me the ritual . . . of your profile . . . unequaled. Kiss of light,
nuptials blush . . . on night medieval, flower pale . . . of
evil . . ."

Why of evil, she who was all beauty and translucence? But
neither he nor she were surprised that the odd word should have
filtered into the poem. The actress again remembered the dangers
which had always filled her life, she thought of the fragility of love
and couldn't restrain a tear from falling; she thought it'd been
born rose-tinted, just as the mother-of-pearl comes into being the
color of rose at the bottom of a dark ocean, which inspired him
to say, "Mother-of-pearl, the mirror where mermaids their own
reflections see, in your haste to weep, transformed into pearls
. . . your tears emerge from the sea . . ." She for the first time
in quite a while deflected her gaze from the object of her new or
old passion, slowly she drew back a few steps, afraid she'd be
unable to breathe if she continued contemplating him. She regretted having done so, because when she looked at him again he
was already undressed and altogether nacreous. An instinctive
feminine reaction forced her to endeavor to get away from the
place, but he took hold of her forcefully around the waist, as he

said with ironic reproach, ". . . only once your lips exquisite
. . . illuminated with a kiss my desire, it was the light flutter of
a butterfly's visit . . . I've been always a slave and just briefly a sire
. . ." and only then did she become aware that brisk air was
nipping at her flesh, she was surprised that it had become cool so
suddenly, but she didn't suspect that he was undressing her, she
was distracted thinking about she didn't know what, and when he
spread the organdy over the grass so she could recline on it
comfortably, for fear of seeming either simple-minded or simply
an easy woman, and not knowing how to absolve herself, she
feigned frivolity and declared ". . . Mistress Mirth, at this moment all that wraps me is a zephyr." At which he added, after
promising her he'd be gentle, now that he saw her covered entirely by his own shadow, ". . . the pallors of a magnolia invade
. . . your woman's face tormented, and in your divine eyes green
as jade . . . you betray that you're . . . infatuated . . . you betray
that you're . . . infatuated . . ." And thus it was that no more words
were heard, the swans and the jasmine contemplated the scene,
perceiving nature to take its course, which at this hour was
the color scarlet, or garnet, or carmine, or pink, or vermilion?
Suddenly words again were heard, not from their lips, but
sprung from the very air, ". . . a swan laments, the afternoon
departs . . . cloaked in red? or crimson? its triumphal chariot's
descent . . ."

When at last it became dark, it became time as well for declarations of love. "He," as she preferred to call him, suggested visiting
the silver lake, not far from the gardens and called thus because
at this hour the moon polished its waters. But He couldn't hold
back, and before sighting its shore the bitterness that filled him
began to spill forth. He wanted her to know everything about his
life. He told her of his ex-wife and the only thing that still
succeeded in bringing some tenderness to his existence, his
daughter, whom he seldom saw. The actress wanted to know
everything about this little girl. He answered that she was a
prodigy, intelligent but also sensitive, and that he was afraid for
her, so vulnerable as she was, she would suffer greatly in this

mockingly, ". . . I was born . . . under a moon of silver, free of all anguish and fear, and was born . . . with the soul of a buccaneer . . ." and seeing lights that flared and died in the grass and over the water, she brandished an imaginary sword, to finish them off. It was a matter of tiny luminous insects, and their blue lights sparkled against the black of the sky. He declared, ". . . on the lagoon, there are reflections of the moon, a stillness which only crystal knows," and she decided that it was her turn to bestow encomiums on Him, ". . . divine enchantment, free of all worldly tarnish, crystal within which my life reflects its anguish . . ." but then He, like a child disconcerted by indulgence, changed the subject, ". . . flickering of fireflies which, with their light, embroider spangles on the night . . ." which stirred tenderness within her without reason and moved her to embrace him with all her might. They both fell on their knees, as if giving thanks, and without letting each other go they turned their gazes to the lake. He said, ". . . they are the nets of silver . . . a lace so fine, butterflies that sleep . . . in the sapphire night . . ." and she, remembering His overflowing emotion in the dark grove, concluded, ". . . how the moon shines on the crystal lake! just so shine your eyes . . . after they've wept . . ." In silence they took the walk returning to the estate.

Attentive as always to the unexpected, she noticed fresh footprints in the sand which didn't correspond to their own. He didn't see them, she preferred not to trouble him and remained silent. But to avoid the path which led them to the house she suggested they take another, to break a new one in the thicket. He wanted nothing but to please her. Thus they left the lake, populated at that time only by fireflies. And the fireflies could hearken to the voice springing anew from the air, ". . . nights of serenade, of silver and organdy . . ." and the voice gradually became a lament, ". . . plenilune of glory, history which dies! . . . illusion which is lost . . . and will never be revived . . ."

The first light of day awakened the lovers. He got up to draw the curtains. The room remained penumbrous, despite which she detected a strange cast to his gaze. It wasn't long before she knew

world. The narrow footpath grew more and more dark, verdan
trees bordered it and blocked the moon's illumination.

The actress suddenly realized the disquieting situation in whic
she found herself: she was walking toward the unknown with a
unknown. She hesitated, would it be advisable to turn back, givin
the excuse of a headache? No, it was already too late, if h
belonged to some enemy faction he could eliminate her righ
there in complicity with the night. She made one more calcul
tion: "If during my whole life caution has been my ally, well, i
time to become her enemy, what happiness have I gained fro
such distrust toward men?" She interrupted a passionate spee
of His and asked his forgiveness, "What is it that I am to forgive
"That for an instant I distrusted you, there as we passed th
palm trees. You know . . . those plants bring back bad memori
and I thought you might have led me here . . . to kill me." H
embraced her and in the darkness she couldn't see that tears we
falling from his face. But in kissing his eyes, she noticed. Th
foliage hid the moon, no one could see what the couple was doi
in the darkness. Only by touching their bodies could one ha
found out.

At some point in the night they resumed their walk, the lak
gentle waves could already be heard when the actress decided
tell him something of her life. Her greatest shame. She too h
a daughter. The company had forced her to put the baby up
adoption. And she hadn't fought it, although nothing would h
changed regardless of how much she had fought it. And not o
had she allowed this crime to take place, but she hadn't car
How could it be that someone, she herself, could have be
capable of such wretchedness? The actress was silent, He for
part decided not to add anything, they descried the lake,
banks of fine white sand, the fishermen's nets raised high in
air, immobile. She sighed.

He reproached her for her inclination toward melancholy. T
silver mirror, as she called the waters, reflected back an unu
image of herself; her hair was disheveled, hence she rippe
flounce from her wide skirt and quickly concocted a turb
reminiscent of the world of piracy, and to end her sadness c

the reason, "My dear, a true love, such as ours, has no room for imperfection. To conceal something, not to confide in the other, that to me is already a serious imperfection, for that reason I want immediately to confess something that troubles me. And it's this: I don't understand how you could allow your daughter to be adopted and not have regretted it later. I would have died of shame in your situation. And that strange reaction of yours fills me with fear, one day would you perhaps renounce me and remember me no longer? That's why I beg of you that on our return to Hollywood we visit my analyst. Placing yourself in his care would enable us to uncover the unknown, we could even undertake joint analysis, as a couple, and so from the start we wouldn't hold secrets from each other. I would know everything, absolutely everything, about you and you about me. Do you promise me you'll do it? That way you'll give me positive proof of your love. Realize that for a simple mortal like me, to receive the love of a deity like yourself could very easily appear an unattainable illusion."

The actress felt her blood grow cold, she recognized perfidy and how well it sounded with the voice of an enamored man. He of course wanted to put her in the hands of the enemy, to force her to reveal all her secrets to fraudulent doctors. And if she resisted, she presumed, his accomplices were hiding right here on the estate, the footprints in the sand were theirs. She feigned yet another seizure of tenderness and promised to surrender to the analysis. He rewarded her with a predictable coupling. She feigned pleasure, meanwhile she worked out a plan. If she remained with Him one moment longer she might take a false step and reveal her distrust. If He realized this He would gag her in order to hand her over to his accomplices, hidden in the thicket.

All moans having quieted, the beauty said she had a tremendous appetite, she had a notion to go downstairs to find something to eat, but she wanted it to be a surprise for Him, it was her imperious fancy to decorate the breakfast tray with jasmine from the garden they'd just visited. He agreed but asked her not to be too long. She donned a dress and ran barefoot down the stairs, unfortunately she had asked her hosts to disconnect the telephone lines and to leave her there isolated from the world. But she remembered that not very far, across the grove of trees by the chapel, there meandered a narrow highway. Someone would pass and she would ask him to take her to the nearest town. There she would rent a car.

She crossed the patio, if he was spying on her from the balcony she could point out that she was headed to pick flowers, but she confirmed that the curtain remained closed. She set off toward the highway without further ado, she was certain that he was an envoy sent by some power, it made no difference to her which it was, and was preparing to abduct her for dishonest purposes. Yes, to put her in the hands of one analyst, and a thousand scientists more, to vivisect her, to wrench from her that innermost secret.

The highway was really a thoroughfare of a secondary order, possibly one vehicle would pass by each hour, or not even that. She thought that perhaps she had made a mistake, she set off walking, to distance herself as best she could from that house, from that trap. Suddenly she thought she heard something, several yards behind her. No, it couldn't be. Yes, there was an engine. She turned around. At the bend in the road quickly appeared a car of the latest model. There were two people riding within, a man at the wheel and a woman in the back seat. She signaled for them to stop. In turn the vehicle accelerated. No, it couldn't be. The car was attempting to run her down. She hastened to one side and managed to dodge them. She succeeded in seeing that the woman's face was covered with smallpox scars. The car turned around. The most beautiful woman in the world began to run in the opposite direction, veering off the road. The car also went off the road, within a few seconds it caught up to her, and smashed her as it might have one of those little birds which at times collide against the windshield. In agony, she allowed herself a moment to think sad thoughts, a few seconds which seemed to her forever. She thought that no one would weep for her, no one in the world. She was saturating herself with this grief when she seemed to hear His voice. In fact it was He who ran along the highway desperately calling her. Immediately the car's engine could be heard starting up again, the screeching of the tires against the cement, another dry knock, another broken scream. Not far from her, He lay immobile, with his eyes open.

She, breathing her last, confirmed her fear, He hadn't betrayed her, He was innocent, He had truly loved her, but hadn't survived long enough to weep for her.

8

—May I?

—Yes . . . come in . . .

—Were you resting?

—No, it doesn't matter.

—But you've kept your room dark.

—The light bothers me.

—Were you sleeping?

—I already said no. . . . I thought you were supposed to take the plane yesterday.

—You thought I'd be in Quilmes by now.

—Yes . . .

—Ana, you seem tired to me. I'd best come back another time.

—Why didn't you go?

—There was trouble, they telephoned me, and I had to postpone it.

—Sit down . . .

—Thanks.

—Tell me.

—Anita, forgive me for the other day. But I lost my temper . . .

—It was my fault.

—I think I'll be here for a while, in Mexico.

—Really . . . ?

—They called from Buenos Aires. Because they raided my house, and it seems they've done a lot of damage.

—And your family?

—No, nothing, the scare, that's all. Now they're at my mother-in-law's house, they shut everything up and took off. That's why it'd be better if I didn't go back for a while.

—I'm really sorry.

—But I don't want to make trouble, don't worry.

—On the contrary, and I don't know if they've told you . . .

—What?

—I haven't been well, Pozzi.

—Oh, no, I didn't know anything about it.

—Yes, it seems that something in the treatment didn't go right with me. They're investigating the problem.

—What a nuisance.

—Yes.

—You were resting, I'd better leave you alone.

—Don't be scared, cancer isn't contagious.

—What do you mean?

—A joke, Pozzi. I was making a joke.

—. . .

—And why are you caressing me? why so affectionate?

—Don't pull my hand out like that, you make it seem as if it disgusted you.

—Look, right now what I feel toward you is envy, because you're healthy and I'm not.

—Don't play practical jokes, Ana, explain to me what the doctors said.

—They tell me that it was a mistake in the diet. But that the tumor was benign and that what I feel now has nothing to do with what they removed.

—And that's what it must be, nothing more, something that will pass quickly.

—I'll be the one to pass quickly.

—What are you saying, convalescence always brings some complications.

—Don't treat me that way, or do you think that I don't notice? It's all well and good that I be patient with them, when they come in with these stories, but I'm not going to put up with it from you.

—. . .

—I feel sick, they operate on me, and within four weeks the same symptoms as before are back. I'd have to be very stupid not to be able to figure it out.

—Didn't you say that to them?

—Yes, of course I said it.

—And?

—They placate me, they tell me that everyone who's sick imagines things. But I'm the one who feels the pains. In short . . . if you don't believe me I really don't care, see. So what's the point of continuing on this subject.

—Whatever suits you.

—. . .

—Do you want me to leave?

—No. . . . Please, would you raise up my bed a little, it's this button. . . . That's it, thanks.

—Is that good, or should I raise it more?

—No, it's good this way. And do you think you'll stay in Mexico?

—Well . . . if I go back, what security can I have?

—That didn't bother you before.

—No, before it didn't. But it's clear that now I've already ended up on some blacklist.

—But your work is legitimate, isn't it? A lawyer who defends a prisoner, it doesn't mean he's committed the same crime.

—Yes, but a lawyer who defends only political prisoners, and those in opposition to the government, you can imagine that it doesn't come out looking very favorable to them.

—But is there any way they could accuse you of something?

—No, not at all.

—Are you sure that you're not hiding anything from me? Because I'm tired of these twists.

—I'm not hiding anything. Of course, they imagine that I come in contact with people in the underground.

—They must think that the guerrillas are paying you. . . . And they'd be right.

—No, I always made do with other work that came my way, at the firm.

—And this trip, who paid for it, would you like to tell me?

—Well, this, yes, but it's the first time, and just for expenses, that's all. And to defend those prisoners I never charged a single dollar.

—But just the same they're accusing you. On what basis?

—Ana, could they by any chance accuse you of anything? and look what they did to you.

—I was asking just in case you'd been hiding something from me.

—. . .

But anyway this trip to Mexico will seem suspicious to them, or won't it?

—When you left, things were still more calm. But now they've already gotten more organized, once you set up a death squad, who's going to control it?

—And it's your very Peronists who set it up.

—If I go back I'd have to go under cover. That's the only way. To enter the country under another name, with completely false documents, do you understand?

—Yes.

—Once they stigmatize a guy, he's got to be very careful right away.

—You won't be able to go back, then.

—So the two of us are out of luck this time.

—Don't make those foolish remarks. I'm the one who's out of luck. You'll adapt to this place right away, you know that the Mexicans are very accommodating, at the University, I'm sure they'll offer you something.

—I don't know . . . it's awful, this situation. And afterward to have to bring the family.

—Would you bring them all up?

—I suppose. The youngest ones won't even get to finish the school year. And to give my wife time to rent the house to someone who can be trusted.

—Oh, Pozzi, you're always the same, you figure out your plan in the twinkling of an eye.

—What of it, does it bother you?

—No, but you know, people are different here, and in comparison the Argentines really make me laugh, with that mania of trying to anticipate everything, and to control everything. You'll see here, how different it is.

—In what sense?

—That people let themselves live more in the present, they aren't planning everything that's coming, like we do. They don't worry so much.

—Isn't it that they're a little irresponsible?

—That could be, but that way life has more flavor, as they say, there are more surprises, more spontaneity, or not?

—Did you fall in love with anyone?

—No, unfortunately I didn't. It didn't happen with me. Look, they couldn't be any more different, especially from you.

—In what sense?

—In the benders they go on . . .

—And what's funny about that?

—Well, I mean that they get drunk, and they go a little crazy, do you know what I mean?

—They lose control.

—That's it! That's the expression I was looking for. And it's great, that way you can get to know people better. They aren't reined in all the time, hiding who knows what.

—You're being hostile, Ana.

—I'm just talking about different modes of being. Each one is whatever it is, with its good side and its bad side. With a Mexican you tell him to meet you in a certain place at a certain time and you never know whether he'll come or not. But if he comes it's because he wanted to, do you know what I mean?

—Whereas an Argentine will come because he promised he would.

—Precisely.

—Like responsible people, adults.

—Whatever it is, but you Argentines annoy me with your complications.

—But if I'm not mistaken, the first day that I arrived you said exactly the opposite, that Mexicans were well educated but that you never knew what they were thinking.

—Yes, but in another sense. They know what things they want to hide from you, they're more crafty. And Argentines conceal things out of habit and they think that it's normal. They conceal because they're repressed. And I don't know, I don't understand, in the end everybody conceals things, then. I'm contradicting myself.

—There you go.

—But that happens to me with people who don't want to understand, like you. The closed ones, those who already know everything. And who only manage to confuse me.

—Ana, not even ten minutes did the peace last.

—It's that I don't care anymore about keeping the peace. I'm going to tell you what I feel and that's all. I've already kept quiet long enough in my whole life.

—. . .

—I'm determined not to keep quiet anymore, and to speak everything even if it's displeasing, do you know what I'm thinking right now? that it makes me furious that this should have happened to me, and not to you or to someone else.

—That what happened? how do you know that you're so sick?

—They can't lie to me. Just last night I felt bad, they brought me into intensive care.

—. . .

—My blood pressure dropped, all of a sudden. It was very serious.

—Forgive me if you're offended by what I'm about to tell you, but I find you looking very well.

—I looked so worn out that I put on makeup, that's why. I was scary-looking . . .

—Tell me about how agreeable those Mexicans are, that way I can get annoyed.

—Yes, it's better that you should take everything as a joke, you have no choice.

—We'll see, tell me.

—For instance, here they all sing, who sings in Argentina? tell me about it.

—It's better if we don't talk about Argentina.

—Why?

—If I can't go back, I don't know what's going to happen with me.

—It's that important to you?

—Yes.

—Because of your family?

—No . . . I could have them come here. It's everything else. My work, the people in jail, Buenos Aires, all of it.

—Buenos Aires?

—Yes, that too. You can't separate one from the other, don't you think? The people and the place, you can't separate them.

—You like it, that place?

—Yes, Anita, I realize that now.

—But you're looking really good, I think Mexico agrees with you, I've never seen you look better. You look terrific.

—Why do you say that?

—Because it's true. You look rested.

—It must be because I sleep. For years I haven't slept as much as my body was demanding.

—One can tell.

—. . .

—I envy you, Pozzi. That you should want so much to go back. There's nothing really important to me back there, or here either.

—. . .

—You stay silent.

—Really, Ana, you don't think about going back?

—In a coffin, I might.

—And Clarita, don't you want to see her?

—She's better off this way.

—And your mother?

—Why should I disturb them, the two of them are better off like this.

—There's really no guy here, whom you've liked?

—Is it possible that you can't get it in your head, that not everything has to revolve around a man . . .

—I didn't mean that.

—. . .

—What are you thinking?

—Pozzi, are you sure my face is looking better?

—Yes.

—Better in what sense?

—I don't know, I just see you well.

—But what? my skin?

—Yes.

—And the shadows under my eyes don't look ugly?

—The shadows aren't really obvious.

—And my gaze? don't I have the gaze of a sick person?

—I wouldn't say so.

—. . .

—Ana, I have to go back, I can't resign myself to staying. With all the things that are happening there. I feel . . . it seems to me . . . that it's bad for me to stay here, instead of going back and doing something.

—To me that government is the real Peronism, of torturers and Nazis.

—It wasn't the Peronism that I was working for, and you know how hard I worked.

—Pozzi, you imagined Peronism as you pleased, and you got married to it without knowing it first. And only now is the beast baring its fangs to you.

—You must have heard someone say that.

—Of course, you think I'm incapable of arriving at an opinion on my own, as empty-headed and frivolous as I am.

—. . .

—You're sure it's true about the raid?

—Of course, why do you ask?

—Because it could be that you're staying here to convince me, to help you in the thing with Alejandro.

—That's absurd.

—I'm afraid that that's the reason.

—I swear it to you, on my sons. The matter with Alejandro has already been thrown out.

—In truth?

—Didn't you hear me? I've just sworn it to you. It's an insult what you're saying.

—It's not an insult. I'm telling you what I feel, it doesn't matter to me anymore whether I please anyone. Why should I make a good impression on you? what can you give me? You can't bring me back my health, and that's the only thing I care about.

—Anita, now I understand what's going on. You don't believe you're going to die. If you were really convinced, you wouldn't have the energy to say another word. What you are is in a rage for some reason, against yourself, and you don't know how to avenge yourself, like a kid.

—Yes, and you're so very adult. Very Argentine and very grown-up. What you are is . . .

—Tell me, I'm listening.

—What you are is . . . a dupe, a dreamer, who got mixed up in this whole mess because of I don't know what . . . because you're a romantic. Just as I got involved in that business of marrying a man whom I didn't really know. And you're also irresponsible, because you collaborate with people who resort to guns without knowing what they're doing. As irresponsible as me, who brought my daughter into the world just because, that's all. So the two of us are the same, dreamers! Irresponsible people.

—I've already explained very thoroughly what my opinion is on the matter, if you didn't understand it, I'm very sorry.

—But it's better that I tell you what I have on my mind. Because that's all over with, believing in wounded soldiers in trenches, and the nurse from the Red Cross. And the blind martyrs who get released from prison, and me bandaging their eyes, so the gashes wouldn't be visible.

—What are you talking about?

—I understand myself.

—But I don't.

—It's something very sad, and why should I depress you even more. Sad especially for me. If one is no longer able to imagine something beautiful, what else is there? If in this world you can't imagine beautiful things you're lost, because they don't exist.

—I'm sorry, I don't agree with that.

—Better for you.

"Four in the afternoon + bare trees + dying light + trek toward work + pleasurable sensation of bundled up clothes + sensation of day that will depart never to return again + fear of finding patient disagreeable + sensation that something either very good or very bad will happen." The young woman marked those premises on her portable computer but held back the process by not pressing the key which within seconds would provide her the requested answer. The park could be seen deserted, by crossing it diagonally she would very shortly reach the square gray building which for a year she had frequented, under obligation, five times every week. The young woman mentally rebuked the architect responsible for the lack of visual inducements in the "Hall of the Citizen." She fully agreed that the Supreme Government shouldn't allot a budget adequate for superfluous expenses, but perhaps those countless smoky, nearly black panes of glass could have been of a greenish, or even pinkish, tinge for the same price. Regardless, they would still have hindered what took place within from being seen outside. In addition it was debatable that the place should have the appearance of a hospital, when its function was something entirely different.

The young woman, registration W218, added one more premise to those already marked, "dissatisfaction before the needless severity of public buildings," and pressed the button for the final tally. Answer: "natural insecurity before the challenge implicit in the fulfillment of duty." W218 breathed deeply, from her diaphragm she was filled with an ample yawn, the same as was produced every time she achieved full satisfaction, physical or moral. She was on favorable terms with herself, something now common among the young women born before the year zero of the polar age. A successful educational method had permitted them to recover within fifteen years of activity, human elements which had been seriously damaged. W218 proved to be a good example, because she had been born before the Great Turn of the Page, as the year zero was called, thus being classified within the final lustrum of the atomic age, a problematic division of the Registry.

What lengthened the walk was the roundabout way that the young women in service should take to enter the building. Residues of false modesty of years gone by. The leaders, on the other hand, asserted that the anonymity of the conscripts added charm to the performance. Along with her weekly card she found the day's order. She was required to present herself immediately at dressing room 3. With joy she punched her card in the clock at the control point, it was the fifth and final day of her week's service. Dressing Room 3 signified clothes in the style of 1948, that is to say, patients between sixty and sixty-five years old, the youngest ones admitted for the treatment of Division A. It was a style of clothing that only a tall slender figure like her own could carry with elegance, due to the full, very long skirt, and shoes without heels, inspired by the slippers of classical ballerinas; a skull cap of flowers embroidered in white would function as headgear. The day's orders also stipulated that her name for that occasion would be Dora.

At five in the afternoon W218 should enter Lounge 12, and thus it came to pass, punctually. Lounge 12 simulated a tearoom with subdued lighting, and a profusion of white undulating rubblework along the border of the walls and orchestral box recalled the decorative use of meringue in confectionery. Nevertheless, what was sought was a reminiscence of 1948, and at the third table in the second row, awaiting the young woman, was a representative from the opposite sex with whom—as instructed in the day's orders—she had made an engagement over the telephone without the two having ever met before. In order to be identified she was carrying a red carnation in her right hand, which was gloved in white lace. The ambient music reproduced a selection of songs by Charles Trenet. The gentleman stood up when he saw her approach and gallantly pulled out her chair to seat her, "I had never made a blind date, and now that I see you . . . I regret that I've been so cowardly." W218 looked at him, seldom had she perceived such sadness expressed in the manner of combing one's hair, that wave that made the hair from the nape of the neck extend to the forehead to cover his baldness.

"Do you know, miss . . . or may I call you by your name? It's Dorita, isn't it? So . . . let me tell you about myself. I'm in my last year of law school, well . . . it's not that I'm so precocious, I'm already twenty-five years old." W218 didn't remember very well which of her two patients of the day this was, she had read both files closely the night before, but she'd forgotten to review them that afternoon before leaving the house. She remembered that one of them was a sixty-two-year-old widower, alone in the world, and yes, as a matter of fact, he happened to be a lawyer. The other was a man from the countryside, sixty-five years old, whose wife was confined in a hospital for cancer patients and was undergoing extensive treatment. "I love this new music, Dorita, one can see that France isn't dead, because such infectious, joyful music indicates that this nation has come back to life again from the ashes of the war, don't you think?" The young woman tried to remember how far back the old man's widowhood dated, and, failing to do so, felt guilty for not having duly prepared her day's assignment.

"Look, Dorita, these orchestras are always like this, they make you wait for hours between one piece and the next. And people aren't inspired to step out onto the floor and dance to the phonograph. I don't either, I should tell you, although I'm not a bad dancer; I do especially well to the rhythm of a foxtrot, and I'm not like those other youths who are put off by a waltz. I don't consider it old-fashioned." Slowly the members of the orchestra of young women climbed onto the dais, once settled in they adopted thin, sleepy smiles; with the first wave of the baton they attacked with vigor the guaracha *Cumbanchero.* "I should tell you, you're light as a feather . . . Dorita. When I saw how tall you were, well, two or three inches taller than me, not so much, right? When I saw that you were as tall as you are . . . I didn't think we would do so well on the dance floor."

Half an hour later W218 believed the time which had elapsed was sufficient, the illusion of healthy, youthful flirting had been fully achieved, and it was time to go on to the well-known second part of the program. "Nicolás, forgive me for saying this . . . the dance is very beautiful, but I must return home. It's that I'm expecting a very important telephone call, and I can't stay any longer. Well . . . my home is very near here, if you'd like we could chat for a little while longer as I wait for that call, what do you think?" The gentleman's gaze became somewhat more somber than was normal for him, the appropriate vouchers covered the price of tea, with almond pastries, and in the hallway they took the elevator to the fifth floor. The room simulated a one-room apartment decorated with school pennants, a racket, a pair of crossed maracas and a calendar devoted to young women in bathing suits drawn in such great detail that they almost appeared to be photographs. "Perhaps you'll think it's bad that a girl should let a fellow into her apartment, without there being anyone else around, I mean . . ." The length of her speeches varied with the patient's boldness, and confirming the average time limit, he in turn interrupted with a kiss so impassioned that she was barely able to hang up their coats. She asked him to take a seat, he sat for his part and with an introductory sigh she lowered her gaze. Regulations dictated that the engagement finish two hours after having entered the mock apartment, "What are you going to think of a girl who gives in this way, and on the very first date. I should never have let you in my apartment because . . . as soon as we started dancing, feeling myself in your manly arms, I began to lose my head . . ."

The patient's performance could be considered within the classification "average 62," that is to say, appropriate for a sixty-two-year-old male, so that W218 shouldn't make too great an effort for her partner to achieve that much longed-for sexual satisfaction; the young woman even decided to skip established speeches since she considered them absurd embellishments, such as "You're very strong, you're hurting me, have they never told you that you have muscles of steel? be gentle with me . . ." and above all, "No, no, that frightens me, I hardly have any experience, don't take advantage of that . . ." Whereas she did use, with very good results, the following speeches, also suggested by regulation with the intent of establishing the mood of the mid-twentieth century, "I had never felt the things that you're making me feel, never, never . . ." "now that you've gotten what you wanted, who knows whether you'll ever want to see me again . . ." and "please swear to me . . . that you'll tell no one, not even your closest friend . . . about what's gone on between us . . ."

At eight o'clock in the evening W218 once again entered the tearoom. The day's orders stipulated that the second and final patient on the day's agenda would be seated at the first table in the last row. The young woman would have recognized him even had she not known this piece of information because his demeanor as a hayseed from the countryside was all too apparent; above all the face weatherbeaten by the outdoors and his uncomfortable relationship with clothes somewhat tight for his corpulence distinguished him from the others in attendance, "You're a beautiful young woman and I an old man of sixty-five, why should we kid ourselves. . . . Others prefer to play-act that farce, I don't." This time the orchestra struck up the bolero *Cowardice*, "I know that you must find me pretty disgusting, and for that reason I would appreciate it if you'd disguise those feelings and not make me feel like a dirty old man. . . . But the truth is that we old men also feel the desire to be with a woman. And I have my wife, who's younger than I am, three years, but the poor woman is confined in a hospital, and she'll be there for a long while, if she comes out alive, poor thing. . . . And I feel tremendous grief over that, but just the same I'm seized with this enormous desire, which comes over me . . . to be with a woman, and when I presented myself at the Ministry I didn't think they would accept me, but they realized that yes, that I also have the right. Actually, we've got to admit that this government really works, all the economic problems have already been solved, no one is poor and no one wants to be rich because of the administrative difficulties that it incurs. Everything works. And now, that they should care for people's souls seems to me only fair."

The young woman wasn't troubled by the close embrace with which her dance partner led her, if it meant pressing their cheeks close together and having him speak into her ear rather than face to face, as sensitive as she was of her interlocutors' bad breath, "I know that others must speak flirtatious compliments, and who knows what other foolish remarks. And it's not that you don't deserve them. But I know that kind of dough-faced old man, in their hearts what they're thinking is that you're a . . . prostitute, like the ones they knew when they were young, that's what they think. But not me, I understand these modern times, and that sex, as they say now, isn't anything bad. And you, what you're doing is a great deed, you girl conscripts from the valley of Urbis. Of course the ugly ones save themselves and get sent to work in the fields, but you bring life back to us, look, I'm not exaggerating, to us poor old men you give life back." W218 believed that interjecting any of her prescribed speeches would be futile and limited herself to say thanks each time that it happened. Once in the room, her work, quite the contrary, proved to be hampered by the brutal way in which she was treated, and she had to threaten her companion with calling the guards. Indignant, the man began to get dressed, but he immediately reconsidered and begged the young woman's pardon. She felt sorry for him and allowed the patient to complete the treatment, believing that the aggressiveness was a product of his fear of impotence. In fact, the treatment's execution proved laborious and in the end, in attaining his elusive orgasm the patient couldn't restrain a negative exclamation, "Whore, whore!"

The man dressed in silence, W218 entered the bathroom to freshen up her light makeup and above all her coiffure. The man rapped on the door with his knuckles, "Excuse what happened. . . . I'm leaving now, and don't bother coming out because I remember where the elevator was." Footsteps were heard, then the door to the common hallway as it shut once again. W218 then realized that she'd been put in a position that troubled her conscience. In such cases she should set forth a detailed complaint on the same page as the patient's classification; those from Division A were entitled to a monthly date and if they didn't behave properly they would be reduced to quota zero, as she believed would occur in the present case, if she explained what had taken place very possibly the subject would receive no further sexual therapy, and if she didn't report him she would put another of her colleagues in danger of a subsequent attack by the hostile patient. W218 told herself that perhaps she was being too conscientious, but seconds later she attributed her kindliness to dilatoriness toward writing the report, which presented obvious enough difficulties in formulation. It was twenty minutes short of eleven o'clock at night, her hour of departure, but because of the report she would be delayed.

Her evaluation proved to be "subaverage 65" and the report took her more than half an hour. The park was illuminated at night, the young woman crossed it attempting to overcome the bad humor that such delays brought upon her. She didn't consult the computer because the situation lacked mystery, what annoyed her was that those problematic clients almost always cropped up in the second shift and forced her to leave late this way. Trying to cheer herself up, she remembered that it would only take less than a month for her to complete the first half of her conscription, while in the second year she would attend, according to regulations, to Divisions B and C, that is, to crippled youths and deformed youths respectively, all of whom were beneficiaries under the statute for sexual services, as should be the case. After those thirteen months passed, well, she would have completed her conscription and could once again take up personal relations, which were absolutely prohibited in the meantime. There was talk that the young women coming from this sort of service enjoyed great prestige among the young men their age, but W218 feared that this would prove to be another of the many beautiful precepts spread by the Supreme Government which reflected no specific reality. For example, she doubted that the son of this peasant tonight would differ greatly from his father.

Arriving at this point in her reasoning she always told herself the same thing, that given her great physical beauty and her kind, communicative disposition she couldn't help but find a man of great worth, under normal circumstances. A real man. A man who would understand her, to whom it wouldn't be necessary to explain anything, someone who would intuitively know her enormous need for affection and at the same her insecurity. Someone who would enlighten her in those moments of doubt. A man superior to all those whom she had known until then. A man, why not? superior to herself. He could be the brains of the pair, while she would bring her pleasant personality, and yes, of course, her much-celebrated beauty. And she would no longer be alone.

What did that matter to her, to be alone no longer? Above all she would use the computer less frequently, she would consult it only in situations of real emergency; it was necessary to bear in mind the Supreme Government's warning about the added load of work that so many consultations represented for the Electronic Assistance Office. She would ask him for advice, she would talk to him of all her problems, to which her companion would listen with as much interest as she would have in listening to his. And he would know how to counsel her, because W218 didn't want a pretty puppet by her side, she sought a being of great intelligence. He should also be good-looking, because that way he would make her forget so many unpleasant men whom she'd had to give treatment to. And very intelligent, what above all would characterize a very intelligent man? W218 told herself that she'd be able to identify him immediately because such people have a natural ability to understand others, even their slightest spiritual complexities, thus fathoming their deepest hidden desires. The only thing that this man would be unable to unriddle would be her nightmares, so persistent, the young woman mused, but yes, of course, she would relate them to him. Finally someone in whom to confide such sensitive secrets! and so disturbing.

Why was she visited in her dreams by that forsaken woman? Without realizing it she had begun to think of her as her best friend, but at the same time it was painful to be unable to help her, as much as the young woman proposed it, it was beyond her ability to succor her. A woman from another age, and other lands, now vanished. In fact, what most distressed W218 during her nightmares was not knowing where this woman had lived, because the landscape where she appeared had been wiped out forever with the polar inundation of years gone by. And the Supreme Government had forbidden the diffusion of prepolar geographic material, it didn't want its citizens to submerge themselves in nostalgia and the consequent frustrations, just as the tropical lands and more had been submerged because of the half-melted ice floes. Elderly survivors used to report that previously the planet had been much more beautiful, and in whispers severely punished by the State they described sensuous flora and crimson dusks. A change in the planet's rotational axis had been enough for vivid colors to disappear from nature, and for the lands lately emerged to know only winter. W218 saw in her dreams scenery that corresponded with those accounts by the elderly. Surely those same stories had given rise to her overflowing imagination, she came to think, and with sorrow she remembered that she still had more than a year to wait before she could find the man with whom she would discuss all this.

Her apartment was small but perfectly heated, a square room where all the furniture rose up no higher than a yard from the floor, the remainder was taken up by the four-fold screen of the teletotal. She turned it on immediately to rid herself of depressing thoughts. Seated on the gyrating chair situated in the geometric center of the room, she took off her shoes and lit up a cigarette. A travel documentary had already begun, one of the genres best suited to the potentialities of the teletotal because they gave the teletotal spectator the illusion of being immersed in the middle of a foreign land without ever leaving the house. There were divisions of the Supreme Government which criticized the isolationist effect of the teletotal; it was argued that since each citizen enjoyed a single-room apartment, he would prefer to remain alone after working hours, able to rotate his teletotalic chair freely, without finding heads in front of him which would obstruct his line of sight.

W218 soon became aware that it had to do with the publicized documentary about the submerged, lifeless city of New York, visited by a touristic submarine. It was particularly amazing how the extraordinarily powerful floodlights from the ship managed to light up a city hundreds of yards below the sea: from the panoramic deck of the submarine the tourists could observe the ex-metropolis of skyscrapers, its elegant neighborhoods, its ghettos and its now-aquatic parks. One of the highlights of the journey involved the entrance—through an immense circular opening—into a movie theater, the biggest one in the world, with an immeasurable dome, where, as a strictly historical and not a nostalgic curiosity, a film from the corresponding period was being projected. W218 turned her chair ninety degrees the better to view the picture, the situation was a unique opportunity to see a prepolar film, forbidden as they were due to their antisocial effects. And despite the turbid subaquatic projection, despite the distortion caused by the oblique focus of the teletotalic camera in this particular take, despite the subsequent color filters, despite everything . . . she was able to recognize the face of that most beautiful woman who in the prepoplar film was visiting a casbah in the disappeared capital of Algiers. It was the face of her friend from the darkness, from the confused, cold tenebrosity of her afflicted nightmares. The film was projected without sound, or the sound hadn't been recorded by the makers of the documentary, so the voice of her mysterious friend couldn't be heard.

Unfortunately the documentary quickly passed to other aspects of the submerged city, such as its ex-airports and ex-railroad stations. W218 turned off the gadget, she folded a portion of the

screen which covered a window overlooking the street, she prepared herself something to eat which she swallowed with difficulty, then tried to sleep. It was already dawn by the time she was
able to induce sleep, she had left the window uncovered but the
light of the polar dawn proved very faint and didn't wake her.
W218 saw her friend once again, but in a landscape different
from that in the film, a landscape of clashing vegetation and
strident colors; the actress took several minutes to arrive on the
scene. In that same setting a man, young and agile, could be seen,
always with his back turned, on watch from behind a tree. He had
a computer in his left hand and with his right was marking
premises: "abandoned little girl + registration W218 + whereabouts unknown + special indications perfect beauty + maternal
heritage already reported"; he pressed the final button and the
response appeared: "attention, dangerous young woman,
equipped with electronic bowels rather than . . ." But the man
didn't have time to read it all because at that moment steps could
be heard, and W218 and he saw the actress appear, desperate,
along an old tropical highway. The actress ran and called out to
someone, not by her registration number but rather by name, as
in ages past, "Where are you? where are you? There's danger,
mistrust him, he draws near only to reduce you to an object of
his desire! and I know you won't be able to renounce him, nor
am I able to renounce him. Oh . . . if only you could hear me
. . . if somehow I knew that you could hear me . . . what peace
you would bring me . . . but you give no sign . . . you're thinking
of him, waiting for him, cooking for him, you're doing any foolishness inspired by him . . . and you consider yourself very clever,
very advanced, ha! but you're the same as all women, if he touches
that soft spot you are destroyed, that weak, putrid spot which you
have between your legs. . . . Anyway I feel such pity for
you . . . because if you don't watch out, they're going to kill
you . . ."

W218 was unable to project her voice to answer her, neither
would her legs obey her to emerge from her hiding place. The
actress continued calling out to that unknown protégée, in ac-

cents with every breath more heart-rending, and in vain, now that an automobile ridiculously antiquated but still very fast rushed headlong upon her. W218 was present, powerless, at the tragedy. In a culminating close-up the actress made one final request, she begged not to be forgotten.

PART II

9

—Listen to this, "Teatro Colón, 1972 Season. Today August 2, at 8 P.M., *I Puritani* by Bellini, with Cristina Deutekom and Alfredo Kraus, musical direction by Veltri, stage direction by Margarita Wallmann. August 3, 6 P.M., recital by pianist André Watts, works by Scarlatti, etc., etc., and 8 P.M., recital by the soprano Victoria de los Angeles, works by Granados, Falla, etc., etc. August 4, 8 P.M., Verdi's *Nabucco*, with Cornell MacNeil, musical direction by Fernando Previtali. August 5, 6 P.M., concert by pianist Claudio Arrau, works by Bach, Mozart, Chopin, etc.; 8 P.M., the Buenos Aires City Ballet, *Firebird, Spiritu tuo* and *Petrushka*. And for the following week, *Manon* by Massenet with Beverly Sills and Nicolai Gedda.

—. . .

—You, Pozzi, you can't appreciate this, but those are opera casts I'm not sure any house in Europe could afford. Only the Metropolitan in New York.

—And what was playing at the movies?

—First runs, let's see. . . . At the Gaumont *Fiddler on the Roof,* at the Monumental *The French Connection,* and at the Loire there's one I never saw, *Made for Each Other,* with Joseph Bologna, who looks a little like you. And *Metello* by Bolognini. . . .

—Almost all gringo movies.

—That's not true. *Isadora* is English and leftist, *Satyricon* by Fellini, *The Escape* with Delon and Simone Signoret, *Tchaikovsky* is Russian, and let me look at the revivals, *Death in Venice* and the Argentine documentary *Neither Conquerors nor Conquered,* about Peronism. And *Kanal,* Polish.

—At the height of a military government, what a contradiction.

—Lanusse was like that.

—He imprisoned a lot of people.

—But if you people made trouble for him, what did you expect from a military government?

—And there was torture under Lanusse, so let's change the subject.

—Listen to this, Pozzi, at the Arizona *Helga and the Men*, there were even porno flicks. And listen to the list of concerts outside the Colón: at the Coliseum the English Chamber Orchestra, directed by John Pritchard, and they're announcing the Loewengath Quartet, the New York Pro Musica . . . at the Municipal *Yvonne* by Gombrowicz, and let me count . . . one, two, four, six, uhm . . . it can't be, thirty-four theaters counting the experimental ones.

—And that city doesn't appeal to you. You don't like it. Don't you realize that it was a unique phenomenon? in an underdeveloped country and lost at the bottom of the southern hemisphere.

—I remember the bad things and that's all, Pozzi. I admit it's a mistake. . . . But that's the way I am.

—Soon we're going back, I have a feeling.

—Whereas I don't, I think never.

—I'm not going to listen to you anymore. Just a few days ago you were dying and now you're better than ever.

—You're wrong to kid around about this. The pains went away, and of course the scare passed too.

—You almost had us convinced that you were sick.

—Those who haven't gone through this don't have the faintest idea of what it is to be sick, with something serious, like what I had.

—. . .

—When any disorder comes up you lose all faith, and you can't believe you're going to get better.

—. . .

—If it goes away later, yes, at last you believe the doctors, and you go through the treatment with the utmost care.

—Today you honestly look good. I'm glad you called me.

—When I started to flip through this newspaper it made me feel like talking to you.

—And where did you get it?

—It came inside the package that Mama sent, wrapped around some bottles. It's even possible that on that day, August 2 in 1972, you'd have come to the house.

—Yes, at that time, yes. . . . I was going to call you today anyway, it seems that the thing at the University is all arranged.

—Great!

—I was waiting to go over and sign the contract, before I called you. But it's all taken care of, or at least that's what they say.

—What subject?

—Social theory, it's a seminar, to start. I'm going to have to prepare myself, I haven't got notes or books here, they're all in Buenos Aires.

—Will you be needing the notes from that famous seminar?

—Yes, those too.

—I've forgotten everything, all you'd taught me.

—Ana, another incredible thing about Buenos Aires: Lacan was hardly known in France and we had already given him all the recognition that he deserved.

—And in other parts he isn't known?

—In 1970? I don't think he was. Now he's starting to be studied seriously in Europe and the United States.

—And the case of Bergman was just like that. It was in Argentina that he was shown for the first time, outside Sweden. In an interview he gave I read that his "Sommarlek" was a hit in Argentina before it was discovered in Paris, which was where it had its international launching, he says that himself. Isn't that phenomenal? I remember that it was forbidden to minors and I couldn't see it, more or less around '54, and I was dying to go, because people could talk about nothing else.

—And this same country produces a guy like Alejandro. It's all very contradictory. It can't be explained.

—But Alejandro is a sick man, he's not typical.

—I'm not so sure.

—You, Pozzi, take note of this, if Argentina ranks highest in the world for people's interest in symphonic music and opera, that's because it has a very elevated middle class, you can't deny that.

—. . .

—Don't make faces, you don't like opera because you don't know anything about it.

—But look, as an example of the national contradiction, there's nothing more hair-raising than the case of psychiatry. Two years ago Argentina had one of the most highly evolved, free psychiatric services in the world. People came from the English school of Cooper to study the phenomenon, those from Antipsychiatry, the most advanced in the world, and some of Melanie Klein's followers, from France.

—And what's the contradiction there?

—Didn't you know?

—No, I don't.

—As I was leaving they were dismantling all the psychiatric services in the hospitals, the free ones. They're going to leave only the insane asylums.

—And why's that?

—The government claims that psychiatrists are subversives, that they have Marxist leanings. So from having an exemplary social service, and a free one, note well, we went on to having nothing at all. From one extreme to the other. And the contradictions can't be explained by saying it's a country of social extremes. On the contrary, it's a middle-class country.

—. . .

—To you, Ana, doesn't it strike you that they've eliminated those services?

—How everything can just go to hell, don't you think? in the blinking of an eye.

—How close all that is. . . . And at the same time so irrecoverable.

—We're like old people, feeling nostalgic over the past.

—But this isn't nostalgia, for me it's worse, Anita. It's as if I had dreamed that whole good period, as if I'd dreamed it last night.

—. . .

—Oh, no . . . just the opposite, it's this business here it seems like I'm dreaming. Argentina a year ago is what seems like reality to me. And this the dream. I remember all of it so clearly that it seems more real to me than this hospital room in Mexico City, I don't know what we're doing here. All that seems more real to me, and at the same time . . . I don't know . . . gone forever.

—Today I'm not taking your hand out. You must have noticed that already.

—I see that you have bottles of liquor for your visitors, but you've never offered me any.

—It's because you never used to drink.

—Now I don't fall asleep if I have a little drink, the way I did in Buenos Aires.

—Could it be the high altitude in Mexico?

—Just now I'm starting to understand a lot of things. I couldn't drink because I was always going around with a shortage of sleep and one drink would knock me out.

—And what else?

—And there I hardly looked at women. And here I look at all of them. It's that there I didn't have any energy left over, quite the reverse. Working so much.

—And studying. Listen, Pozzi, what do you remember of the seminar? How did that business with the mirror go?

—I have to review all that.

—Just roughly, tell me.

—I've forgotten it, how the postulate begins.

—Whatever you remember.

—Well, it began, let's say, with that a baby isn't aware that his feet, his hands, his back, make up parts of a whole, which is his body. . . . And what else? this concept of the whole will be provided by the mirror. But there one says mirror to signify other things.

—Such as . . .

—Well, before that there's the matter of the baby living in anguish with the disappearance of a foot, let's say, a hand, beneath a bedsheet, for instance. Because it's a part, of himself, that's familiar, known, but over which he has no control, because it appears and disappears. And that, this sensation is called "the phantom of the disintegrated body" if it reappears later on in life as a type of anguish, do you see?

—Yes, now I'm starting to remember.

—Such as when one loses control over something, or over a person, which unconsciously was regarded as part of oneself.

—And the thing about the mirror, then?

—Yes, one says mirror, but as a symbol. In reality what gives you back your own image is the sight of others. It's in the eyes of others that one sees oneself reflected for the first time.

—But the sight of others isn't always so objective.

—More than that, they can see you in whatever way suits them, and shape you however they please.

—And misshape you as they please. Yes, these were the things I wanted to remember. It's what made the biggest impression on me.

—But you would have to look at all this more thoroughly. What I'm telling you is nothing more than a start. I like what Lacan says about the unconscious, that it's organized like a language.

—Yes, I remember something about that too.

—Before it was interpreted that the unconscious was like a bag of cats, where everything falls and gets jumbled together.

—Yes, now I remember, that there everything gets sorted out and filed, like in a computer.

—No, Anita . . . hold on a minute.

—I like that, because I'm that way, like a sort of computer. And it doesn't have to make me feel ashamed.

—Of what?

—You were the one who accused me of being like a computer. And now you see, we all have that little calculating device within us.

—Don't trivialize. Those are your stories, it has nothing to do with what I was telling you.

—Why?

—The unconscious is not a memory from which you can retrieve index cards as you would from a file. There is a model of operation, but which can't be grasped concretely, except through the fiction of language.

—How's that?

—It's a model homologous to a language, which functions like a language, but which cannot be known in its totality.

—I don't understand.

—It's a little complicated. Most of all you have to apply the terminology quite carefully.

—Couldn't you explain it to me with intelligible words?

—In this case, it's essential to use a rigorous terminology.

—. . .

—You can't seek to have access to Lacan any other way. The terminology is important. Otherwise one trivializes it. You are trivializing it.

—. . .

—And that about how the unconscious is the other, the Other with a capital "o," I don't know if you'll remember.

—No, that you never explained to me.

—Yes, of course I did. He says that the "I" is that part of the self over which each one has control, that is, the conscience. Later that part over which one doesn't have control, or let's say the unconscious, passing as foreign, crosses over to join the surrounding universe. It is the Other.

—I follow.

—And part of the Other, of the foreign, is really yours, although that part of you is actually foreign to you, because it's beyond your control. And at the same time, your entire view of the universe is filtered through the unconscious. And thus part of your self is foreign to you, but the entire universe is a projection of yours.

—It's confusing.

—Not really. Always two things in play, do you follow? That's why according to these theories you're never alone, because within one's self there's always a dialogue, a tension. Between the conscious "I" and the Other, which is, we would say, the universe.

—How difficult.

—Everything is difficult for you. Or you want to perceive it as difficult.

—I get lost, on such uneven ground.

—You get dizzy?

—No, I get lost. To get dizzy is ugly, that's something else. Getting dizzy makes you nauseous, makes you vomit.

—. . .

—Getting lost isn't ugly.

—But what's all this nonsense? Getting lost yes, and getting dizzy no. What's that?

—Can't one daydream a little, maybe?

—But we're talking about something serious. But with you it can't be done.

—Oh, Pozzi, I've noticed one thing, a flaw of yours.

—What?

—You enjoy being on top. You enjoy being the one who's right and not the others.

—. . .

—And now I realize that it's something very much from back there, from Buenos Aires. They like to disagree.

—What's this?

—You're not even aware of it because you've never lived anywhere else.

—Explain.

—There, if people can contradict you they're happier. They don't like to be in agreement.

—They like to win an argument, that's only logical, human.

—No, wait.

—What?

—Wait a minute, so I can think.

—Think all you want.

—There they like to win an argument. Or no. It's worse. They like to defeat. They enjoy defeating someone else.

—I'm not like that.

—It seems to me you are.

—This is rubbish on your part, Anita.

—I'm no intellectual, no shining light. But it's that looking at the country from outside you'd have to be very stupid not to notice certain things.

—I at least am not like that.

—Yes, you too, and I think that makes you lose points.

—. . .

—We'd best change the subject, don't you think?

—So you'll see that I do operate with a desire to be in agreement, and not just to win, I'm going to tell you something that goes against me.

—Let's hear it . . .

—I didn't know whether to tell you or not, about the fact that my wife knew about you. During that whole time.

—. . .

—I used to tell my wife about some things and not about others. And about you I told her from the first moment.

—I can't believe you.

—Yes, at that time we were coming out of a crisis, and I tried to tell her everything.

—You never told me about it. Or about the crisis either.

—. . .

—Excuse me, but I don't find that amusing.

—I never got the nerve to tell you.

—And why are you telling me now? To make me angry?

—It occurred to me, that's all. Because I'd never told you.

—And with her why did you decide to tell her everything?

—There was a period when I was always going around in a bad mood at the house. I took it all out on her, because of things that were going on at the office.

—That's classic, a man who's a louse at the office is a little lamb at home, and vice versa.

—When I realized that I was tolerant at the office and a louse at home, I reacted. I had no right to put them through that kind of life, especially my wife.

—How were you a louse?

—Bad temper, everything annoyed me. And I thought about it and realized what it was.

—A guilty conscience over hiding adventures from her.

—Just the opposite. I wasn't having relations outside the house, and that's why I was in such a bad mood, because I needed to have them. And I told her that, and she understood.

—Just hold on . . . before I forget: how did you realize that you'd turned into a louse at home?

—Because it seemed that they were starting to be afraid of me. And they were whispering behind my back. Just like they did to my old man when I was little. And before getting married I also behaved like a louse to my old lady.

—And what was she depriving you of?

—I don't know, maybe it was that she had too much patience with me and it made me nervous.

—And to you if they treat you kindly you feel guilty, admit it.

—No, it's that my old lady didn't want me to get married before finishing my career, and she treated her future daughter-in-law very coldly.

—. . .

—There's one thing I would like to know, do you remember when I called you in the office that morning, after the first night we spent together?

—Yes.

—Now I can say it to you, what I was going to say that day.

—I remember that morning perfectly. I got to the office late because we'd hardly slept. And I waited for your call.

—I phoned at one o'clock sharp, Anita, just as we'd planned.

—I knew that call would be important. I couldn't do anything in the office, until you phoned.

—I couldn't do anything either.

—You said some wonderful things to me.

—You don't remember a thing.

—Yes, I do remember. That I was the loveliest woman . . .

—Most beautiful.

—. . . beautiful, the most interesting, and I even think you said the most intelligent, but with other words, so that you'd sound more believable.

—The most important thing was what I didn't say to you.

—I realized that you were about to tell me other things, that's why I got strange.

—Anita . . . I was completely in your thrall.

—I remember that you said you didn't know what good you had done in life to deserve someone like me. And while you were saying all these things to me I had before me my schedule of activities for the month, almost every night filled, with engagements at the theater, all of which had been bringing me so much satisfaction, all my things at work.

—And that's why you didn't want to see me again that very night.

—No, I thought that if I showed myself too available that you'd get tired of me.

—That's really what you thought?

—Yes, this guy is going to treat me like a plaything, I thought.

—That day I was going to ask that we live together. For once in my life I totally lost control, and it was over you. I couldn't conceive of life without you.

—To that degree?

—Yes. But when you told me you were busy that night, and the next, and the next, it was like you'd dumped a bucket of cold water on me.

—And we left it that I would call you if I was able to get free. And I called you two days later, and then it was you who were busy. Do you remember that call?

—More or less, Anita.

—I do remember. It was the time that we went over the commitments of one and the other. The night I was free that

week, the only one, you weren't, and we left it that you'd call me
if you could arrange a special schedule.

—And who called the next time?

—You did, you suggested that I go to the seminar.

—I remember less about that.

—Whereas I think it was the most wonderful time, when we
talked until really late and you . . .

—Don't go on, Ana.

—What's wrong?

—It's going to depress us.

—It doesn't make me feel bad. On the contrary, it makes me
feel good to explain things.

—. . .

—For you, Pozzi, this makes you feel bad?

—Yes, remembering the good things makes me feel bad.
Remembering the bad things doesn't affect me either way.

—Times passed are always better. Maybe it's that in remembering it all appears so much lovelier.

—No, in our case it's like that. It isn't an illusion. It's as if life
was left behind, and it no longer . . . belongs to us.

—I hope to get well, Pozzi.

—. . .

—Put your head here, that way I can stroke your hair. Here on
my shoulder.

—. . .

—Pozzi, one has to be patient. Things are going to change.

—I don't want to think, Ana, I feel good like this, feeling your
warmth, and your nightgown.

—Your hair grows very fast.

—Go on caressing me.

—Do you like to feel my nightgown against your ear?

—Yes, the fabric is fresh, but beneath . . . one can feel your
faint warmth.

—Do you like my new perfume?

—Yes.

—You have good taste. It's the most expensive one in the
world. From the essence of simple violets, although it seems

unbelievable. I had never gotten around to buying it, but last week I asked Beatriz to pick some up for me. I didn't want to die without having worn it.

—. . .

—And just a little while ago I brushed my teeth, after I took the medication that leaves my mouth bitter.

—. . .

—Pozzi, you're hugging me so tight . . .

—I'm afraid you'll slip away.

—Me slip away where, in my nightgown?

—. . .

—I told you that I brushed my teeth . . .

—And what if someone comes?

—They'll find us making out, like teen-agers.

—But if I kiss you, I'm not going to let you go.

—If you press this knob, the blue light in the hall will turn on, that means I'm sleeping, and no one's allowed to come in.

—And isn't there a safety latch, from the inside?

—I never noticed.

—Yes, Anita, there is a safety latch.

—Before going to sleep, I draw the curtains. It leaves the room almost dark, barely semidarkness to let you see something lovely, if there is anything lovely around.

—. . .

—Almost always there's some flower that's been brought to me that day, or the day before. But they have to be very fresh. Even before they've really begun to wilt, I ask that they be removed.

10

"REGISTRATION W218 + CONSCRIPT Division A of Sexual Therapeutics of the Ministry of Public Welfare + recently praised by superiors + physical beauty recognized + prone to nightmares + equipped with electronic mechanism instead of . . ." The young woman marked these premises decisively but hesitated before pressing the button for the tally. She had been waiting outside the manager's office of the Institute where she lent her services, she intended to clarify an error in the most recent week's paycheck. She took a deep breath and pressed the conclusive button, but at that very moment a door opened and she was forced to lift her eyes before reading the response. Beside her there passed, paying no attention to her, a group of officials accompanying a visitor, most likely a foreigner, from the looks of his attire.

W218 couldn't believe her eyes, had she been able to sketch the ideal man she wouldn't have succeeded in depicting him so precisely. Never had she seen him in her dreams, but she was certain that just so was the man for whom her heart yearned. Her heart! apprehensive, she looked at the computer: "response impossible, one of the premises badly phrased or incomplete, devoid of meaning." The conscript let out a deep sigh of relief, evidently the nightmare of the previous eve lacked meaning, and therefore she need concern herself no longer over gloomy phantoms, they represented no particular warning requiring special attention. Whereas this man, so very handsome, was no phantom, much less a gloomy one, but he had passed through her life and she would never see him again. Another sigh, but hadn't he at least provided her the satisfaction of knowing that a gentleman existed so completely to her liking? W218 was highly skilled in the art of extracting positive conclusions from every experience.

The park was covered with snow that night, even her own steps weren't audible. Less still would those of another passer-by be heard, but for reasons unknown to her the young woman swung around to see if someone was following her. Never at this hour had she encountered anyone, her gesture had no meaning. She carefully examined the path which she'd walked, the dead trees and street lights of mercury, their respective shadows, her own solitary tracks in the snow. Absolutely nothing disturbing could be perceived, nor could any sound be heard, except her own cry of horror as she returned her gaze forward. An unknown man was impeding her passage, standing beside a street light which, rather than illuminating, threw a shadow onto his face cast by the brim of his hat.

"Forgive me, I didn't intend to frighten you," he said with the resonant timbre of a baritone. The young woman trembled, unable to take another step. To make things worse, the man spoke with the accent of a neighboring country, her own native land. It was an accent which only reminded her of misfortune, the great catastrophe of the ices, the loss of her family, the orphanage, the crossing with other consumptive children into the high lands of this bordering nation. The man removed his hat and W218 was on the verge of emitting another cry, not out of dread this time. Before her, smiling and inclining his head by way of greeting, there stood the man of her dreams.

The computer slipped from her fingers, the gentleman picked it up, brushed the snow from it with a gloved hand and held it out to the young woman, who stammered, "No . . . it wasn't out of fear, bu . . . only surprise . . ." Her countryman smiled, "Forgive my impudence, I'm here on a research tour, sent by my government to learn the techniques of the Institute which you honor with your collaboration. In hearing you speak I realized that you and I are fellow citizens and I couldn't resist the desire to wait for you here, to exchange a few words apart from all protocol." She inquired where he had heard her speak, "During the tour through the various agencies I had the opportunity to hear you speak, in intimate dialogue with a client." She was caught up with the sight of such emblematic being and paid no heed to those words, she surveyed his features one by one and could find no way to improve them with her imagination: his brow was wide but not excessively so, the eyes—green, an imperative requirement—shadowed by eyelashes full but not creating a languid expression, the nose aquiline but only enough so as to lend it strength, the mustache thick but without covering the protrusion of the upper lip, the lower lip well proportioned to the upper, the teeth perfect but not false, the chin strong or not but covered with a fundamental requirement of the young woman's, that is, a pointed beard, the hair black and wavy but with silver touches of light gray, the spectacles ordinary but sufficient to lend the precise intellectual touch, the shoulders wide but not as those of a brutish rugby player, the legs long but in harmony with his long waist and finally the hands which, being gloved, presented the best opportunity for the young woman's ability to imagine them as she pleased.

"I should add that I'm very favorably impressed with the Institute's operations." Just then W218 reacted, how was it that the visitor had been able to hear her through closed doors? "As you must know, charming compatriot, some of the walls of the rooms allow the viewing and hearing of what takes place between patient and conscript, a convenience which the doctors utilize to examine the alternatives within the therapies administered." The young woman hadn't known it and tried to dissemble, clearly the visitor had perpetrated a serious indiscretion, "I've been very well received by the capable authorities, and I'm being offered every kind of assistance, but in seeing you and hearing you there arose within me a wish for an informal chat . . ." She thought it appropriate to inform him of the impossibility of establishing intimate relations outside the Institute, "I'm aware of that, and that isn't what I seek, rather a simple comraderie. I presume that wouldn't be forbidden, or would you prefer to consult your computer? Do you know something . . . they strike me as somewhat picturesque, the uses that these artifacts have here." The young woman replied that all foreigners reacted in this manner, because they suspected that in this way the Supreme Government would keep informed of all the people's secrets, "And by any chance might that not be true?"

W218 rebutted that if the citizen didn't want his inquiry to remain on record at the Center for Electronic Assistance it sufficed to press a button as soon as the response was read, but note, not after two minutes because at that point it would already have been filed at the Center; in conclusion she added that those, like herself, who had nothing to conceal from the State, would certainly allow their requests to be transferred to the Governmental Archive, as illustration of the nation's problems. "And do you believe that the Center doesn't find out regardless, whether or not that button is pressed before those two precious minutes?" W218 pointed out that was one of the principal arguments of dissident citizens, to which she responded with a simple act of faith in the Supreme Government. The discussion ended there, and after planning an engagement two days hence, that is, on the conscript's day off from work, he removed his right glove to extend his hand to W218. She could then appreciate that the right hand of her countryman was as sensitive as a pianist's, as rough as a woodcutter's, as trusting as a childhood friend's, as strong as a boxer's, as sensuous as a lover's, as furry as a bear's, as manicured as an actor's and consequently as perfect as those of the man of her dreams. Who responded to the name or abbreviation LKJS.

At seven o'clock on the afternoon designated, the compatriot called at W218's door. The young woman awaited him dressed in a pair of blue overalls, her plan was to take the tourist to a popular restaurant at the electricians' guild, among those whom she considered friends. But LKJS's attire proved to be an inconvenience: patent leather shoes, a tuxedo jacket with glossy silk lapels, a white bow at the neck, a black cape lined in satin, a top hat. W218 communicated her discomposure, "There isn't a problem, young lady, everything has been anticipated. I would have been quite interested to carry out your plan, but this morning I received —from a branch office of the government—a complete set of vouchers for immediate consumption, and as you'll realize, it is impossible for me to ignore so kind an invitation. It has to do with . . . uhm, let's see, in the first stage, cocktails at a particular place, followed by dinner and dancing at another, and . . . well, nothing more. Yes, I already know, I know, there will be complications in dress on your part, but that has also been foreseen, within a few minutes a messenger will arrive with everything you'll require." W218 felt annoyed, her plan had been to return from the restaurant to her house bringing some friends for a drink of punch, and thus to forestall the danger of ending the night alone with LKJS.

The doorbell at the entrance rang loudly. A messenger carried boxes both large and small wrapped in extraordinary papers of whose existence W218 had been unaware until that very moment. Already this luxury seemed excessive to her. LKJS noticed this, "No, W218, if you feel uncomfortable with this change of plan, let's leave things as they were. I don't want to pressure you." The young woman felt obliged to look into his eyes, and that instant of renewed dazzlement proved fatal to her. Without answering she began to untie the silk bow of one of the large packages, and, while she struggled with the knot, indelible impressions from childhood came back to mind, such as certain long, ethereal evening gowns of pleated chiffon, of what color? somewhere between lilac and sapphire, lightly caressing a woman's long-waisted silhouette like her own. Of course they no longer existed, she concluded.

The box contained a full-length evening gown, in pleated chiffon more lilac than sapphire, the difference perhaps attributable to the light from the reddish lamp in the single habitation. This style would go well with those colorless high-heeled sandals of transparent acrylic which were used toward the end of the atomic era, thought the conscript in a minicrisis of insubordination. She searched for them in one of the medium-sized boxes and found them. From there she embarked upon the task of opening the largest box, trying to remember the name of a prestigious fur, the most expensive of all, a fur with short hair that ranged from dark to light gray in very expensive undulations. "It's called chinchilla, they are very few, the examples that still exist," LKJS explained, as he held the full-length coat while the young woman prepared to try it on over her overalls, a hasty test. Two packages remained unopened, the two smallest ones. W218 imagined a handbag of

violet beads which she had never in her life seen, and she opened
the package with the certainty—justified, at these high levels—
of finding it. She was mistaken, "This perfume it seems was
famous for its cost, the most expensive of all. In my country we
hold large quantities in the government warehouse, together with
wines and liquors, the loot from successive expeditions to the
submerged nation of France. The fact that this entire battery of
bottles was hermetically sealed saved the exquisite products. The
spoils included the sculptural works of great artists and some
stained-glass windows in the Gothic style." The young woman
opened the flask and it sufficed to smell the fragrance for her to
feel different, for the first time in her life she dug her fingers in
her hair, roughing it up, a gesture typical of a frivolous female.
Without further ado she picked up the dress and the shoes and
directed herself toward the bathroom, "There's still one package
left for you to open, and forgive the request, but I ask that you
be careful with all this, it involves a loan from my embassy."
W218 returned to open the last package, whose contents were a
handbag of violet beads. Smiling, she entered the bathroom with
her dubious cargo. As she emerged she was pale and serious,
seeing herself in the mirror so inordinately beautiful had sobered
her up, it had caused her to descry a superhuman dimension in
her being. "Why do you look at me thus, young lady? do you feel
unsatisfied? Of course the accouterments are not complete . . ."
and he proceeded to withdraw, from the inside pocket of his
jacket, two flat cases of black velvet, "this could not be carried by
a messenger because its value is great." The square case contained
a necklace and a pair of earrings, with an abundance of diamonds
mounted on platinum in the style of 1930, and the elongated case
a bracelet and a ring, also with diamonds and platinum, of a
design similar in style.

The waste of gasoline was looked upon with disapproval by the
Supreme Government, but this was not of any concern to the
visitor and in the automobile placed at his disposal they sped off
at great velocity, with shameful indulgence. They were distancing
themselves from the city, which was situated in a valley of very
high altitude completely surrounded by mountains, and the fall

of the gray afternoon appeared to hasten as they reached the foot of those massifs of maroon and black stone. She had a particular weakness for the settings of the sun but had to content herself with seeing them by teletotal, stowed away as the city was at the bottom of this box without a lid, the valley of Urbis. The automobile climbed the slope and W218 inquired whether the site for the purchase of cocktails could be found there on the dark hillside, "No, in the center of the city. What I'd like to show you now is something else." She hadn't mentioned her wish, was it possible that he'd have guessed this too? They reached the summit and from the impending nightfall they passed into the rosy light of the other slope, the color gray had disappeared, and the black and maroon as well, only then did W218 admit how much she detested them. To disguise her enjoyment she asked random questions of the visitor, "Yes, I'll leave very much impressed by the workings of the Institution to which you belong. If I had more time I would interview that entirely different category of conscripts, those who perform tasks in the fields, work with which no citizen wants to be concerned, I suppose." Other groups were visible, couples in the majority of cases, dispersed along the scenery. They were all bedecked in exclusive formal attire, "I know that the citizens of your country don't have access to these paths, because of the restrictions on gasoline. Well then, those whom you see are either foreign diplomats or local government officials, mostly the latter."

They descended from the automobile, W218 carried herself in her sumptuous finery like the most distinguished, worldly woman of the surpassed atomic age, she intuitively dropped one shoulder and ignored those around her as if she saw no one. To return to the official subject, the young woman explained that there were other tasks, much less publicized, carried out in the city under the compulsory civil service, such as the cleaning of homes and the care of children, "Yes, I did know that. Now, then . . . doesn't it seem to you, W218, that it's unjust to keep in mind the sexual needs only of the disqualified masculine sector? by chance wouldn't the older women, the crippled or deformed young women, have the same needs?" She responded without hesitation, explaining that the Supreme Government had plans for reform of this sort, but it wouldn't be realized for several decades hence, there were other emergencies which preceded them, such as the defense of the frontiers, which occupied all the nation's male conscripts. By all means, sexual therapy for women was planned, and it would come to pass after the services of free cosmetic surgery, foreseen within the none-too-distant future. Immediately afterward, and with diminishing conviction, she added that after sensible studies, they had come to understand that the sexual needs of a woman were much more minor than a man's. These words, which she had uttered with conviction so many times in the gray, maroon and black scenery of the city, sounded false in her own ears, there in the rosy-tinted foothills. Finally W218 felt obliged to lower her head, for fear of offending, as she murmured, "My personal opinion . . . is that women can dispense with these activities because they have far greater spiritual resources, particularly at an advanced age. In addition, with so many men dying in war, what other consolation is left them, poor things?"

They decided to return to the city before the spectacle began to fade. Soon they arrived at a somber ministerial building, they crossed a deserted passageway after slipping away through the usual side entrance. A silent elevator conducted them to a concealed cabaret in the penthouse which simulated, or was, a grove of coconut palms beneath a starry tropical sky, with the sounds of maracas and bongos. W218 had to hold her countryman's arm because her legs threatened to buckle out of excitement. She could do no more than ask him whether this decor was based on some landscape from the planets recently visited. He chose not to answer, to circumvent an embarrassing moment for her. Because of the accent the young woman discovered with astonishment that the majority of those present were natives of the country, members of the government. Champagne was being drunk as a matter of course. After the first glassful she looked into the green of her countryman's eyes, "You needn't say anything to me, dear W218, or better said . . . tell me that yes . . . that you too want to remain here, and not to go to another place, the aforementioned restaurant . . ." It was precisely what she wanted, and to dance, to practice unknown steps to the beat of rhythms never before heard. He explained to her that they were from the years prior to 1940 and for that reason outside the repertory of the "Hall of the Citizen." They got onto their feet without further hesitation, "The place which we were supposed to visit next offers a more sophisticated ambience, but it occurs to me that you may have, as I do, an aversion to wild game, and that's all that's offered there, wild boar, rabbit, pheasant, venison." This most unique man shared even her phobias, W218 thought, and immediately turned to cast a glance at other dancers to learn the steps that the woman should take. After the second cocktail they felt hunger, and she couldn't believe what she saw, a waiter carrying an enormous platter of spaghetti, something she hadn't eaten since her earliest infancy because it was banned by the Supreme Government. It was believed to cause deformity, in addition to inflaming gluttony.

It being impossible to eat spaghetti without spoiling the makeup on the mouth and even on the chin if one was careless, W218 managed to withdraw for a brief time from her compatriot's presence, from his intelligent words, his hypnotic gaze, to go to the ladies' room. An eccentric matron was powdering her nose before an immense mirror, W218 confirmed that her own chin was greasy. She opened the beaded handbag to remove what she needed when she discovered that unconsciously she had slipped the computer inside. The matron departed impeccably whitened and W218 extracted the modern oracle, "gentleman exceedingly good-looking + gentleman intelligent + gentleman understanding + gentleman with total spiritual affinity + gentleman ardent + gentleman foreign." Without letting a second pass she pressed the button for the summary, "caution and distrust, necessary to behave rationally and to control all emotion." Enraged, she pressed the button corresponding to erasure, she decided that all that was cited as evidence by the dissidents against the state system of assistance had a valid reason. With one wipe she removed the dab of meat sauce and applied her lipstick; she pulled herself together determined to fight for her new convictions and opened the doors which led to the jungle of coconut royal palms, or its representation in chromium-plated metal, it was the same to her now. She was forced to grab hold of the handle so as not to reel, such was the power of what was offering itself to her eyes: LKJS. W218 let out a sigh of deep-felt satisfaction and she blessed her parents, whom she had never known, for having brought her into a world with such unsuspected delights.

Morning was breaking. She was sleeping, a seraphic smile lit up her face more than the faint, deathly light of the polar dawn. At her side there lay, awake, the man of her dreams. What darkened his face, more than the expression of his eyes, was the sardonic grin of his lips. With the utmost caution, to prevent making any noise, he stretched out his hand and withdrew, from trousers cast beside him on the rug, a box which contained two small plates of glass of the sort used in microscopic analysis. He concealed them within the closed fist of his left hand, in the event that the young woman awakened. Very gently he inserted the index finger of his right hand into her vulva, seeking a vaginal secretion. The young woman registered a pleasurable sensation, but she didn't succeed in waking up. His eyebrows arched in the manner of Mephistopheles and his eyes reddened but not with tears: now they would be able to complete the detailed evaluation of the young woman's personality, based on zodiacal studies, on the analysis of the saliva left on glasses and cutlery, on the examination of locks of her hair which had been cut and stealthily collected at some hairdressing salon. The compatriot removed his finger and smeared the liquid on one of the small plates of glass, which he immediately covered with the other. Thus joined, he stored them in the tiny box. At last he was able to surrender to sleep, certain that his country's secret police would be proud of the mission accomplished.

Friday. How many days have passed without opening this notebook. But it's useful to write, to order one's thoughts a little, and to figure out what the real problems are. I'm determined to avoid worries that aren't pertinent, I won't allow myself to get frightened, and I'm succeeding in this. This morning I woke up with the pain and in spite of it I didn't get scared like last week, because now I know that it's a stage in the evolution of an illness, no, how ugly that sounds, the evolution of a convalescence. Last week I was so sick and later I rallied, maybe this time it'll pass the same way, and also this time the pain hasn't hit me with such force. Undoubtedly things are going well. And it's even possible that the pain attacked me because yesterday I took that little liberty with the treatment. What a way to say it.

Later. I stopped because the pain got worse and they had to give me a sedative. And afterward that two-hour nap also helped. It's been days since it attacked me with such force. What a mistake that was yesterday. I thought it would do me good, that it would make the blood circulate better, some hope! With the doctor there was never any talk of discontinuing sexual activities, which was logical, since there was nothing to discontinue. It's been so long since I've done anything like that. I didn't feel a thing. It might have been because of those medicines. What could it have been? I remember many bad experiences, but this one was different, I didn't feel recoil, I didn't feel pleasure, I felt absolutely nothing.

The strange thing is that I didn't have to force myself to do it. I felt desire. I felt so much tenderness toward him at that moment, he seemed so beaten down, poor thing. If he was in my arms I could comfort him a little, how could I not have done it? Afterward he left ever so happy. Although it's not necessarily so that I did it out of tenderness. No, there was a moment when I felt, what was it? vertigo, a very strong desire for him, a desire to let myself fall, where? a chasm opened up and there came over me a desire to throw myself into the unknown, him, unknown? no! what would the unknown have been in this case? . . . But what an unpleasant feeling remains afterward, when one feels nothing. Really I grew myself into a void, the void which is inside me. I have to admit it, it was a mistake, which won't be repeated. But will I sometime feel that marvel of other times? Never again will I do it if I'm not crazy in love with someone.

Someone. Does he exist? Yes, about this, better not to doubt, because if not, let me die now. Without that hope. But where is he? I'd have to go out and look for him, not just wait for him to appear. What an awful thing that's just occurred to me: I'm waiting for Prince Charming. Like a fifteen-year-old girl. If instead of saying that I was waiting for Prince Charming I were to say that I'm looking for Prince Charming, it'd already sound a little better. But where do I find him?

The more I think about that criminal proposal of Pozzi's, the more furious I get. It hadn't occurred to me that in this way I could endanger Clarita, for instance. If I agreed to get mixed up with them, the Argentine government could uncover my involvement and retaliate against my child, or even against Mama. Especially against Mama, who, poor woman, already has a record, thanks to Beelzebub, what wouldn't they be capable of, those mafioso Peronists who govern or misgovern us? So that I, by helping a movement so dubious, like the Peronism of the left, would have put my family in danger. That's the first thing I'm going to say to Pozzi's face when he appears.

And that he not go on annoying me with his nonsense about Buenos Aires, the Queen of the River Plate. I'm bored of this queen. Of course it's a paradise for the arts, or was, I don't think by now there is any money left for the budget at the Colón, the way they're robbing the country blind, those scoundrels. Before, one didn't know where to begin, concerts, operas, movies, theater. Even television held a certain attraction, with so many politicians telling lies at all hours of the day, when Lanusse lifted the censorship. Shows and more shows, to spend the entire day and night watching shows, seeing what others do, actors, singers, musicians. Those are the great moments that are lived in the Queen of the River Plate. From an orchestra seat, that is, or in bed making love? in the dark. Would that be a great moment too? What a coincidence, it had never occurred to me, because during shows the lights are out as well.

But what performances. What quality. What variety. And what unforgettable moments. Wagner sung by casts worthy of Bayreuth. Verdi deserving of Parma's Teatro Reggio. And movies and more movies. To choose from. It wouldn't be unfair to say, the best moments of my life, with the exception of that period with Fito, have been spent in a box seat at the Teatro Colón. And like me almost everyone else, I'm sure, watching love films. But what foolish remarks I'm making. Women are the ones who spend their time watching soap operas and love films, not men. Well, but they're spectators too, aren't they? of detestable soccer games and boxing matches. How disgusting the world of men, enjoying those fights where both contenders finish with their faces bloodied. How disgusting men are. And I say that my life depends on finding a man, the right one. How crazy I am. How stupid. And the worst thing is that it's the truth. Without that fantasy I wouldn't care if I lived one minute more. Why am I so foolish? who has put that in my head? or is it in our nature to need romance? what romance, if nothing lasts?

Then, thinking it over, it could be a great discovery by Argentines, or by Argentine women, I should say, to get involved with those shows, since one can't have such wonderful love stories in life, at least to have them in one's imagination. Although it's wrong to judge everything according to what happens to me, there are women more easily contented. There are women who don't have to imagine odd things to feel pleasure. Or not? or are they all the same as me? Because to shut your eyes and imagine things while a man is embracing you, it's as if you were watching a show, it's always the same, or isn't it? the same as being a spectator, I mean. That must be why sex is better in semidarkness, because then the room is like a theater. But maybe that's reality, that always in life one has to be a spectator. But no, that's in my case, or the case of many women, but it can't be the only truth in life, there has to be something more!

I'm embarrassed to be a spectator, I want something more. I understand Pozzi when he says that he got involved in Peronism because from the inside he'd be able to do something to change what he didn't like. So at least he's trying to do something in life, by taking action. Or he has the illusion of being involved in something. But I couldn't have that illusion, if I were in his place. Because I don't trust those guys, as much as I'd like to. Everything they're proposing is so mixed up. How can he think he's going to change all that? He has faith, he's very much a fighter. To change Peronism from within. What a task. I can't even change myself.

Not even change him, to my liking. That wouldn't be bad. What is it that I'd change? I think that if he had political ideas that convinced me, that made me enthusiastic, I would respect him more. But what political ideas would inspire me if I don't have any? Marxism appeals to me with the idea of equality, but later on in practice it seems to be trouble. I would like Argentina to develop, for its standard of living to rise, for there to be a great deal to parcel out. In some way that's what Pozzi wants, a socialism of national characteristics, he calls it, but how can he associate with people who have such bad track records for that? To change Pozzi, but by any chance can people after a certain age be changed? who would have been able to alter Fito? They're already the way they are, and there's nothing to be done about it. Mama was right, one has to accept them as they are, because none of them are perfect. And a woman who accepts Fito has to accompany him to all those dinners with executives, and a woman who accepts Pozzi has to get mixed up in that mess of collaborating with terrorists. How beautiful it is to be a woman, how many agreeable options are presented to us, either to yield to one side or yield to the other. If we want to live as a couple with a man who will make us happy at night, not making us feel nothing. Such a lovely plan. Such justice. The brute who goes to sleep after having enjoyed himself as he wished, and the noble sacrificed female who goes to sleep with the satisfaction that she's been useful though she may have felt a virtuous nothing.

Without intending to I've confessed all my egoism. Since I have problems now I'm wishing that all women were in the same situation. Let's hope not, poor devils. Let's hope that at least they can imagine they're being ravished by an evil sultan, and all those tall tales that help us at times. And that in this way they'll be able to be spectators in some romantic adventure. But thinking it through, when one imagines things while someone else is doing others, one isn't entirely a spectator. How confused I'm making myself. Beatriz said something else, that it's more like acting out a role, a character that you choose for yourself because you like it. A character with whom you feel comfortable. If I was with Fito and I imagined that he was a big man and he'd abducted the little girl who was me, at that moment I, more than a spectator, was a fraud, I was passing myself off as someone I wasn't. Well, I'm exaggerating, what I would do would be to play the drama, like an actress. This reminds me of that question of Fito, the impression he gives of always acting on a stage. But he's so happy with the character he plays. The poor thing is an absolute nothing, he contents himself with very little, with quite a small character. Then deep down isn't he that way? he's one thing and the character another? Who knows. . . . Also, it could prove to be that in the world everyone is a blank which has to choose some character which he likes. To amuse himself with something, to fill the hours or the void which he has within, I don't know. And that's where each one's cleverness must lie in knowing what he wants. Could it be that? Whether one wants a blue mask or a green one. For me there's nothing worse than when they tell me that I don't know what I want. I'd like to kill Mama when she tells me that I don't know what I want, that my mistake in life is to want to be different. At this very moment the blood is rising to my head just remembering. She's sure she's right, that I'm the fool who doesn't know what she wants. Of course, what she's really saying, in other words, is that I'm the fool who can't find her character. Because everyone else finds one except me. But it's true, Pozzi is the leftist, the martyr, and he's delighted with his character. Beatriz is a feminist, and delighted. Mama is a lady devoted to her friends, another success in life. And Alejandro? it seems to me that he's like me, he doesn't know what he wants. But that's not true, I know what I want, I want a man worthy of my respect! Then my character is that of a woman who seeks a man worthy of her respect. But perhaps this isn't a character, or is it? but a character that I have very little desire to play. Then the cleverness lies where? in not thinking? in playing only certain characters? in finding the character that you'd like to play? But I haven't been able to find it. I remember what happened with Pozzi yesterday and it makes me as embarrassed as remembering that greasy kiss at the restaurant. There's nothing worse than regretting something you've done.

But I'll say one thing, wouldn't it be nicer if everyone was who they are, without playing a role? wouldn't it all be more spontaneous, more fun? But it's been proven repeatedly that it isn't, because I've already called the muster for those who act out the drama, and they're the ones who are delighted with life. The two who come off the worst are poor Beelzebub and me, those who were left without a role, those who got there last when the masks were being handed out. And am I being fair in saying that Beatriz plays a role? No, she's more flexible. The problem exists in the Argentines, it seems to me. With the Mexicans the problem is another one, do they wear masks too? No, here in this country that's curious, because there are people completely out of character, I see them and I can't imagine who they might be, whether they're guitarists, whether they're senators. And there are guitarists who look like senators and senators who look like guitarists, and even some trapeze girl who looks like a socialite and the other way around. Here the problem is another one. But it's a thing of theirs. And they have the good taste not to be aggressive, that has to be admitted. With them the problem is that they all wear the same manner of expression, that of courtesy, of generosity, I would almost say of compassion. They pity me because I'm exiled, or do they pity me because I'm sick? might they think I'm going to die? They see me growing thin and taking sedatives more and more, it's logical that they'd think the worst, they have no way of knowing that I'm under special treatment.

II

"Eyes Full Of tears + strange heaviness in center of chest + interminable wait for letter + . . . " rather than going on with the doleful premises she chose to press the red button which canceled the consultation. Her suspicions were on the increase regarding the discretion of the Center for Electronic Assistance. Also increasing was her need, now nearing despair, for her countryman. The afternoon was predictably gray and cold, there within the apartment all the window panes were covered with fog from the steam heat and at the top of the window frame one after another drops sprouted, then rolled down the smooth surface of the glass, as they would down a cheek. There was still an hour left before she departed, bound for work, she had spent the morning waiting for the postman who in the end had brought her nothing, and since then had begun her wait for the next day's mail.

She lit up a cigarette, forbidden during the two years of conscription, and counted the days which had passed since the sudden departure of LKJS. He had been summoned by his government for unknown reasons, thus interrupting his goodwill visit. Several days before the fact the young woman had submitted a request to the Ministry of Public Welfare, to which she was subject, for permission to leave the country for a weekend, on a sojourn to the neighboring country where she had been born. Was it possible that her request had given rise to suspicion? Because her plan, and that of her lover, was not to return. Suspicion of desertion could cost her a trial, and even years in prison. No, she told herself, she was filling in the blanks pointlessly, no one could be accused of a simple bad intention not brought to fruition. Or could one? there had been reforms in the penal code that she was ignorant of, very much under attack from the dissident sector.

Worst of all, he had bade her that unexpected farewell by telephone, from the airport, and because of LKJS's evasive tone the young woman had inferred that he was unable to speak openly. The sole positive point in the conversation had been the promise of return, at any cost, to complete his research and to see her. W218 seemed to be somewhat relieved, she could breathe more easily, without that affliction in her chest. Perhaps the mentholated cigarette had opened her respiratory passages, but it was already the last remaining one, her lover had forgotten them there. No, she corrected herself again, it was the thought of him that comforted her. Yes, that brightening up which had occurred in her brain was produced by the memory of him, and nothing more, she argued. The young woman didn't suspect that the tobacco contained a good dose of the enemy's malice. Suddenly she was able to remember even the most remote detail of any moment spent with him. Every one of them magical moments. And the explanation, in her view, was so simple: the undeniable attraction to this Apollonian man's body was combined with the peace, the expansiveness, the satisfaction of knowing that everything that pleased her would also be pleasing to him. There would be no differences of opinion, or discussions, or renunciations, or sacrifices by either of them. Everything that was proposed by one was a fountain of delight for the other, the caprice of one was a discovery of new forms of pleasure for the other. From the second day of their romance they had ceased to consult each other before making decisions because all conjecture was superfluous.

"It's incredible, but true. I, a man, you, a woman, that is, two different conceptions of life, I thought and action, you sensibility and . . . and more sensibility, and in spite of all the differences . . . we agree on everything. Do you remember when you told me that you, as I do, preferred string instruments? well, then, from that moment I began to know you. . . . Dearest, the first thing we will do on reaching my country will be to listen to music unknown to you. They say here that music isn't censored, and they lie, my love, they lie. Just as you rippled to those tropical

rhythms on our first night, which those hypocrite high officials
reserve for themselves, you will likewise ripple to a sort of music
you do not know, that which is sung, and is forbidden here
because it contains a narrative element. Oh, how joyous we will
be in that marvelous land . . ." She then had proceeded with
complete sweetness to reveal unsuspected subsoils of the national
reality, "My love, you must take into account the tragic essence
of this country. The fact that it was the first to emerge from the
waters doesn't prevent it from being the coldest and most desolate. Those ghostly branches of dead trees attest to this, the final
evidence of an extinguished vegetation. Would you not agree,
perchance, that they should be removed? They bring me anguish,
for the same reason that the Supreme Government decided to
forbid all prepolar artistic expression with the exception of music,
because it isn't figurative. Also literature depicts scenes of yesterday, and for that reason it too is forbidden. For us, my treasure,
everything that reminds us of the past proves nostalgic and hence
pernicious. We must build a new nation on a new foundation, it
isn't advisable to imitate the past, because we will not succeed."

W218 inhaled another puff of smoke and in her memory there
resonated once again his stentorian voice, "How I adore you! just
as your beauty overwhelms me, so does your intelligence. And
this, for a man, proves difficult to admit. How you understand and
love this land! . . . but you have to see whether she loves
and understands you in the same measure . . ." The foggy windows obscured the streets. The cigarette had burned almost completely, she was forced to extinguish the stub in an ashtray.
Within a few minutes the pleasant intoxication began to abandon
her to the point of becoming detached from her and foreign,
whereas the knot in the middle of her chest was growing tighter
and tighter. W218 tried to focus on the good memories, "Dearest
. . . you ask me how it is that I am able to know everything about
you. I know everything about you for the same reason that you
know everything about me. And that reason . . . needn't be
named, why should it? perchance aren't we aware of it? Like you,
I don't care to speak in the morning until well after an hour has
passed since I've awakened. Like me, you prefer to do those things

of least importance—such as going to the bank, to the post office, to the hairstylist—in the morning. The same as you, I enjoy resting for a while after lunch, taking off my shoes, reclining on the blanket and dozing for a good half hour. Like me, you prefer confronting tasks of greatest substance in the afternoon, when your creative potential is greatest, which is simply the result of a problem of low blood pressure. The same as you, I enjoy going out for a short time in the evening, or watching a good teletotal broadcast. Like me, you enjoy making love at night. Like you, I like to speak during lovemaking. Like myself, the fantasy-laden, affected forms of love offend you, you prefer the simplicity of a natural embrace, while looking into each other's eyes. And a mistake it is to say simplicity, because the infinite can never be simple: you are reflected in my eyes and I in yours, and in that reflection of you which is in my eyes, there appear your eyes, within which in turn I am reflected, the one in the other multiplied to infinity, thus filling the space with ourselves, our own infinity filling up the other infinity, that of the people, and at last there is no room for them, because we have no need for them." Whereas W218 hadn't confessed her feelings at those times, simply his embrace made her invulnerable, it lifted her above the dangers destined for mortals: observing the perfection of his features was enough to feel close to a being of another sort, superior.

Next the young woman tried to remember the melody of one of those joyful rumbas. No, it proved impossible. She looked at the easy chair where he preferred to sit. She looked at the box of cigarettes, now empty, she held it gently in her hands and kissed it as one would a child whom one didn't want to wake. She looked at the weeping windows.

At that exact moment she had a revelation. If he didn't return she would be unable to survive the grief. After one has known bliss it is impossible to resign oneself to having lost it. No one could ever replace this man, therefore if he didn't return life would have lost all meaning. If she didn't dare to take her own life she would be reduced to waiting for death. From far away the chimes of a bell tower could be heard, they reminded her that it was time to prepare herself for work. She blessed that obligation, she could no longer tolerate the solitude of her room.

"*Order of the Day*, Notification Attached. Registration of the Conscript: W218. Department of Services: Division A. Date: 10 Glacial Year 15. Text: Be thus notified that in forty-eight hours you must be prepared for a journey lasting three days to the neighboring Republic of the Waters, acting as guide for a group of crippled youths. The decision to choose you took into account your birth in that republic, and the proximity of your transfer to Division B, given that in the current month a year will have passed since you were recruited for services at Division A. It is sought in this way to bring the conscript into contact with her future beneficiaries, promoting the familiarity necessary for the future performance of her work. It is asked that the person notified sign the gray copy of this message. Signed, Chief of Personnel Division A, R4562. *Miscellaneous:* Dear colleague, we are pleased in this way to reward your very felicitous performance in the Establishment. Of course, also influencing your election was the request which you had made for permission to travel to the republic of your birth for one weekend. As you can see, we are also able at times to act in this manner, as in a family. Let's not tolerate those injudicious dissidents saying that all is mechanical and cold in our Ministry. Regards, and enjoy the journey, R4562." The conscript had to catch hold of the clock where she punched her card, she feared falling over from emotion. For several minutes she was unable to stop her tears of joy.

Immediately afterward she was forced to hasten her pace because it would take some time to make herself up for the day's encounters, all of them to take place in premises that feigned a masked ball in the Opera, an effective recourse for patients who were receiving treatment for the first time. While she dressed in her disguise of Columbina, the melody of one of those rumbas found the way back to her memory. Amid tears and smiles she danced before the mirrors in the dressing room. The makeup was smeared with all that weeping and she drew closer to the mirror to make herself over completely. She let out a loud chortle of laughter in noticing that the beauty mark painted on her cheek was dyeing a tear black. Trying to control such euphoria she breathed deeply many times. As she held the little puff of white powder for the first time she found the strength to admit an occurrence: on the last day spent in the arms of LKJS, even if for very few seconds, a strange shadow had fallen on the love of both. She patted the snowy powder on her face, held the black pencil between thumb and forefinger and with all her concentration directed herself to draw the beauty mark once again, "Dear girl, look into my eyes. I must make a superhuman effort to confront this subject, but it is essential that I do so. Yes, ridiculous as it sounds, after these sublime hours of love, I'm afraid of losing you. You know that I anticipate all your wishes, isn't that so? and it doesn't surprise me, because he who loves reads the thoughts of the person loved. Well, then, I've read yours, but you haven't mine, and . . . this fills me with doubts, with horrible fears . . . could this signify that perhaps you don't love me, or is it a peculiar coquetry which makes you behave as if you didn't penetrate the poor miasma of my mind?"

With a pink wig of short curls, and a purplish three-cornered hat, the headgear was complete. W218 then donned the mask, why did he demand that she read his thoughts? what was it about love that permitted one to anticipate the wishes of the other? Surely he would have left his address at the Ministry, on the occasion of his recent official visit. The following forty-eight hours seemed forever to her.

Avenue of the Aurora Boreal number 300, an address so easy to remember that she hadn't even made a note of it. The young woman was tempted to pinch herself in order to believe it, now that it was there, before her eyes, the white plaque with the number inscribed in black. How differently she had imagined the place. It wasn't a house, but an enormous government building. And how differently she had imagined the City of Aquarius, nothing had anything to do with her nebulous memories from infancy. From the airplane she had had the first definitive impression, from within the snow there emerged gray buildings, and the only contrast was provided by patches of humidity which stained some of the walls black. She had kept calm until reaching the gloomy façade, but in crossing the threshold her heart began to palpitate unrestrainedly. She thought perhaps that the minutes and yards were few which separated her from her beloved, governing bureaucrats guided her to the office of personnel. Half an hour later she was back on the sidewalk, desolate and cold. No one knew LKJS, and she was assured that from this ministry, that of matters dealing with public health, no visitor had been sent recently to the neighboring country. The cold of the street chilled through to her bones, she took several steps aimlessly, not knowing how to get her bearings. Immediately she fell lifeless into a faint.

When she awoke she was in her hotel, a passer-by had picked her up and from the documentation in her purse had known where to take her. It was the floor maid who was now wrenching her from her deep sleep, knocking on the door with a plate of hot soup. She asked the young woman how she was feeling. That one did not respond, she was still engrossed in her nightmare. As if her distress over the afternoon's failed search wasn't enough, a terrifying voice had plagued her during her sleep. She looked at the waitress without seeing her, "Who is the little girl's wet nurse? Tell me, please, who is it?" The waitress answered that she didn't know and withdrew as soon as she was able. W218 shut her eyes, she wanted to return to sleep so as not to think of the incident at the ministry, but she was also afraid of slipping back into the same nightmare. A blind nightmare, in total darkness a voice had uttered these words which signified nothing, over and over again, "the little girl's wet nurse . . . the wet nurse . . ."

With the arrival of night, all the activities of the disabled group were completed and the young woman slipped away along the hallways toward the service exit of the hotel. Something had returned to her memory—a lie?—that her love, or simply lover? had told her, "From my window I see an oak tree, perennially green." Why had he said something like that? First of all, an oak was a tree with deciduous leaves, and lastly, in the City of Aquarius all vegetation had died during the thaws, and the polar age had not seen the growth of a single blade of grass. Why hadn't she asked LKJS the reason for such a fantasy? Simply because his presence had seemed sufficient to justify whatever license nature might have taken. If nature had been capable of creating him, then it shouldn't be surprising if in front of his house there stood the only living tree on the continent.

She saw a taxi pass, hailed it, but the driver was too young. She waited several minutes until she saw a driver pass who was older than sixty years old. Before stepping into the automobile she asked whether he knew the city well, "Like the cracked palm of my hand, where would the little lady like to go?" She explained that she sought a house before which grew an oak that was perennially green. "You are mocking this city. Here there isn't a single tree living. Young people nowadays don't know what the word means, even if there is in this country a cult of nostalgia, and even if a memory of the past is hoped to be kept alive. But since it is the official attitude, new generations reject all memories that prove alien to them." The young woman repeated her lover's exact words to the old man, "I don't know how to answer you, young lady. Perhaps he was just having a hallucination. All trees are so erased from our weak memories that there's even a new neighborhood where the streets have names like Path of Pines, or Promenade of Larches, or Willow Lane, so that the town will not forget." She asked whether one of those streets wouldn't make a reference to an oak, "There may be, although I don't remember it."

It took half an hour to reach the remote residential neighborhood. The homes were all spacious, with yards where in the place of plants there were swings, trapezes, seesaws and other gadgets for children's play. Each street relied on a post at the corner which displayed a sheet of wood at the height of two yards. Upon it were depicted the name of the street and a drawing of the respective tree. Soon they found a certain "Oak Lane," only three blocks in length. W218 bade the driver farewell with a generous gratuity, forbidden in that republic but always coveted by all public workers. The elder man offered to wait for her, it would be very difficult in this area for her to find other means of transportation for her return. The young woman looked at him mockingly, she was certain she would be spending the night within one of these houses, "But what if you don't find whom you seek?" They agreed that the auto would wait five minutes stationed at this corner. W218 was prepared to knock on every one of those doors, there were lights in some of the houses, from the exterior, typical family scenes could be seen. The young woman lucubrated before undertaking her inspection, why had he said that from his window he could see an oak? perhaps because the house was situated on the corner, and he was able to descry the plate with the drawing of the corresponding tree. She immediately looked at the plate on this corner, and yes, the drawing represented a green oak.

What a way to glorify reality, she thought; he demonstrated that it didn't disturb him to lie so long as it would draw her to this city. But the houses on this corner had the windows closed, they appeared uninhabited. Whereas on the next corner there were lights, and if he wasn't there she would proceed to the following corners, there were four in all, the search had been simplified noticeably. She signaled the driver to approach and had him take her to the next corner. One of the more modern dwellings had lights burning on the ground floor, the enormous picture windows would have allowed her to see even the most minute detail of the interior, but due to the cold they were somewhat foggy. W218 saw children of a very young age and decided not to draw any closer to see better, clearly they weren't dealing with the home of LKJS. Climbing into the automobile to move on to the next corner, she threw one last glance carelessly at one of the cloudy windows. She seemed to distinguish a familiar silhouette, a man's. She descended again, and traversed the first yard, between seesaws, sleds and swings. The snow stifled the rustling of her steps.

LKJS played with two small children, a pregnant woman came and went. W218 couldn't believe her eyes, she drew even nearer to make certain. One of the children saw her and pointed her out to LKJS. W218 ran toward the auto, the unmistakable voice thundered forth threateningly, "May I help you in some way, madam?" She paused, not daring to turn and show her face. In barely a whisper another tense message reached her, "I beg of you, dissemble. We are being watched. The secret police . . ." The young woman finally looked at him straight on, she feigned to be searching for the home of some friends, "It must be on the following block, madam, I believe I've heard that name," and immediately added in a distressed murmur, "At ten in the morning, at the Central Library, the Reading Room . . ." W218 thanked him and got into the taxi. Never had she imagined that LKJS would be afraid of anyone, but the voice had indicated profound terror. The driver congratulated himself for having waited for her, "And now back to your hotel?" W218 asked herself whether this kind old man might not be a spy, "Forgive me, but if you look at me silently and choose not to tell me where you'd like to go, I can't read your thoughts." Read your thoughts! that hateful expression again. Yes, to the hotel, where else could she make her way in the black of the night? the black night, everything enveloped by black, the streets, the sky, the interior of this frozen taxi. Black. What else was black on this night? what other thing had been invaded by the color black? No, it was impossible. But yes, that had been what alarmed her most in her encounter with LKJS, his eyes had ceased to be light green, and had become black! She was certain, it was the reason that his gaze was another's. Eyes not green but black. Black as night, as the cold, as solitude, as the tears which an exorbitant pain will turn to ice within the darkness of the chest and which will not be released. Black tears, locked in, captive.

At this late hour, the service entrance to the hotel was being watched by a guard who would not let her pass. She made her way to the main entrance. It was snowing copiously. Beneath the marquee, keeping company with the concierge in livery, there smoked one of the wardens from her group. W218 retraced her steps. Crossing the street she saw another enormous modern structure, one of whose entrances was illuminated. She sought refuge there. It appeared to be yet another division of the Government. The signs indicated "Lending Room," "General Archives," "Reading Room," and there she ceased to look, she made her way to the nearest room and asked a woman of an advanced age what the place was, "It is the Central Library, young lady, where we welcome readers throughout the entire night."

The little old lady was dressed in vivid colors, her wig was blond and straight, "But young woman . . . you look so much like someone. . . . Perhaps you may not know it, but many years ago there was an actress, the most beautiful of all, whom you very much resemble." A cold shiver siezed W218 anew when she learned where she was, because once again, in that very place— it made no difference to her under what circumstances—she would see LKJS. To conceal such great emotion—her chest pounded and her nostrils quivered—she asked the little old lady who the actress was of whom she spoke, "Only the oldest among us are able to remember her. For me it is an unforgettable face. You will see, all of us who were young girls in that period fantasized we'd be movie stars, and I was no exception. I dyed my hair platinum blond, and the closest I got to the screen was as an usher. But don't think it was in a crummy neighborhood theater. It was at a first-run one. There are levels and then there are levels. And something occurred with her that did not with any other actress. . . . When she appeared in her first scene of every movie the audience invariably let out an 'ah . . .' in astonishment. It was a face so lovely that it didn't appear human."

W218 immediately knew how to pass the while, until the watchman became neglectful at the hotel entrance. It was indicated very amiably to her where the archives could be consulted, old newspapers and magazines. An ancient librarian recommended a series bound in black and white leather. In all frankness she didn't see so great a resemblance between herself and this actress, but it did prove to be a face previously seen someplace. It didn't take her long to realize where, one of the photographs showed her sumptuously clad on a visit to an Arab quarter. W218 felt chilled to the bone. It dealt with that film which had been projected in the submerged city, as part of the touristic documentary viewed by teletotal. Afterward she came across the actress photographed in early youth, in her few European films, and there the resemblance did appear undeniable. It was an article describing the life of the star, who had been born in a country by the name of Austria. A curious anecdote told of a particular caprice of the luminary's, because of which she had turned down one million dollars to play the lead in a story entitled "I Read Thoughts." She had died in Mexico in a puzzling roadside accident and she'd been survived by one daughter, of whose whereabouts she was ignorant. Whosoever was able to find her had been offered sums of millions, issuing from the estate of the star's first husband, presumed to be the father of the child.

The orphan dropped the heavy volume, as if it were charged with electricity. She read no further, could it be that she, W218, was the lost daughter? No, the actress had died more than twenty years before her own birth. She ran to the librarian and asked that she help her find information about a . . . wet nurse, stories of famous wet nurses, if there were any, "Couldn't the young lady provide me with any additional information?" W218 ventured to say that the person could have been involved in international intrigue. Without further ado the octogenarian dedicated himself to the investigation, after shrugging his shoulders meaningfully. There were peculiar wet nurses, but not international ones, would she have any interest, by any chance, in a so-and-so without a name, known only by one initial, with a sad criminal dossier? W218 asked what was her nationality, "From a European nation which was called Austria."

The young woman asked to see everything that could be found referring to the subject. Only one police report was found, with pious tones, where it described how a wet nurse, or simply a domestic servant, had attempted to murder the daughter of the household, on the day of her twelfth birthday, plying her with poison. The woman, many years in the service of this family, whose name was omitted out of respect, had acted in a fit of madness, because of which she had later strangled herself with her own braid, in the cell of the lunatic asylum where she had been locked away. There was, transcribed as a curiosity, the text of the suicide note found beside the corpse of the unfortunate wretch: "Goodbye, it is my destiny, as it was my poor brother's, that I should leave this world because of having lost my mind. Uhm . . . ha! that's what they'll believe, but he was nothing but a mere servant whom the Professor, in order to conceal his own villainy, had passed off as a mad scientist . . ." W218 continued reading, with growing fear: ". . . there was no other woman but me in the house, the Professor hadn't wanted anyone to occupy his mother's place . . ." ". . . he had prayed that they would permit him to pay in the afterlife for the sins of his mother, who would thus find peace at last . . ." ". . . the garden of white lilies seemed like a very precious jewel that night, but when I became aware that we were not alone, that cold shadows had crept behind the oleanders and jasmine, it was already too late . . ." ". . . a daughter, conceived under the worst auspices, that of a love not reciprocated . . ." ". . . the most beautiful girl who ever existed. But today I tried to kill her, now that it's only a question of a female, and what can one hope for from a woman? with her, the first cunning scoundrel who proposes it will do what he pleases. How ashamed I am to have had a daughter and not a little male, who would avenge all the humiliations that I've endured in my life, because of having this weak point between my legs, which makes me an easy prey of the first dog that knows how to smell out my foolishness. And the only thing that gratifies me is never having heard her call me 'Mama,' because I don't love her, and I wish her not to love me. Yes, I disdain her as much as I disdain myself, a servant to one man and to every man . . ."

W218 folded the paper up again and placed it in its file. Only then did she discover another newspaper clipping, a small one, in the depths of the envelope. It was an abstract from the chronicles of Nazi crimes gathered at the end of the Second World War. According to that source, the search for the descendants of the wet nurse constituted part of an unsuccessful scheme by the Gestapo, which was interested in the person who had been designated "the sorceress of thought-reading." The young woman made an effort—superhuman—and got on her feet. She departed from the Archive Room without making acknowledgment to the librarian. A sign indicated how to reach the Reading Room.

There she would encounter the man of her dreams at ten the following morning, beneath a dome illuminated by neon. Now she was convinced that he only longed to make her happy, because only he would be able to help her resolve the dilemma of her enigmas. The assumed logic of said rationalization succeeded in calming her.

At last she understood, hence his insistence on the subject of guessing, or not, the thoughts of the beloved one! He loved her so much that he'd been able to sense the danger with which she was threatened. Yes, she would confide all to him, and he, enlightened with the love he had for her, would thwart all interference on the part of Evil. He loved her, otherwise how to explain, on the other hand, the way he had been able to guess even her slightest desires? It had been for fear of losing her love that he hadn't spoken the truth about his children, and his wife, whom surely he was now on the verge of divorcing. It was midnight, only ten hours remained before concluding all anguish.

Now there was no caretaker in front of the hotel. In her room, under the door, she found a note announcing that the visit to the City of Aquarius was declared finished, due to the prevailing bad weather and the negative effect which this had had on the disadvantaged members of the group: the return flight had been moved forward to the following morning, on the plane departing at ten o'clock. W218, for the nth time that day, was forced to grab hold of something so as not to lose her balance.

12

—What a scare you gave me!

—Do I look that different?

—You're another person, Pozzi.

—Better or worse?

—I don't like how it looks.

—May I give you a kiss, without a mustache?

—And your hair, why so short?

—I'm going to Buenos Aires.

—I don't believe you.

—Yes. I fly to Chile, and from there I enter through Mendoza, by train.

—And you don't want to be recognized?

—New papers are being made up for me. My name will be Ramirez, what do you think?

—The bandit in *La fanciulla del West* is called Ramirez, but he's the dashing hero.

—And I'm not the dashing hero?

—. . .

—Do they kill him in the end?

—He's saved, they're about to hang him and the girl rescues him in the end. The soprano.

—How are you feeling?

—I have pains, every day, at around mealtime. It seems they'll go on for a while, a result of the operation.

—Ask them for painkillers.

—I have to really nag them, they're opposed to giving out so many sedatives.

—You'll just have to put up with it for the time being, then.

—The truth is, I never imagined it was going to take so long.

—If you get impatient it'll be worse.

—In the mirror I see myself looking awful, but I don't know if it's just my imagination. How do I look to you?

—You've got shadows under your eyes, but it's probably from being shut up in here for so long.

—It's madness that you're going, Pozzi.

—There's no sense in my staying.

—I was sure that by now you would have signed the contract with the University.

—No, I'm restless here.

—It's much worse that you're running those risks. You're crazy to go.

—There's no need to exaggerate, Anita. The thing with the papers is just a precaution for the entry, that's all.

—And afterward?

—We'll have people there who know who's being watched, and if it's necessary to hide.

—And if it turns out that you need to hide, what's the point in your going?

—It's that I can go on with the work, defending those prisoners. There's no need for me to appear in court, I can do all the other parts of the work, which are really tiresome, the petitions, for instance. And another lawyer would present them as his own. That's all, I'm not going to get mixed up with anything having to do with guerrillas, you know that's not where I'm involved.

—What I don't like is that they already have a dossier on you, if they raided your house there had to be a reason.

—Half the population has had its house raided, that doesn't mean anything.

—Do you believe that?

—Of course, distance makes those things seem bigger than they are.

—I admire your courage. I just wish you wouldn't go.

—How did you feel . . . after the other day?

—I don't know.

—How can you not know?

—. . .

—I felt great.

—Not me. I felt worse, to tell you the truth.

—It can't do any harm . . .

—. . .

—Don't take my hand out . . . I want to touch you.

—No, Pozzi.

—You used to like my mustache.

—Seriously, I don't feel well.

—Whatever you say.

—Listen to me about this one thing. If I'd agreed to your proposal, about calling Alejandro, wouldn't this have endangered my family? Clarita, and Mama.

—I don't think so.

—I do think so. They would at least have questioned Mama. And don't forget we already have the precedent of what Alejandro did to us, I don't know what kind of record the police would have kept.

—No, I don't think they would meddle with an old woman, or a little kid.

—You don't think so, and I'll have to be satisfied with only that.

—It's common sense, that's all, what can they get out of your mother or Clarita? It's obvious that they're no threat to the regime.

—But they might think I'm mixed up in something.

—They know very well who's involved and who isn't. And you in this case would only be calling someone who had been a friend at one point, and in a way a protector.

—I'm not convinced.

—. . .

—When would you go?

—Tomorrow.

—Please don't go.

—Your hand is so delicate, so cool.

—It would do you good to stay here, my sweet. Really, you could go on studying, you've got a good head on your shoulders, you could explore all those things that interest you, about Sociology, all of that.

—But what's most urgent are those matters back there.

—I was fantasizing that you'd stay. Here you were going to change . . .

—Why do you want me to change?

—You have promise, I think. If you stayed here longer, you would see things from back there under another perspective, and your beliefs would change.

—I have no interest in having my beliefs change, what are you talking about?

—Yes, I don't want to offend you, you have many great qualities, which I have a lot of respect for, really, but this stuff about Peronism. . . . If you stay here maybe it'll pass . . .

—You're crazy.

—And if you turned yourself into an authority on your subject, you'd be able to return within a few years and be useful in another way.

—Your proposal is totally absurd. The country needs me now, and I know I could be of use right now. And I'm not speaking vaguely, the things I have to straighten out back there are concrete things. The people who are under arrest, the people who have disappeared, it's imperative to help find them, to get them released from prison.

—But if they've held up banks, or kidnapped someone, how can you get them out of jail? wouldn't that make them ordinary criminals?

—I'm talking about very different cases. Journalists, teachers, people who think and who won't stay silent, and who are prisoners for that reason. And those are the people who are waiting for me, because by means of protests something is achieved, we'll be able to get someone out of that hell.

—Yes, you're right, I've always respected that in you, but . . .

—I believe that it's my responsibility, Anita. I'm incapable of turning a blind eye.

—But it's that there might be other people who would do it,

this sort of work. Who wouldn't be on a blacklist, as you are.

—There aren't any other people, we are very few who can do this work.

—I'm afraid that you may be exaggerating. You have too strong a tendency for sacrifice, don't deny that. You always have. There was no need for you to work while you were still at law school, but you got it into your head that you had to work, and who can stop you when you get an idea in your head?

—I'm like that, Ana. I always felt that way, that I had more than enough, and could give something to those who had less.

—You are like that, but couldn't you change, possibly?

—I've already told you I don't want to change.

—Of course, you like your role too much, that of a self-sacrificing person, a martyr.

—To me it isn't sacrifice, it's a sense of justice, that's all.

—If you stayed here you could be useful later on, dead you won't be of any help to anyone, is it possible that you're deaf to everything that's said to you? can't you listen to others just for once?

—What about you? By any chance do you ever listen? I've assured you that the thing with Alejandro would be easy, without risk, and that you'd be doing a great service for your country.

—If I called Alejandro you would stay?

—Yes, of course . . .

—. . .

—Anita, it would be tremendous.

—. . .

—Maybe we could even call him tomorrow morning, after I speak to Buenos Aires.

—No, Pozzi. It's because of Clarita and Mama that I can't do it.

—You're crazy, they would never meddle with a little kid and an old lady.

—What do you mean they wouldn't? by any chance wouldn't it work as extortion against me? and to make me talk!

—They wouldn't dare.

—Of course they would! You know the sleaze that's in this

government, the criminals that have gotten in there. And in spite of this you insist, Pozzi. You're acting in bad faith with me.

—It's only because you fear for yourself, that's all. It's because of yourself that you won't do it.

—Well, it is me. It scares me. Furthermore, if at some point I wanted to return to Buenos Aires, now I'd no longer be able to.

—Anita, let's put a stop to this nonsense.

—What nonsense?

—Pay attention to me, this is too serious, there are lives depending on what we decide, really valuable lives, I'm trying to tell you.

—My life is important. And yours too.

—My life is less important, Ana, than those of the two men we want to get out of the country.

—Enough of this obsession of yours with sacrifice. Now it's become mania.

—Not at all, Ana. It's my reality, I don't care what happens to me, if it's for something that's worthwhile.

—And what about my reality? do you want me to be wedded to sacrifice too?

—It would be a way of doing good, while you still can.

—Why do you say while I still can?

—Enough of these lies, Anita, please. You know what I'm talking about.

—What? you think I'm going to die?

—You know it, better than I do.

—I don't know anything of the sort. I want to get well, that's the only thing I know.

—You know they didn't operate. They opened you up and closed you up again, because in that condition there was nothing they could do.

—That's not true.

—We're not playing, Ana. We're not adolescents. These could be the last days left for us to live, we can't stop facing reality. If we have time to do something positive . . . we must do it!

—I never believed you'd be capable of saying something like this . . .

—But it's time to really speak quite seriously, Anita. No matter how many lies I tell you, I won't be able to bring you back your health.

—You mean to say that I can't be cured.

—The likelihood of your being cured is minimal. They were trying to get you in condition for another operation, because the tumor is in the stomach but also in part of one lung, it's already ramified.

—. . .

—But after the last consultation they came away undecided, they think it may be useless to try and operate again.

—To operate they need my consent. And they haven't said anything to me.

—They spoke with your friend, with Beatriz. And she spoke to your mother.

—Mama knows?

—Yes, and she authorized it. And she guaranteed the expense.

—Why are you telling me all this? The whole thing is just a fiction of yours.

—It's terrible, Anita, but that's how it is, we can't change things.

—But I didn't know . . .

—You really didn't know?

—No.

—But didn't you notice you were losing weight, and that the pains were getting worse every time?

—I wasn't aware of that.

—But wouldn't you prefer to know?

—No, Pozzi.

—But this way you can at least decide, choose, I don't know how to say it . . .

—Decide what?

—What you're going to do with your last days. For these few days you can do what you might have been afraid to do all your life.

—I don't like what you're saying, Pozzi.

—Since I've known I've felt tremendous sadness, Ana. You're

a part of me, the part that's pleasure, I don't know how to explain it, the part that's luxury. You were my luxury, Anita. But it's not up to me to change the way things are. The only thing that I can do is to ask that you accept the reality, and to do the most you can with what you have left to live. And I hope that a miracle will come to pass, and that everything will be mended. But . . .

—If I help you with the matter of Alejandro . . .

—Tell me . . .

—. . .

—I'm listening . . .

—If I help you, my death will have meaning . . .

—Don't say it like that. I don't know, it all sounds very bad, but it seems to me that it's your life . . . which . . . well, I don't want to say it. These are things that are so . . . important, it frightens me to handle them . . .

—Yes, I understand what you're trying to say.

—. . .

—What cruelty, Pozzi.

—. . .

—How cruel of you.

—Don't take it like that.

—You must feel like a real man being capable of uttering such cruel things.

—You don't understand me . . .

—Only a man would be capable of such cruelty as that.

—. . .

—A woman wouldn't be capable of it.

—You see, what you go on doing is telling lies, deceiving yourself. You have no right to say that, because you despise women.

—That's not true, Pozzi.

—You don't even love your daughter, or your mother. For that very reason.

—It's not true, I do love them. They're all I have.

—Do you see that you can't even admit things that you know are true? They aren't here because you don't love them, you don't

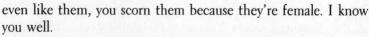

even like them, you scorn them because they're female. I know you well.

—I don't want to see you ever again, in my life.

—. . .

—Even if there are only hours left to me, however long it is, please let me never have to see you again.

—I never wanted to do you any harm. I swear it to you.

—. . .

—I believe it's better for you to know the truth.

—Thanks, Pozzi.

—After you've thought about it, you may well come to understand my intentions.

—Your intentions were good, thank you.

—. . .

—I would rather be alone now, if you don't mind.

—Yes, of course. You'll see that in thinking it over . . .

—Not another word, I beg of you.

—I'll call you tomorrow.

—No, please, I never want to hear from you again.

—I love you very much, Anita.

—. . .

—'Til tomorrow.

—. . .

13

MONDAY. SOMETIMES THERE's nothing better than a good scare. When we see ourselves facing a serious danger, even if it's not for real, as in this case, we appreciate the things we have. Now I realize just how attached I am to life. Therefore with joy, happily, I'm going to stop thinking foolish thoughts.

Doctors always say that if a patient has a positive outlook he gets well more quickly. And it must be true, because someone who's depressed starts not carrying out the treatment to the letter. Now I'm going to follow it with the utmost care. And very probably the process will speed up. It's during moments of crisis that one must maintain one's presence of mind. And I'm going to maintain it. The point is to let this moment pass, because of the pain, which is what can be most frightening. And later I'm no longer going to be frightened by anything, because some uncomfortable treatment is bound to take place, but that's the least important thing. The more one asks the doctors the worse it is, therefore I'm not going to ask them anything, about the sort of nonsense which that heartless fellow talked about. It's nonsense that they would have to operate again, first of all the doctors would have asked me, whether I agreed, whether I had the money to pay. Especially that. There's nothing better than making things clear in writing, because with just thinking one can get confused. Whereas by jotting things down everything becomes clear.

That stuff about them talking to Mama couldn't have happened, moreover I don't believe they would accept the guarantee of payment just like that, verbally, and nothing more. And from Argentina, with the difficulties there are in getting foreign currency from there. All specious arguments on his part so I'd help

him with his scheme. It's clear that he was resolved to do anything, even to give me this horrific scare. But putting everything
in writing helps me see things more clearly. As tremulous as my
grasp is I can still make out what I've written. And I don't have
to stop doing it, continuing to make notes on everything. For the
few hours that I'm really awake, because luckily this cure has the
advantage of making me sleep a lot. All the while that I'm undergoing this treatment I'm resting, I don't feel pain, it's much
better like that, that they've increased it so much.

The only thing I regret is that with so few hours in the day
when I'm completely lucid mentally, I'm left with very little time
to think of all those plans I'd like to carry out, once I'm out of
the hospital. First and foremost is to be attentive to my health.
Gymnastics, I have to find a place where they'll set me up to do
gymnastics, and to correct my tendency to stoop. And to find
another job, little by little to get closer to my interests, to be closer
to music, even if it means the same kind of work in public
relations. And to figure out how to make a little more money, to
be able to travel. And outside of Mexico to be able to buy clothes,
to restore my wardrobe a little, because at these prices here it's
impossible for me to dress as I'd like to.

What I should not do is sell my jewels, whatever bad memories
they bring me. Might they have brought me bad luck? It's stupid
to think about that, on the contrary, it could be they've brought
me good luck, and that's why the operation turned out well. I'm
not going to sell them. On the contrary, I plan to accept them
if I receive any more as presents. Yes, it's clear, I won't be able
to pay for trips with my work, and Mama, poor thing, with her
devaluated pesos won't be able to pay for such a luxury for me
either. I would have to allow myself to be invited by some guy.
But would I be any good for that kind of thing? I think I'll never
allow myself to be touched by any guy, unless we're dealing with
that superior man. However late or early, he'll arrive. One has to
know how to wait. Even before I've quite left this place I'm going
to begin a new life. No more of that worrying over nonsense, I'm
always going to be positive, I'm not going to give importance to
unworthy matters, the way I used to do before. I'm going to be

content just having my health. Yes, I make this solemn oath, I am going to content myself with just being well. I thought I would fill more pages, but this discomfort in a while will become unbearable. But it's all transient, already in a few more days I will no longer feel the pain, it will lessen, the way it increased. Just like when you get a cold, the aches and pains keep adding up, the fever, you know the next day you'll be worse, and the fever reaches its peak and right away at that point improvement's on its way, you know the following day you're going to feel better, until you're well. And just from knowing that today he's taking the plane to Buenos Aires, I already feel better. And tomorrow, just from knowing that he'll already be there, thousands and thousands of miles away, I'm going to feel even better.

I'm never going to understand them, to me they are creatures from another planet. How someone could stoop so low, to me is beyond all comprehension. How irresponsible, how beastly. I've heard of cases where sick people have tried to kill themselves in finding out that their illness has no cure, and so I, had I believed that lie, might have even tried to kill myself. Didn't he consider the consequences of such an act? It's that their pride is stronger than everything else, and if one challenges them they're capable of doing just about anything. They don't know how to lose, they see themselves as having been born to conquer the world, that's why they get so angry when one blocks their path and won't let them pass. At that moment I don't know what kind of rage comes out from inside of them, something like a vulture bursts forth from within their chests. They frighten me when they're like that. I don't know why they scare me so. It must be because this vulture doesn't care about anything or anybody. It's an ugly bird that only knows how to attack, without weighing the consequences. When I told Fito I was leaving him, never would I have imagined that someone could become as enraged as that, he said everything that came into his head so he'd destroy me. Never had I seen that madman's face he wore, or yes, there were times I'd seen him angry, but not with me, when his team would lose the game. Every Sunday, that time bomb at three in the afternoon, the soccer game. I knew that it was advisable for me to leave the house

at that hour, especially if he was staying to listen to it on the radio
or to see it on television. If he was going to the fields it was better,
because on his return trip home he would already have let off
steam.

I'd better call the nurse, it'll take her a few minutes to get here.
Well, and it's a being like that with whom a woman has to spend
her whole life? and in addition, to love him? what do those guys
have inside? and one has to feel frustrated if by her side she
doesn't have a monster like that? And yes, it's true, we feel
frustrated if we're alone. But why? from pure masochism? And it's
not because of that nighttime pleasure, what pleasure? because
once we know what worthless scum the guy is, already we no
longer feel anything. Or do other women continue to feel things?
That can never be known because those things don't get asked.
And if one is so rude and impertinent as to ask, no other woman
will answer.

Actually I don't know if it was suggestion or what, but barely
after they'd given me that shot, the pain had already eased this
time. I don't want to sleep, I want to go on a little more. I think
they win because they cause fear. And they cause fear because
they have greater strength, physical strength. Papa was tall. Fito
too. But the man who scared me the most in my life was as short
as a pygmy, that professor of Latin and Greek at the University,
what a sadist! and what a hysteric! And it wasn't his fist I was
scared of. Then it isn't the physical strength. Well, yes, they also
instill fear because of their physical strength. Then what? I believe that they frighten because one knows that if it's not with the
strength of their arms, it's with the vulture within that they'll
scare off the poor fool who sets herself in front of them. They win
because that murderous rage comes much more easily to them
than to a woman. Yes, there I'm sure I'm right, because men who
are married to women who are neurotic, hysterical, are scared of
them. Because he who gets angry first wins. Then men win because they're hysterics. One is afraid of them quite simply because
they're hysterics, neither more nor less. But in that case what's
the reason that one comes to fall in love? could it be that they're

able to give us a feeling of support, of protection? or because seeing them so hysterical makes us feel sorry for them? In me they don't inspire pity, they inspire anger. Although they really deserve pity, if one thinks that they have to live with that ugly bird living inside, under their ribs.

But the world is theirs. Even the Pope is a man, the politicians, the scientists. And the world is like that. The world is created in their image and likeness. Everything so dehumanized, so ugly, so rough. Although Papa wasn't like that, he didn't like football, or those boxing matches with those faces beaten to a bloody pulp, anyone would think it was still the age of gladiators. At home with Papa on Sundays there was no need to leave, and we listened to music, the live broadcast by radio of the matinee at the Colón. But on Sundays he wasn't always there. And this is true, I must admit it: once in a while he liked to go hunting. He wanted to take me with him, and he got irritated because I didn't enjoy it.

I slept a while, I feel my mouth dry. Maybe a piece of candy will get rid of that feeling of thirst better than so much mineral water. One time I went along with Papa. Just that one time was enough for me, aiming at those poor rabbits, and afterward finding them with their hearts still beating, their eyes open. The sensation of killing. I wanted to use the rifle, and I pulled the trigger, but without the least aim, and it seemed a lot of fun to me to load the bullets. But when at last they killed the first rabbit, and I went to find it, I will never in my life forget it. I'm crazy, and exaggerated as Mama says, but it seemed to me that it was like finding a wounded soldier in the trenches, from the First World War. And one is hypocritical, because later one will eat hare with great enjoyment. But that's something else again. And if there are people who, to earn a living, have to work in a slaughterhouse, that too is another thing. But that there should be people who enjoy killing those beasts, that they should do it as a sport, I can't understand it. And Papa was one of those.

It's quite evident that's their world, the world of soccer, of boxing, of hunting. . . . But I'm not expressing myself well, when I say their world, what I mean to say is . . . I don't know what

word to choose, maybe the word is inanities, the inanities they
have in their heads, but which they won't acknowledge. Their
interior world, it seems to me that's the expression. Because what
is it that they like so much about soccer? It must be that they
identify with the strongest kicker, with the swiftest runner, with
the one who deceives with those famous stutter-steps. For Fito,
to stutter-step was a verb of the gods. Everything competitive, to
stutter-step the most, the most of this, the most of that. And in
boxing? they must identify with the one who hits the most, of
course, with the one who punishes, I've heard boxing champions
being called punishers. And let's not look for the reason in the
hunter's enjoyment. . . . Best not even to think about it. And
that's the beautiful internal world of men. Their internal landscape, the sweet landscape of their souls. And the truth is that it
very much resembles the real world, full of wars and violence of
every sort. The resemblance is undeniable, how curious. But how
dumb of me, it's no secret they're the ones who build the world!
in their image and likeness. A world of wars, of hysterical attacks
between nations, of the exploitation of the weak. Because that's
how the leaders are, what's the difference between Hitler and a
hysterical husband who comes home drunk and abuses his family,
and who quarrels with his neighbors? It's the same.

I can't imagine a world governed by women. Because what we
have in our heads are dresses, and curtains and tablecloths, and
boots by Dior, and wallets by Gucci, and scarves by Hermès, and
watches by Cartier, and handbags by Vuitton, and coats of leop-
ard skin and of ocelot and of horsehide and of mink and of
chinchilla and of sable, and platinum bracelets and emerald neck-
laces and drop earrings made of anything that's precious, and
French perfume, and Persian rugs and Chinese vases and let me
just die if I'm lacking a lacquered folding screen also Chinese, and
antique furniture colonial-style if it's a country house. What else
do we women have in our heads?

I think a little about it and more things occur to me: love
poems, schmaltzy concertos by Rachmaninoff, and paintings by
Delacroix, and the bossa nova which I'm not sure is still fashion-

able, and the latest dance which I love, the hustle, because it's those things that fill our heads, and what would the world be like made in the image and likeness of woman? It would be well decorated, at least. But it's bad that I dump dirt on myself, for being a woman. We're not just full of these frivolities, there's also a real sensibility. A world created by women would have to be like the duet with Fiordiligi and Dorabella in *Cosi fan' tutte*, a world where everything is charm, grace, lightness. There's nothing like the music of Mozart to suggest a world of harmony, into which one would have been brought to enjoy every minute of our existence. If men had more music in their hearts, more Mozart, the world would be different. But we women took hold of everything that's beautiful, everything ugly fell to men, we seized all that's good. And they're delighted with the garbage that befell them.

But Alejandro never watches football, and hates boxing and everything that has to do with violent sports. One of his projects in the government was to propose the abolition of auto racing. And he adores music, he's full of music, inside him not one more note would fit. And in spite of this he is what he is. That means that everything I've written in this notebook this afternoon doesn't make the least sense. I must admit that I don't understand anything about what's going on, neither to men nor to others. But I don't pretend anything, I don't pretend to understand anything, I'm resigned to the luck I've had, that this very dangerous operation that they've performed on me had very good results.

A pleasant, sexless voice announced the departure of the flight over loudspeakers. W218 was at the head of her group, pale and disheveled. She had spent the night awake, tortured by a quandary: unable to appear at ten in the morning at her appointment in the Reading Room, because just at that time the flight to Urbis would be taking off, the only way to see LKJS prior to that involved another visit to the street of the Oak, which would put him in a compromising situation. It was at dawn that she came to a decision, by then exhausted from swinging like a pendulum between two unsatisfactory possibilities. As was predictable in her, she chose to make the sacrifice, to endure the anguish of not seeing him and to depart without further ado.

The passengers proceeded to embark. The young woman almost didn't have the strength to take those few steps. Now not only would she pine for her love, she would also tremble with fear, deprived of his protection. Everything designated her as having descended from those unfortunate women, the wet nurse and the movie star, and he knew she was in danger. How else to explain his obsession with the reading of thought? Surely his love for W218 allowed him to sense the impending danger. She could very well be on the verge of falling into a snare of espionage, laid by enemy governments.

She took her seat inside the apparatus, exchanging smiles of circumstance with the contingent of excursionists under her charge. She secured the safety belt and leaned her head against the seat's back, seeking assuagement for the muscles at the nape of her neck, which were comparable to wires twisted and taut. The passengers were already seated, only the steward and the stewardesses remained on foot, one of them proceeded to close the door of admittance when the steward on board signaled her to halt. W218 happened to gaze for an instant at the face of the commissary, he in turn looked at her. W218 heard within herself the voice of a man, "Attractive, although somewhat sad, I will offer her a free drink to cheer her up, and on arrival I'll ask for her telephone number." It was a voice unknown to her, and it echoed peculiarly to her ears, as if issuing from loudspeakers. W218 decided that due to a lack of sleep she was hearing nonexistent voices, as did madmen and saints. She looked again at the stewardess. This one remained beside the door and attentive to what was taking place outside the plane. The stewardess suddenly smiled, evidently someone was approaching, someone who merited an elaborate smile. W218 shut her eyes, she disliked the servility which certain jobs prompted. Her own work was even worse, but it was a question of an obligatory civil task, and of brief duration. With direct association of ideas she moved on to examine dates and remembered only then that the next day she would turn twenty-one, full legal age. The most recent events had been

overwhelming to the extent of making her forget what day it was.
She opened her eyes again. It wasn't possible: in addition to
hearing voices she was now seeing apparitions. The late-coming
traveler, to whom the stewardess was indicating a seat, was LKJS.
Or someone identical to him, a double. Identical but without that
brilliance, or halo, or magnetism which was exclusively his. The
gentleman expressed his appreciation to the obliging stewardess
for her attentions, next his eyes seemed to search for someone.

On descrying W218 the gentleman's eyes turned as sweet as
the nectar from a honeycomb, honey dark and shining. Immediately it passed to feign the indifference appropriate to a passenger
traveling alone. She caught the message: during the journey they
should behave as if they didn't know each other, someone could
be watching them. Regardless she couldn't avoid looking at him
from time to time, certainly, he was very handsome, but . . . was
he the man who had wrested her heart, and who had come to
crush it, from clenching it so closely in a fist? Although this man
resembled LKJS like two drops of water, his presence didn't move
her, it didn't stir her with passion, it didn't transport her to a
world of reverie. Something requisite was missing.

Turbulence soon struck, the airplane was shaken, the steel of
its framework rattling. W218 shut her eyes, the atmospheric
storminess absorbed her spiritual turbulence and for a moment
she felt only fear of dying in an aerial accident. The airplane
surmounted the dense layer of clouds which had produced the
jolting and was reinstated in unruffled air. She reopened her eyes,
and saw that now his own were shut. This man was LKJS, now
there was no doubt. There issued from him an irresistible charm,
it was useless to feign indifference, the young woman only
managed to join the palms of her hands as in prayer, she grew
dizzy in this resplendent voyage to which he invited her, he
carried her to other limits, remote and fearsome this time, she
thought that a leaf at the mercy of a hurricane knows its most
prized adventure simultaneously as terror. Everything about him,
every eyelash, the caprice of every line on his forehead, every pore,
subjugated her. Suddenly he opened his eyes, he intimated a wink
of complicity. W218 took apart her gesture of prayer, she became

once again master of herself, the spell had been broken. That man
was not LKJS. Or was he? What she saw was a perfect doll, but
without a soul, no doubt about it. A certainty which was inexplica-
ble and at the same time absolute. He continued observing her,
now with a disconcerted expression. She searched for the very
center of his pupils, and as had happened in looking at the commissary on board, she heard a voice within herself, this time also
as if originating from loudspeakers, somewhat imperfect in trans-
mission. And it was the voice of LKJS, "Damnation! could it be
possible that I've forgotten to put on my green contact lenses?
There's nothing worse than hurrying, and this imbecile is liable
to notice it." The young woman fainted, but seated as she was
with the seat back reclining somewhat, and her security belt
fastened, she gave the semblance of sleep.

A stewardess brought her out of her dormant state, to announce that they had already landed in the airport of the city of
Urbis. W218 looked immediately toward the seat of her would-be
assassin, he was already on his feet and had turned his back toward
her, while he arranged something in his traveling bag. The young
woman no longer remembered what had caused her to faint, nor
the swoon itself, but, although not knowing why, the nearness of
LKJS perturbed her negatively. As she unfastened her security
belt, she noticed that someone had dropped a note on her lap,
while she slept. "My Love: dissemble, however much you wish to,
dissemble. I knew you'd be unable to come to our rendezvous,
simply because my love for you allows me to read your thoughts.
I have followed you because I couldn't endure the anguish of
knowing you to be suffering on my account. I know what stirs
within you, that suspicion of having been deceived. I have followed you to prove that my adoration for you is true. Anyway I
beg that you be patient, don't greet me, don't address me before
these people! I fear I've been followed by spies from my government, I have fallen into disgrace, later on I will tell you about it.
At the airport exit I will put them off the scent, I know how to
go about it. Therefore, a little before midnight I will be able to
come by to see you, at last without fear that they're following me.
Await my visit, with an embrace and a kiss, your Love."

The first thing that W218 did upon arriving at her apartment was to search in the medicine chest in her bathroom for a small blue tube. The conscripts were ordered always to take it with them in case of problems with their patients, it sufficed to squeeze the tube at its base for a fluid, aimed into the nostrils of the consignee, to stun him for ten minutes. The young woman continued to search without finding an explanation for such a defensive stance, the farthest that she got was to think that LKJS's double could appear at her door, with unforeseeable intent.

It was already five minutes before midnight when she heard steps on the stairs. She had been perfectly groomed, made up, perfumed and attired since half past ten. The twenty-five cigarettes smoked since then had made her eyes somewhat bloodshot and her mouth pasty. The doorbell rang. She raised the peephole to see who she was dealing with, him or his double. Green eyes gazed at her with infinite tenderness: W218 was unable to resist their power and remained for a long while contemplating them, in that awkward position. She was about to turn the bolt of her lock, without ceasing to watch how he waited calmly, silently, when that voice could be heard anew, his own voice, but badly transmitted and uselessly amplified. W218 heard it within herself, echoing in her own brain, "What is this mangy bitch waiting for to open up? might she be waiting for me to knock the door down? these females from this shitty Urbis, what they expect are males of the old-fashioned sort who will take care of everything for them. But she ought not provoke me too much tonight because it'll even come to blows."

The young woman opened the door and from his mouth there flowed words of love. But although she could scarcely make it out, within herself there resounded other, very different ones, "She continues enamored, she didn't notice the oversight with the lenses. It will suffice for me to satisfy her ordinary carnal needs one more time, to calm her down. Tomorrow I shall fly back and just by returning to see her once a year we'll have her under control until she reaches her stinking thirty years old." The young woman didn't know whether to employ the blue fluid now or to allow him to make love to her. She chose the latter, justifying it to herself that in this way she would give the traitor more time to unfold the richness of his perfidy.

LKJS reported that the government of his country had considered immoral his behavior in Urbis, due to his affair with W218. Because of that he had been called to reincorporate himself into his customary work in the City of Aquarius, despite which he had embarked on that plane this morning, impelled by passion. The clock bells struck twelve, W218 placed her index finger on his lips as a sign for silence, she counted with gloating satisfaction the twelve tolls. She had technically thus turned twenty-one years old. She heard next the voice from within her, it sounded clearly and without interference, the transmitting mechanism now operated perfectly, "Only a woman in love could believe my licentious deceptions." He began to undress her, she asked that he not speak for several minutes, because to her there would be no music more sublime than his breathing, and his incidental panting.

She then looked fixedly into his green eyes and devoted all her attention to the pronouncements of the truth, "What agreeable work is mine, I enjoy women and I enjoy lying, so I feel very much at ease. It will suffice that I take great pains in the rendition of my service for her to remain faithful all these years that still remain, nine visits in total, that is, if my superiors don't decide to abduct her prior to that and place her under observation in some prison in Aquarius. For the remote possibility that her mental powers should develop before that as yet distant birthday. Oh . . . sexual pleasure, you are the realm of my work, thanks to you I make my living and support my family. And if there's something for which I rebuke myself it's to make a victim in this fraud out of a colleague, because the poor girl also earns her daily bread with her genitals. And what discipline is hers, never has she complained about her work, she has served as an instructive example for me, could it be due to this that I am performing my mission so well? How dangerous it would be that someone could read my thoughts, it's noteworthy that such a thing could come to pass, the wave of masculine sexual desire as a singular conduc-

tor of that ray of light which penetrates the darkness of the mind,
her gaze. A woman who will read the thought of every man who
craves her sexually, and allows her to look into his eyes. A danger
to this planet of men, my planet. For that reason she must be
eliminated, or at least kept under control, the control of men. It's
even possible that we could use her in our own plans for territorial
and economic expansion. It will be possible to deceive her, notwithstanding her overgrown perceptions. Poor little one, what
pleasure I'm giving her, at times it brings me pity, poor girl, how
generously she's opened the way for me which leads to her own
destruction. And she's so pretty, and so sweet, a gentle little ewe,
what pity I feel leading her to the slaughterhouse. To defile my
own penis with her blood. . . . But it befell her to be a victim,
nature is cruel and if I don't subordinate her it will be she who
will subordinate me. My little ewe, caress after caress, thrust after
thrust, kiss after kiss, I accompany you to your beheading. . . .
Allow me to kiss you, thus, on your brow, where are held all your
thoughts, innocent and good. . . . I feel sorry for you . . . my poor
little female . . . you remind me of that poor doll which my
daughters hurl constantly onto the floor, the rag doll, the filthiest,
the one which never breaks and for that reason they mistreat her,
and when they cannot find her they ask that I look for her, behind
some piece of furniture where they cannot reach, my poor little
girls, they too, little females, poor souls, better not think of that,
but it's for my own home, my own family, that I must sacrifice
you, and because I pledged that oath thus . . . so many years ago
. . . along with those other males chosen . . . the strongest from
every scholastic classroom . . . that designated evening, every boy
selected, at the hand of his father, dressed in a premature man's
suit, stiff collar, tie, hair severely cropped, every boy entered that
darkened precinct with a candle in his hand, hundreds of candles
burning in the enormous hall; the boy-men sworn in there received the teachings, our supreme order for survival, 'Boys of
today, men of tomorrow, males of the world, be united. You have
been selected amongst millions of boys of today because you are
the pride of the nation, the strongest, the attacking and trium-

phant penises of tomorrow. Well then, we have called you together here to initiate you in the practices of the Command, you shall be received into the Cenacle of Power. The instructions necessary for your deportment are simple, and your pride as superior beings shall dictate them to you. But you must be implacable in your mission, above all you shall never mention this ceremony, and later, the first commandment, you must spread the doctrine amongst your brothers the males of the secondary class, and the next commandment, you shall crush with contempt the natural enemy, the female. Like all inferior creatures, she is resentful and cunning, but her natural weapons will be useless if the arm which brandishes them trembles with insecurity and fear. For that it is compulsory to behave in complete solidarity with the male world. For that it is indispensable to come to an agreement amongst ourselves, and to decree them unworthy of our trust, without the slightest hesitation. Boy of today, male of tomorrow: humiliate the female, be convinced within yourself that she is inferior to you, and thus she will begin to convince herself. Consequently disdain her, and thus there will be no need for you to tell her that she is inferior, much less to prove it to her. She is not stupid, damned creature, but make her believe that she is, because if not, the kingdom of this planet shall be hers.' The little boys trembled with emotion, the candles which they held threw tenuous flickering flames, some thought of their mothers and sisters, but all hesitation was eliminated quite suddenly, because the Command ordered each father to place his hand on the penis of the son and to fondle to the point of awakening his yearning. . . . Yes, I swear. . . . Yes, I swear. . . . Ah . . . ah . . . yes . . . yes, I swear . . . I swear by this immense pleasure which I give to you . . . ah . . . ah . . . and that which you give to me . . . my ewe . . . a shepherd and his ewe . . . alone, forsaken in the darkened meadow, inside this hut . . . until one very cold day when I will slaughter you, to warm myself with your pelt . . . and you don't even thank me . . . I who have just given you the best of me, and you lie there, silent . . . as if you deserved everything . . . and as if perhaps you didn't deserve that I should one day behead you and wrench off your pelt . . . and you begin to tremble now, who knows why, but I like to watch you tremble . . . at last I see you tremble . . . from fear . . . which is what every woman ought to do before her male . . . tremble in fear . . ."

W218 had the blue tube concealed beneath the pillow, she lay her hand upon it.

14

—You must forgive me, Beatriz. It's the sedatives . . .

—But when I speak to you do you hear me? can you understand me?

—Yes, but for me to talk . . . it's difficult . . . a bit.

—But the pain has been alleviated, hasn't it?

—Yes . . . I'm also a little stunned by the news.

—When did your mother call you?

—Just a moment before . . . I called you. We had barely hung up . . . and I called you. I couldn't be here . . . alone . . . with that news.

—You did well to call me.

—It was yesterday, they called her first from the . . . manager's office, of my apartment. . . . Yesterday in the afternoon.

—Slowly, Anita, don't push yourself, I'm listening.

—She didn't know whether she should call me. . . . But . . . when the news broke this morning . . . in Buenos Aires . . .

—Yes.

—I had wanted to rent . . . the apartment. I didn't remember . . . that he . . . had kept . . . a set . . . of keys. Because already for some time before coming . . . here . . . we had stopped seeing each other.

—What apartment, Anita?

—The one I had . . . in Buenos Aires.

—When?

—The apartment . . . is mine. Mama . . . bought it for me . . . when I got separated. After all . . . I was her only . . . heir.

—And you lived there?

—Yes . . . I lived alone. And when we were seeing each other . . . Pozzi and me . . . I gave him keys, years ago. . . . My mouth is so dry.

—Would you like something?

—Yes . . . water . . . from that bottle. . . . Thank you.

—I'm going to have some too.

—Beatriz, you too have been affected . . . by this . . . . One can see it in your face.

—And the apartment was empty.

—Nobody lived there. But it was . . . just as . . . I left it. With my things.

—But what was his plan? what did he tell you?

—He told me that he was flying to Chile . . . and that from there he would cross by train . . . into Mendoza, which is near the frontier, and is already Argentina . . . where the Andes begin . . . but he must have changed his mind, because I don't know how he arrived . . . so quickly. . . . They probably followed him . . . who knows. . . . He was with two others, who fought off the police . . . while two others got away.

—Then this compromises you, in a way.

—Beatriz, let's hope that . . . it would compromise me. That would mean . . . that I'm going to be alive. That the operation. . .

—One must have faith . . .

—The worst thing . . . is that I . . . wished that he'd die. . . . Some day . . . I'll tell you what he said to me . . . . He made me angry . . . so angry . . . . And Mama has such hopes, she knows everything, the doctors . . . keep her . . . informed. They call by telephone . . . once a week. At Fito's house . . . was it you . . . who gave them . . . the telephone number?

—Yes, Anita. The doctors talked to me.

—Mama . . . wants to come. . . . But again I told her no.

—Tell me more, about what your mother told you.

—She . . . called me, because if I . . . found out from the newspaper . . . it would have been worse. . . . Today the whole thing was in the newspaper. And they labeled him . . . a terrorist, Mama said. . . . He swore to me . . . on his children . . . that

he wasn't mixed up in that. . . . Who knows how it happened . . .

 —. . .

 —I had wanted to rent it . . . the apartment. After all . . . I
didn't expect to go back for ma . . . many years. . . . But Mama
. . . Mama . . . opposed it. And in part, she was . . . right . . .
because back there it's very hard to evict . . . a tenant. . . . And
she . . . says that going over to . . . air it out . . . once a week gives
her . . . the impression . . . that I'm coming back . . .
soon . . .

 —. . .

 —I . . . really insisted . . . that she rent it. . . . But she would
say that it caused her . . . too much sadness. And she never paid
attention to me . . . though each month the money . . . from Papa,
and the pensions . . . brings her less and less. . . . And the expenses
from the empty apartment keep going up.

 —Now I'm starting to understand.

 —That's why she . . . is in touch with . . . with the . . . the
managers . . . of the building. . . . And I think . . . that as for Pozzi
. . . they followed him . . . from the time he arrived in the
. . . country. I already know . . . that you . . . toward the Peronists
. . . aren't sympathetic . . .

 —Anyway, I feel sorry for him.

 —Me, too . . . very much . . .

 —What can you do, Anita. It was also a choice, a free one,
wasn't it? on his part.

 —But it's that his intention . . . was so good . . .

 —Was he a terrorist, or not? Do you know for sure about that?

 —He swore to me . . . on his children . . . that he wasn't.
. . . But I think . . . that inevita . . . bly, he had to come in contact
. . . with people . . . that did . . . go around . . . armed . . .
and . . .

 —Don't force yourself, it'll do you harm.

 —. . . He . . . according to Mama . . . resisted . . . the police,
if not . . . maybe . . . they wouldn't have killed him . . .

 —. . .

—According to Mama . . . the newspaper says . . . that
he . . . was armed. But when they want to get rid . . . of someone . . .

—You know, Ana, it's also possible that he wouldn't have been
armed, but that those who had met up with him were.

—Those people . . . in the manager's office asked . . . the
neighbors . . . of my apartment, and no one had heard anything
. . . steps, or voices, until that night. . . . He had told me that when
he arrived . . . there'd be people who'd be informed who would
tell him, if there was any need . . . to hide, or not. . . . And they
probably told him that there was, and he didn't know where to
go . . . and it occurred to him . . . that place.

—Had he been there before, after you'd left to come here?

—Where . . . Beatriz?

—To your apartment.

—No . . . as far as I know, no. . . . But now everything . . . is
possible. . . . Never, Beatriz . . . will I be able to know for sure
. . . what happened . . . with him.

—But you must have a feeling, nearing a certainty, your own,
intimately, of what happened . . .

—No . . . I feel . . . great . . . confusion.

—. . .

—I . . . would resign myself . . . more readily if I knew he'd
been armed . . . and that then he died . . . because he'd asked for
it, really. . . . But if they killed him . . . because he was a decent
guy . . . and because he defended those prisoners . . . it devastates
me.

—I understand.

—But on the other hand . . . I don't want . . . to remember
him as a . . . terrorist . . . as they say in the newspaper. I want
. . . him to have been . . . just as he used to tell me that he was.

—. . .

—But in this case . . . they killed him . . . without the slightest
provocation. . . . He's a martyr, then . . .

—You knew him well, Ana. You should know, in some way.

—. . .

—You should have an intuition, deep inside, of how it really was.

—I don't know . . . Beatriz. . . . It seems to me that I'm . . . so used to thinking whatever I please about people . . . about each one . . . that now if I want to think it over seriously . . . I can't.

—I think, since this is all so recent, that the shock won't let you see anything clearly, for the moment.

—I don't know . . .

—. . .

—How it falls to pieces . . . this country. So much effort . . . poor Pozzi, so much work, so much studying . . . to end up this way.

—. . .

—You don't know, Beatriz . . . what the majority's like . . . of the people there. What an effort they make, what a desire they have . . . to improve themselves. The people there . . . consume daily newspapers and books . . . about politics, and they are . . . informed . . . about everything. And many who are already beyond their youth . . . beyond their thirties I mean . . . go on studying, they work and continue to study . . .

—. . .

—And they have that sort of . . . impatience, to emerge from that . . . underdevelopment . . . And just the same everything ends up badly . . .

—It's very hard to change the structure, Anita.

—But when the effort . . . is so great . . . it should be rewarded . . . with results. . . . And on the other hand . . . what happens . . .

—. . .

—There are so many people there who have . . . two jobs. . . . They leave the house, in the morning, early. . . . The entire day, that eagerness . . . to live a little better . . . but then . . .

—Your friend was like that, wasn't he?

—Yes . . . he supported his family with his work . . . in a firm . . . of lawyers, commercial, and afterward . . . he defended . . . the unprotected areas . . . as much as he could . . .

—That's extraordinary.

—And he kept studying . . . he was full . . . of curiosity, of what the world . . . had . . . discovered . . . lately . . .

—You told me about that.

—But just the same . . . in something . . .

—I'm listening . . .

—. . . in something . . . he was wrong.

—. . .

—. . . or wasn't he?

—. . .

—But if it was a mistake . . . it was only one . . . and with only that . . . it was already enough . . . to destroy everything.

—. . .

—Whose death will have . . . more meaning? . . . mine . . . or his?

—You shouldn't talk like that.

—. . . What do I do . . . for my country . . . here . . . so far away . . . ?

—Anita, I think it's bad for you to be so hard on yourself. Later, with time, we'll know more about what he was doing, and you'll have more grounds to evaluate him.

—Do you think so?

—Yes, you'll see that you will . . .

—I don't want to remember him . . . badly. Though he was so . . . cruel to me . . . I was forgiving him . . . in a way . . . thinking that . . . that it was . . . an invention of his . . . that I was sick . . . so that I'd help him . . . with his plans . . .

—. . .

—But it was true . . .

—You don't have to see it that way. Your illness . . .

—In talking today . . . with Mama . . . she without meaning to . . . confirmed it for me . . . Because I . . . I told her . . . that there was no need to be alarmed . . . about the first operation . . . that it had brought no results . . . because it hadn't been an operation, they had . . . opened me up . . . and nothing more . . . because they hadn't . . . found me . . . in any condition . . . to operate.

—. . .

—And she . . . poor thing . . . didn't deny it . . . she told me
that she knew that . . . but that I didn't have to be . . . frightened,
and you could tell . . . that . . . she could barely talk . . . from the
effort not to let her sorrow show . . . and the worst thing . . . is
that she asked me to . . . let her come . . .

—. . .

—But I didn't . . . I didn't want to, with the excuse . . . that
I wanted her to . . . look after Clarita. . . . But I promised her,
that if there was danger . . . that certainly I would . . . call her
. . .

—About Clarita, did she tell you anything?

—Yes, that she's very well . . . very tall.

—. . .

—How the rain just keeps coming . . .

—Don't you want Clarita to come?

—Beatriz, tell me . . . when is it going to stop raining? It's
torture.

—It should have already stopped, at the beginning of the
month.

—. . .

—When I was driving the car here, luckily it wasn't raining as
hard.

—How long . . . the rainy season . . .

—Before it wasn't like this, Anita. It began a little later, in
June, toward the end, and it ended in September.

—. . .

—It's already October . . . and it's still going on.

—. . .

—Before it wasn't like this, it would rain for a while in the
afternoon and that was all. Now it starts in the morning.

—Luckily . . . for these two months . . . of rain I was spared,
being sick in bed.

—You know, Anita, the climate has changed here, before it was
hotter, because the rains didn't last as long.

—. . .

—The traffic is going to be awful, on the way home.

—. . .

—But I think that in two more weeks, the season will be over at last.

—How I'd like to be well . . . by then . . .

—At the most, it'll be two weeks, I think, of daily rain, and after that it'll let up.

—Beatriz . . . when Mama gave me the news . . . at that moment . . .

—. . .

—I myself find it hard . . . to believe it . . . but I was gladdened about poor old Pozzi's death . . .

—. . .

—It almost made me laugh . . . that he would have died . . . him first . . .

—. . .

—And I think it's . . . fairly common, that people feel well . . . with the misfortune of . . . others . . . . But it's a second, that's all, later right away one feels . . . sadness.

—. . .

—Why is it . . . that one should feel something so . . . pointless?

—I don't know, Anita.

—The first thing, the most . . . spontaneous is to be happy . . . that it happened to someone else . . . and not to oneself . . .

—I think it's logical, after the last stance that he took with you. It's only human to react that way, I think.

—Logical . . . ?

—Yes, Anita, and human.

—For myself I feel ashamed . . . to be like that . . .

15

THE TRIAL AGAINST the young woman accused of murder hadn't stirred particular interest on the part of the general public. The boxes in the hall where judgment was being pursued could be seen almost empty. The appearance of the members of the jury—all of them men—with the verdict was awaited momentarily. The accusation was homicide, but there were extenuating pleas such as self-defense and temporary insanity. Only the murderess knew the truth, and the victim, of course, still battling between life and death in a hospital in Urbis. The murderess saw the members of the jury enter, preceded by their spokesman wielding an envelope, which he handed to the judge. Like a bolt of lightning in her memory, the accused remembered everything which had taken place and made one final self-examination.

"I endeavored to kill my countryman LKJS, but I shall never reveal why. If there is justice in this world they will allow me to be set free, and in the opposite circumstance I prefer to go to jail rather than be placed beneath a microscope like a bacterium recently discovered. If I have learned anything from this whole story it is that above all there's my dignity. My dignity . . . although I don't know very well what the word means. How strange it was to see him there defenseless in my monohabitation, I had taken advantage of the minutes of his stupefaction, the result of the blue tube, to seat him in a chair and to bind his feet and hands, in addition to gagging him. My intention was to continue listening to the voice of his thoughts, which he was unable to silence. . . . 'How mistaken I was about this girl, I believed her to be frivolous and snobbish, and what a surprise I've had. Why did I presume her to be thus? could it be because deep within myself I disdain whosoever loves me well? which means that I consider myself unworthy of being treated well, that I scorn myself, that I long for the sentence requested by my mediocrity. She fell in love with me, yes, with the exception of the false green of my eyes, it was I with whom she became enamored. Also there were other devices I made use of, none of which was fundamental. But I hated her for loving me so. Yes, she once told me that my spirit of sacrifice was unhealthy. Whereas she, if treated well, reacts favorably and, important point, is not suspicious, she always expects the best from people. This indicates a deep democratic sentiment, since she doesn't wish others to be below her level; she, on the contrary, delights in the practice of equality. But don't let it happen that she realizes she's being deceived, because then her blood boils with rage, and what better proof of that than my actual situation as ridiculous puppet bound to an armchair. And who knows what she plans to do with me . . . if I could only read her thoughts! How the hell she discovered my imposture I do not know, I attribute it to the foolish carelessness with regard to the contact lenses. If I could only turn back the hands of the clock, then I would confess all to her in good time and she would pardon me: without interrupting my assaults, saturated there by that ceaseless waterfall of our delights, I would confess all, and she without interrupting her moans would forgive me. But now it's too late, it's impossible that she would become aware now of the tumble which my heart has taken. If she were only able to read my thoughts, but many years will pass before that happens, although that doesn't cease to be of some comfort, knowing that some far-off day she will discover that I admire her and respect her.' . . . And these last words of his were what caused my sudden dash forward, I was unable to stop myself, I ran in search of a knife and . . . nervously, out of breath, I cut his fasteners. I let the knife fall on the rug. How impulsive and foolish, I believed that in this way I was giving a start to a tale of requited love. Unfortunately what I then read in his mind destroyed my last illusion, yes, now I know it, that very short-lived illusion, for those few seconds it was the last one in my life. Although he hadn't altogether regained his freedom, his soul cried out the inevitable, 'I cannot

betray my country or my children, I must now escape from this
place,' but no, he neither escaped nor will he escape, because
notwithstanding his leap like a tiger—to obtain the weapon hidden in his clothes—I continued to hold the winning cards: at my
feet lay the knife and before he was able to turn his face back
toward me I had plunged the serrated blade into his back. Wrath?
self-defense? temporary insanity? who will decipher the enigma?
what a hieroglyphic, this woman's heart of mine . . ."

The members of the jury were now seated in their places, the
judge made the envelope rustle unnecessarily as he opened it, and
he asked the accused to rise. This one lowered her eyes, she
repudiated the dirty thoughts which might be stowed beneath
venerable white hair. The sentence did not surprise W218, she
was condemned to life imprisonment but was granted her request
to be transferred to the far-off hospitals of Ices Everlasting as a
voluntary conscript, rather than carrying out her penalty in an
ordinary prison. The voice of the judge was dry and haughty,
when he finished reading the will of the jurors he ordered the
young woman to lift her gaze. This one refused, she said that it
sufficed to have listened. The voice of the judge changed, suddenly it became compassionate and broken, "Good God, young
woman, your request is so unusual that I feel obliged to ask you
whether you really know what awaits you in the desolate regions
of Ices Everlasting. Confined there are only the beings who have
been damned forever by society or by nature. I am referring
respectively to the most dangerous political prisoners and to the
ill who are highly contagious. What you propose is to continue
your obligatory civil service in a pavilion with the latter of these,
but it is fitting to raise the question, do you realize, unhappy
creature, that in this manner you are condemning yourself to an
imminent death?" W218, without lifting her eyes from the floor,
let there be heard a feeble yes.

The train station could be observed to be severely patrolled,
torrential rain was falling that morning of the perpetual Urbisan
winter. One of the waiting halls was shut off to the public; in one
corner, watched by two guards, languished W218 as the sole
prisoner. Martial paces could be heard, there entered, preceded

by innumerable guards, a group of political prisoners, also destined for Ices Everlasting. It was composed of men of different ages but all sharing the same look, one without hope, since their eyes were like dried-up plants. One of them had in the past had green eyes, now they were the color of the barren soil in some parts of Urbis. Everything seemed to be dark gray in Urbis, all that managed to emerge from the cement, the rocky earth and the trunks of the ancient trees blighted by the frost.

One of the guards began to distribute goggles with lenses the color blue, another explained to the convicts that the following morning they would enter the frozen zone, where they'd be unable to look at the landscape without protection due to the fact that all was a dazzling white during that month, the remainder of the year there was nothing but night. One month of the color blue and eleven of the color black. The guard who was distributing the goggles found himself with one pair too many and only then remembered that they were intended for another convict. It sufficed to take a quick look around the room to spot the consignee, half hidden by her two ruthless guardians. He had to cross the entire hall to reach W218, the floor of thick planks creaked under his military boots. All followed him with their glances, they got as excited as would stallions in discovering the mare. LKJS, just another convict, recognized her immediately, despite her hair being close cropped and her eyes sunken due to grief. The convicts began to hurl obscenities, in gesture and in word; the guards celebrated with boisterous laughter each outrage. One of the prisoners, the one furthest along in years, whispered into a guard's ear how great it would be to permit them a farewell to the flesh, it would be an hour before the train departed and they could possess the wench one by one, including those responsible for keeping order. The guard responded with a negative none too resolute, he looked at the colleague beside him, a smile began to take form on lips cracked from the cold. After speedy reflection he brought his hand to the crotch of his trousers and in a loud voice he told his colleague of the improper proposal.

LKJS managed to hear him and immediately fell to his knees, beginning to sob with his head sunk down in his chest. Until that moment the clamor had been on the rise, so the wailing proved inaudible. One of the vociferous convicts crouched next to LKJS to ascertain what had seemed to him impossible, a man crying? he made a sign to another of the renegades and grew quiet. Little by little the affronts diminished, in the hall there resonated the sobbing of a man repentant. The young woman, who until then had not dared to look at the group, discovered at last to whom belonged that inclined brow. One of the guards took the arm of the convict and respectfully invited him to get to his feet. He disengaged him, lifted his glance toward her and on his knees continued his silent supplication.

Only W218 was able to hear it, despite her being at the greatest distance, "I don't dare ask forgiveness, because I know I don't deserve it. What I seek is a little sanity at this instant, to say a word to this poor young woman . . . which will help her to bear her load. I will receive my punishment, a sentence which will last for the rest of my days, but I know that she, generous as she is, will not be consoled by knowing this. In addition, if my life is finished it's because I asked for it, whereas she was a victim of destiny. What word could I extract from my bitter heart which would make her forget even if only one of my iniquities? what may I offer her in addition to my repentance? It's true that I did not inform against her to the authorities, that I didn't mention her superhuman powers, but that was simply so as not to implicate my own country in the case, so as not to implicate the entire network of espionage. I sacrificed myself because my superiors ordered me to do so, and not for her sake. For that reason and for no other I feigned a passionate drama without greater motive than the spite of a girl seduced and the violence of a philandering tourist. And there is no place for spite and violence in this modern society. Hence my enormous debt against my poor dear little victim. For her I have done nothing, except to lead her to a martyrdom. One word, if only one word were to occur to me, one deserving word, one sweet word, since it will be the last one between us. I cannot tell her lies, I cannot tell her that I loved her more than anyone, because I have greater love for my wife and for my children, and for my country. Toward her what I feel is something else, the sentiment which most denigrates, as much her as myself . . . pity. It causes me infinite pity to see her reduced in this manner, it causes me infinite pity to know what she has already suffered, it causes me infinite pity to know what awaits her still, and to remember her sorrow day and night is to feel once again the blade of the knife plunged in the back, the stroke which smothers and bleeds you completely, such as the one she delivered to me. But now I am no longer the man of then, I have changed, it doesn't comfort me to know that she too is condemned forever, it no longer relieves me as before to know that others suffer, something within me has changed, I don't want to be above others, I don't want my suffering to be lessened if that of others is not, I want to do no more wrong to anyone, I don't want to exploit anyone, I don't want to be superior to anyone, and that, in some strange way, was what she taught me, she was the one who changed me. But if I were to tell her . . . she wouldn't believe me. . . ."

The sobs seemed to lessen, but it was unclear whether he was aware of what he had achieved, the taming of the wild beasts. Imploringly the young woman looked at her two guards, these lowered their heads in the semblance of a response. She drew closer to the kneeling man, she stroked his brow, she dried his tears and into his ear whispered words which she didn't entirely believe, "I don't lay the blame on you, we have been the playthings of forces superior to ourselves. You are not culpable for the cruel orders which you had to obey . . ." and afterward added, this time truly with total conviction, "In spite of it all, I continue to remember you as part of the best period of my life, when I worked and awaited the ideal man. And if it was I who succeeded in altering something in your soul, if you believe that I succeeded in giving you something important . . ." The young woman was unable to complete the sentence, the guards had decided to reestablish order and separated the pair for the last time.

The armored train made its way amidst the snow, pursuing a night which it wouldn't succeed in reaching. On the contrary, the white brilliance increased inexorably. W218 had been entrusted to a female warden specializing in railway transport, and there was

no longer any need to fear the assault of the prisoners, who were
crowded together in another coach. At midnight they were ordered to don their spectacles and all became blue, the same as the
skin of those partners in the political struggle who remained in
Urbis, stretched out on slabs of marble at the morgue. After a
little more than twenty-four hours' travel the convoy paused on
a blue pampas, to the eyes there was visible solely a platform for
descent, the remainder of the station was subterranean. For the
same reason neither could the prison be seen, several miles hence.
The contingent of prisoners disembarked onto the platform,
guarded by their wardens.

The men watched the blue train which was now setting off.
W218 waved her hand from behind the small window, the warden had not permitted her to open it due to the prevailing cold.
All the prisoners there on the platform looked alike, covered as
they were by their cowls and coats. Some of them descried the
young woman in her compartment and saluted her with hands
seemingly voluminous in their gloves. One of them brought his
hand to his heart as if to express tenderness, W218 thought that
perhaps it was her acquaintance. She didn't dare call him anything else, neither friend, nor lover, nor great love. But why was
he among the political prisoners? had he perchance not been
condemned as an ordinary criminal? W218 then knew she would
never be certain of what had taken place with him. The blue men
grew smaller in the distance, the warden took pity and lowered
the small window so the prisoner could lean out, the men were
now barely dots, dark blue, and in another instant they dissolved
in the pale blue immensity. What tone of blue? W218 didn't
think of the blue skin of the dead, she could not allow herself, her
heart would not have been able to endure any more anguish, for
that reason she breathed deeply and leaned her head against
something comfortable, the back of her seat. Then she decided
it was the very shade of blue of some children's eyes in Urbis, and
for the first time in many years she remembered the live hydran-
geas of her most tender infancy, and it occurred to her in last term
that her unknown mother would have at some point lifted her

from the crib to lull her to sleep on her lap, dressed in that same blue.

The management of the Hospital for the Contagious saw itself facing serious difficulties with the arrival of W218. The presence there of one sentenced to life imprisonment, moreover an ex-conscript from the special services, and to complicate matters further destined for avant-gardist contacts with the patients required adopting measures as uncommon as they were delicate. First of all it was decided not to make known her position of prisoner, W218 would be considered yet another nurse, the fact that the hospital was completely isolated in the middle of an ice floe resolved whatever problems of vigilance and of possible escape. As to the nature of her encounters with the patients, very few employees outside the Management were notified of the experimental character with which they were invested. Finally, the Management ordered that the patient beneficiaries be told that the young woman had been vaccinated in a special manner and consequently they should harbor no feelings of guilt with respect to her. Such a vaccination did not exist.

One additional complication was the fact that the health of W218 was very weak. Before undertaking her activities it was ordered that she take a complete rest for three weeks. Her room was underground, like the rest of the building. The solar light, which could be depended on for only one month out of the year, had been excluded from all ecological calculations. Good nourishment and rest brought strength back to the conscript, and one hour before putting an end to her obligatory vacation, she asked to go to the earth's surface. The month of light had already passed and she was interested in seeing what a black polar day was like, she felt a visceral fear toward the unknown landscape, but curiosity prevailed. A nurse accompanied her, they had to traverse long passageways and take more than one elevator. The nurse treated her with cordiality and a sense of comradeship, she was unaware of the reasons for the presence there of W218. She told of her experience of three years at the sanitarium, and of her plans to be transferred one year hence. In one year's stay at Ices Everlast-

ing one earned five times that earned in an ordinary place, and
she would apply her important savings toward the education of
her children, whom she had seen so seldom these years, of sacrifice not in vain. She added that her husband had suffered an
accident and was unable to work normally, he took charge of
caring for their home. Finally she said that the accident had
brought them closer together even than their children had, and
she counted the days which still separated her from her joyous
family reunion. W218 said nothing, she understood that the
nurse had no way to gauge the significance of her words.

They finally arrived at the face of the earth. The day was not
the blind shaft which she had imagined, the day was black but
the stars were sparkling, at ten in the morning, and that brilliance
succeeded in granting a soft luminescence to the crust of ice
which completely covered the area. The nurse explained that
when there was a full moon the luminescence increased, in two
weeks they should emerge for a look once again.

The location for the first appointment was a room just like all
the others, with bed, light table and washbasin as the total fur-
nishings. W218 trembled just as she had the first day of her
conscription at Urbis, momentarily her first patient would enter
the room. She asked that the attending nurse be anyone other
than the one who had accompanied her on her walk. The one
chosen entered with the patient, only then did W218 think of the
excess of light which the single lamp emitted. She didn't glance
at the patient again, she asked the nurse that the light be changed
for another more subdued. According to the nurse the doctor had
ordered that the lamp remain lit, because in this way the patient
would be able to indulge in the contemplation of her extraordinary beauty. The nurse withdrew, W218 began to undress and
placed one of her garments on the lampshade. A calloused hand
caressed her. One short exchange of glances was enough to hear
the man's thoughts. It was a religious prayer, an act of thanks for
the riches received, which finished in turn with a request, "I ask
that this young woman as beautiful as she is generous honor my
request and that she not open her eyes whilst I am with her, I
don't want to importune her even further, I'd like to help her in

whatever way possible, and if she doesn't see me it will all be easier for her, because the only thing in me which does not cause revulsion is the touch of the skin and thus she will be able to pretend she is with someone healthy . . ."

The young woman stretched out her hand and grasped a linen cloth provided for personal cleanliness, with it she blindfolded herself. The sick man kissed her tenderly on her cheek and placed himself on top of her, without interrupting his mute prayer, "The doctor had told me that we were dealing with an exceptional creature, but it was difficult for me to believe it. Now she is before my eyes and I return to thinking that God brought me into the world to enjoy supreme pleasures. This moment which I am experiencing, together with the most beautiful creature in the world and symbol of all that is most desirable, justifies all the penury and sorrows which marked my existence. Thank you, Lord, for having given me life, for having permitted me to know to what degree your creation is sublime. . . . And forgive me if each time I give you thanks for something . . . in passing . . . I dare make another request of you. This time it is not for me . . . it is for her . . . I beg of you, although it surely be unnecessary, that you recognize the greatness of her spirit, and that you reward her deservedly. For myself I ask nothing more, soon I will die, like all those afflicted with this misfortune, but it will be with my heart restored with the sweetness from this gift I am receiving. It is for her that I ask that you protect her, that you assist her in her arduous journey, that you allow her to meet the counterpart whom she deserves, a man of the same worth as she. Because every woman needs a companion, and hers must be as noble and giving as she, strong, so he may support her during the inevitable stumbling blocks in life. He must be . . . an ideal man, just as she is an ideal woman. But who am I to tell you, my Lord, what you should do. Perhaps you have already granted her what she deserves. Perhaps she needs no one, her valor, her integrity, her generosity, perhaps it has already been made evident to her that the ideal man whom she longs for . . . she carries within herself. The one capable of all the sacrifices and of all the demonstrations

of courage is herself, even if she not find the courage in acknowl-
edging that, accustomed as she is to her humble corner in the
semidarkness."

W218, blindfolded, could not read the thoughts of her companion.

16

THREE MONTHS AFTER the start of her work, W218 began to show signs of contagion. The doctors had predicted that the first symptoms would appear after having performed the first month of contacts, so that the services rendered by the sentenced one were considered triply valuable in terms of number. With regard to the quality, the beneficiary patients refused to discuss the experience, due to the profound respect which the person in question had inspired in them.

During the first days of her malaise the prisoner remained in her private room, but when there was no longer any doubt that they were dealing with the mortal infection, she was transferred to a room of sick women with the same disease. To her left there was a septuagenarian, isolated in an oxygen tent, nearing death. To her right there was a woman of nearly forty years old, in stable condition. This same one explained it to her, the day W218 arrived in the pavilion, "It's better that you talk to me, that way you won't hear at your left the labored breathing from bed 27, it's going to make a very bad impression on you, this struggle her lungs are having under the tent, the poor thing doesn't want to die. I have seen many die, and now I've grown accustomed to it. But listen to me, don't go thinking that I am a cruel or insensitive person, it's nothing like that, in the past I would faint if I saw a drop of blood, but one grows accustomed to all things, it's a distinctive quality of the human being which I cannot quite comprehend. But it's a good thing that it is that way, because it seems I'll be here for a long time. I don't know whether they've explained to you that some people are able to endure a long time, those who've had a slow incubation of the illness. And that's the case with me, it seems we have developed antibodies which slow down, though do not stop of course, the advance of the disease. Whereas those who have undergone a very intense exposure to the contagious disease die quickly, like your neighbor on the left. But don't grieve for her, don't put on that face. Worse off am I, and I would almost venture to say you too. Because she has a daughter. . . . After all, the fact of having a daughter isn't everything, because I have one as well. But let me tell you about that. I too have a daughter. But it's as if I didn't have one, it's been years since we've seen each other, years before my falling ill. I'll explain, I was one inclined to fall in love, and for a man I abandoned my home, nothing mattered to me anymore that had to do with them, with my husband and daughter. Well, no, I'm deceiving you, it wasn't because of a man, it was . . . it was . . . due to a simple desire for travel, to know the world, for independence. And I abandoned my home and my country. When I repented it was already too late. Pardon me if a tear escapes me. When I realized my mistake it was too late, my daughter didn't remember me and even to myself she was a stranger to whom I couldn't think of what to say. Whereas your neighbor to the left, she told me her story before getting worse. And believe me when I say that she is worthy of envy. No, don't knit your brow in a frown, there's no need to squint your eyes with sadness, in truth her luck mustn't make you grieve. She has someone in the world in whom to continue living, as if reincarnated. She has a daughter who loves her. One night when I was unable to sleep, she got up and sat down at the foot of my bed, she told me of all the beautiful things which she had discovered in the world. She was certain that I too had enjoyed many of them, but that I had ungratefully forgotten them. She was right, I had enjoyed many of them. Whereas the love for her daughter, and that of her daughter for her, how I envied it. Her daughter writes her very long letters, and I have read them. She tells of how grateful she is for all the teaching which she has received, to defend herself better against her enemies, and how she will go on defending all the ideals that her mother has taught her to love. For which reason you, my new friend, should not grieve for her, yes, I already know it's horrible to hear her struggling in this way so a little oxygen may enter her lungs, but it's her body which is struggling, not her soul, which has already surrendered, the daughter has gathered her mother's spirit and holds it close against her breast, she will cherish her in her memory as long as she lives. And look at her now, look at her, don't be afraid, she is dying now, don't you notice her relief, even in her tormented flesh? Now, now . . . don't you see the profound satisfaction which her eyes express, her lips almost smiling? that is her final grin, she is already dead, what relief for her flesh, she is dead within her wearied flesh, and her spirit lives on, far from here, from this desolation, her spirit lives on in a young body and full of hopes . . ."

A very ingenious play of lights depicted, through false picture windows, the dawning of a sunny day. The sick women in the pavilion opened their eyes to another day, some had already forgotten that they were at the bottom of a polar basement and they spoke of the prevailing good weather. The amiable chatter was interrupted by the appearance of two nurses guiding a stretcher. They were bringing a patient already known in the pavilion, she came to occupy bed 27. The others looked at one another with forced resignation. In a whisper, the neighbor on the right explained to W218 that they were dealing with a sick woman whose conduct was quite reprehensible, disposed to nervous excesses; she had spent the past week in a room or cell in isolation, after an attack of rage against the poor woman who had expired the previous night, because she was bothered by her labored breathing. As she heard these words, W218 followed with her eyes the new neighbor to her left, who in her turn was casting quick glances at her, hostile and curious ones. She was a woman over sixty, with her hair graying and wild, and large black eyes embedded under violaceous eyelids. W218 did not perceive malice in those eyes, which defied the entire pavilion. When the nurses finished making up her bed and situating her toiletries on the respective light table, the much-feared woman removed a ring and gave it to them as a gratuity. It was the only thing left to her, of little material but certainly of nostalgic value, a ring corresponding to the hippie style of her youth, thirty or more years before.

Night was beginning to fall. The light which was entering through the picture windows was turning pink, lilac and finally bluish. Now was the time to switch on the little lamps on the tables, whosoever wanted to. The feared one was about to turn on her bedside lamp, which was on her right side and hence beside W218. She then noticed that the girl was trembling with fever, she did not turn on the light out of respect for another's suffering, "My poor little thing, such a young girl and so beautiful and here among crazy old women. Please don't tremble anymore, and don't be afraid of me . . . that above all. It's been a long time since I've been in this pavilion, I'm the most ancient toad in the pond, and I'm not liked because all of them here are resigned to dying, except for me. Look . . . it would be better if you come closer, that way I can speak more softly, and I won't get you mixed up in any trouble. Well, and now that no one can hear us, let me tell you. . . . What makes these moth-eaten old women most furious is that I don't consider myself defeated, and I have even made attempts to escape. . . . Yes, more than once. Because of that they think me crazy. Of course, they don't believe anything other than what they see, but I believe in other things as well. Do you know . . . we are many hours away from the nearest village, isolated by the ices, but notwithstanding this, I believe, it is possible to escape. This that I'm telling you is known by all who have spent a long time here, but they won't admit it. And it's that one of us . . . managed to escape. She was desperate to return to her country, she didn't come from Urbis like you and the others, she came from a country very distant from everything and which was at war, a very futile and bloody civil war. And she would suffer horribly because she had a daughter there, scarcely a little girl. She had told me many times that she was going to attempt to flee, one night while all were asleep. And she did it just that way. One night she disappeared. She got away in her nightdress and nothing more. She was a young woman, of course, and as beautiful as you. And I know what happened, they have told me about it, I can't

tell you who, but I know what happened. She emerged on the
surface of the earth, almost naked in the polar cold. And they set
off to search for her but they were already unable to find her. You
know how implacable the horizon of Ices Everlasting is, one sees
the frozen crust for hundreds of miles around. But notwithstanding a full moon, its silvery light shimmering on the ground, no one
was able to descry her. And it was that the cold, the madness, the
wind, the daring, the ice itself, the yearning to see her daughter,
the stars, all together made it so she disintegrated into thin air.
That was why no one was able to follow her and force her return.
And in the meantime within her country the men were fighting
in the Town Square, brothers were killing each other, and there
in the very center of the square, where there stood a white pyramid, she appeared anew, the air restored her flesh. She lay beside
the pyramid, asleep, barely covered by her nightgown, barefoot.
The roar of the cannons awoke her. She was not afraid, just as you
were not afraid of me, I who am as ugly as the slaughter which
she witnessed in opening her eyes. And she got to her feet and
asked, raising her voice as much as she could, where was her
daughter. But no one knew what to answer her, the shooting grew
more severe and the soldiers were being ordered to load up with
more and more gunpowder. Suddenly a strange gust of wind arose
and the nightdress was lifted, showing me to be naked, and the
men trembled, and it's that they saw I was a divine creature, my
pubis was like that of the angels, without down and without sex,
smooth. The soldiers were paralyzed with amazement. An angel
had descended to the earth. And the shooting stopped, and the
enemies embraced one another and cried, giving thanks to the
heavens for having sent a message of peace. But a little further
away thunderous cannon blasts could still be heard and I asked
to be brought there. Once again the air disintegrated my flesh,
I disappeared from the square and was reconstituted at another
locale, at the foot of smoldering ruins. And there too, as the troops
saw me, the bombardment ceased, and what could be heard was
just my voice, crying out for my daughter. And it was only then
that I felt fear, because I was close to her, yes, but I could also

be near her dead body. A profound silence descended, and afterward were heard the paces of a multitude, serene and full of affection, which was coming toward me. In the lead was a man with his eyes bandaged, whom I thought I recognized, and whom I had thought dead. At his sides there marched children of both sexes, all of them maimed by the war. I prayed that my daughter were alive, and that she would even be one of these innocent victims of the violence, anything so long as I would find her alive. The blind man who led the people spoke to me, and now I knew who he was. He gave me thanks for my incredible deed, but because of the sadness in his voice I realized he wasn't bringing me good news. He asked that I forgive him for having told me I was a frivolous woman, unconcerned with the fate of the people, and that in the name of all, the nation was grateful for the miracle of peace, heaven had chosen me to demonstrate the path to salvation. I didn't know what to answer, because although at those moments I was the incarnation of Good, within I was no more than a poor mortal tormented by the fear of losing the only thing that she loved on this earth. The bandaged man was silent and afterward, in a voice broken with emotion, the report began. Forgive me, but I cannot repeat it for you, or can I, I believed he was about to tell me that my daughter was dead, but . . . why was this fool crying? could it be perchance from happiness? because I heard in the distance the voice of my little girl who was telling me that she loved me very much, and that she was proud of me, and finally she appeared, and the wind lifted her little skirt and there was no doubt that she was my daughter, because she too was a pure angel. And only then did I realize why nothing was more important to me on this earth than she was, why I loved her so, because she would be a woman whom no man could humiliate! because she would not be a slave to the first scoundrel who sensed that weak point between her legs, a slave to the first dog which knew to smell out her folly! And it must have been out of joy that my head became jumbled, it was from joy that I went mad, and for that reason I wanted no one to see me, and I vanished from there, and am here once again, but don't pay any attention to your neighbor in the other bed, she doesn't like me because she says I'm crazy, and that I'm dangerous, no, I never did anything to anyone, and it makes me furious, that's all, when they tell me I've lost my mind because my daughter died, which isn't true, she's alive, and she loves me . . ."

The sick woman in bed 27 was left exhausted after her account, she lay her head on the pillow and fell asleep. W218 looked around her, the other sick women fixed mocking eyes on bed 27. On the other hand, W218 herself had the feeling that the story was true, and after getting up with difficulty, she stretched out her arms and tucked in the ancient one.

—I don't understand what you're saying. . . . Forgive me, Anita, but I don't know what it is you're asking me . . .

—Who are you?

—I'm Beatriz, don't you recognize me?

—What Beatriz?

—Beatriz, your friend.

—Is that you . . . Beatriz?

—Yes . . . how do you feel?

—Half asleep . . .

—It's the anesthesia. You rest now, you'll be more awake later on.

—Anesthesia . . . ?

—Yes, they operated on you.

—When . . . ?

—This morning, and just now you're starting to wake up.

—They operated on me . . . ?

—Yes, and we're all very pleased.

—I don't understand.

—We're very pleased with the results.

—I don't understand . . .

—Yes, they removed the tumor, and the branching wasn't what they had at first believed. They were able to remove the whole thing. It was in the lung, the part that had spread.

—They got it all?

—According to them, the limits were well defined, not what they'd expected.

—They're not lying to me?

—No, Anita, the doctors were very surprised. They were able to remove all of it. They have hopes that there won't be a reappearance of . . . shoots.

—. . .

—Don't you believe me?

—. . .

—They don't anticipate other . . . branching, they're very optimistic. And they want to give you radiation.

—And I'm going to be cured?

—Yes, and you have to make plans.

—Plans . . . for what?

—I don't know, for the future . . .

—. . .

—At least for someone to go clean your apartment, because in ten days you'll be discharged from here.

—To Buenos Aires?

—Your apartment here, in Mexico City. Which is where your doctors are, where you're going to continue with your treatment, and you're going to be cured completely.

—It can't be . . .

—Yes, it worked out very well and was very much in time, Anita.

—But always . . . there's danger.

—Danger. . . . There's danger for all of us. Yes, they're going to give you radiation, but as a method of prevention, that's all.

—They aren't . . . saying it . . . to trick me?

—No, sometimes things turn out well, Anita, though it's hard to believe it.

—I'm afraid that you're deceiving me . . . or that I don't understand . . . what you're telling me . . .

—No, it's all better than what was believed. . . . And later on a call should be placed to your family in Buenos Aires, you'll tell them yourself. That everything turned out better than they had hoped.

—Me?

—Yes, of course, I'll bring the phone closer to you and you'll speak for yourself.

—And what . . . do I tell them?

—That you're better . . .

—Beatriz . . .

—Yes . . .

—Ask . . . for the connection, now.

—Wouldn't you rather be more awake?

—It doesn't matter, if I . . . fall back asleep . . . you talk . . . with Mama.

—However you like.

—I ask you please . . . to make it now . . . the call.

—But it would bring your mother greater joy to talk to you . . .

—No . . . it doesn't matter. . . . You talk . . . and calm her down . . . to Mama . . .

—As you like.

—And please . . . tell her . . .

—Yes . . .

—Tell her . . . that I want to see . . . Clarita . . . that she should send her . . .

—Do you want her to come?

—Yes . . . and the sooner . . . better.

—I'll tell her.

—Yes, let them come . . . soon . . . the two of them . . . because I very much want . . . to see them. . . . And that's the truth, that really is true.

—Why do you look at me like that?

—. . .

—Anita . . . what I told you about the operation is the truth too.

—I don't care . . . even though I may have . . . little time, what matters to me is to last long enough to see them . . . one more time.

—You'll be able to hug them, really tight.

—More than to hug them . . . what I want . . . is . . .

—Tell me.

—. . .

—Tell me, what do you want?

—More than to hug them, I want . . . to talk to them . . . and it could even be . . . that we would understand each other . . .

About the Author

MANUEL PUIG was born in 1932 in a small town in the Argentine pampas. He studied philosophy at the University of Buenos Aires, and in 1956 he won a scholarship from the Italian Institute of Buenos Aires and chose to take a course in film direction at Cinecittà in Rome. There he worked as an assistant director until 1962, when he began to write his first novel. Puig's novels, *Betrayed by Rita Hayworth, Heartbreak Tango, The Buenos Aires Affair, Kiss of the Spider Woman* (the last two were banned in Argentina during a decade), *Pubis Angelical, Eternal Curse on the Reader of These Pages,* and *Blood of Requited Love,* have been translated into twenty-five languages. Lately he's written for the stage, and his own adaptation of *Kiss of the Spider Woman* has played in many countries for long runs. He's also authored the drama *Under a Mantle of Stars.* Manuel Puig now lives in Rio de Janeiro.